YOUNG WOMEN.

Jessica Moor studied English at Cambridge before completing a Creative Writing MA at the University of Manchester. Moor was selected as one of the *Observer*'s debut novelists of 2020, and her first novel, *Keeper*, was chosen by the *Sunday Times*, *Independent* and *Cosmopolitan* as one of their top debuts of the year. *Keeper* was nominated for the Desmond Elliott Prize and the Mystery Writers of America Edgar Award. *Young Women* is her second novel.

YOUNG WOMEN.

JESSICA MOOR

MANILLA
PRESS

First published in the UK in 2022 by
MANILLA PRESS
An imprint of Bonnier Books UK
4th Floor, Victoria House, Bloomsbury Square, London,
England, WC1B 4DA
Owned by Bonnier Books
Sveavägen 56, Stockholm, Sweden

Quote on page 46 from *Collected Poems* by Sylvia Plath,
Copyright © 1981 by Faber and Faber Limited

This is a work of fiction. Names, places, events and
incidents are either the products of the author's
imagination or used fictitiously. Any resemblance to
actual persons, living or dead, or actual
events is purely coincidental.

A CIP catalogue record for this book is
available from the British Library.

Hardback ISBN: 978-1-83877-868-2
Export ISBN: 978-1-83877-869-9

Also available as an ebook and an audiobook

1 3 5 7 9 10 8 6 4 2

Typeset by IDSUK (Data Connection) Ltd
Printed and bound in Great Britain by Clays Ltd, Elcograf S.p.A.

Manilla Press is an imprint of Bonnier Books UK
www.bonnierbooks.co.uk

For Jason, who wanted to know what happened next.

*Dedicated to the memory of John and
Audrey Cunningham.*

Half victims, half accomplices, like everyone else.

Jean-Paul Sartre, *Dirty Hands*, used by Simone de Beauvoir
as epigraph for *The Second Sex*

Prologue

I WATCHED HER FILM *last night.* Moitié Victime, *it was called.*

She was sixteen in that movie. You could tell by the way that the director shot the sex scene that he knew that too. Maybe not emotionally, but contractually.

I hunched my body around the laptop, my nose inches from the screen. To see her better. To reach through and grab her.

Her face was perfect for period pieces. She made sense with her hair (chestnut brown here) back in a chignon, Cupid's bow mouth accentuated in creamy red lipstick. Perfect for an ingénue in Vichy France, a double agent. That was her role in this film, and that was always her gift, her magic. The way she worked in every context, not just plausible but perfectly suited. Inevitable.

She looks so young in that film. Deer-limbed and emerald-eyed, afraid in that way that men find sexy. So different to how she was when I knew her. I watched the film once as a forensic exercise, ignoring the parts of it that weren't her, or were at least an echo of her.

After I saw her in the footage of the protest, I watched her film a second time. This time I put on my dressing gown, poured a glass of red wine, let myself stretch out over the sofa. *I watched for the colour palette and the shot composition and the languid, reproachful pan of the camera over the cafes of a small-town square where the Nazi officers sat.*

I treated it as an aesthetic experience. It worked well that way.

Part One

Chapter One

THE FIRST TIME I saw Tamsin her eyes were closed. Her lashes didn't flicker, even as the sirens wailed closer, even when they were so close that we could feel their screams through our bodies. Even as our skulls jolted with the knock on the tarmac of police boots.

The whole time her face was serene, as if she were dead and laid to rest.

I turned my head to look at her, feeling the road's grit scrape against my scalp. Her hair was gold. What they call old gold – the colour of gilded furniture, with just the slightest tinge of olive. Skin strobed by the lights of Piccadilly Circus. In all the shouts and slams and the crashes and the cries, she stayed lying there, unmoving. She seemed, in that moment, other-worldly.

As the police drew level with us we were engulfed by noise. It was then that her eyes popped open. They were green and feline, yellow-flecked.

I must have looked afraid. She looked at me. Grabbed my hand. Then she was yanked upright and her fingers were torn from mine. She went limp, resisting arrest as a corpse resists its own concealment.

Cop's breath on my neck, arms pulled painfully behind me, they half dragged, half carried us away. I couldn't stop my feet from skittering along in obedience. Tamsin was smiling slightly, as if she thought the whole thing was just a little bit funny.

They put us all into the van and slammed the door shut, harder than I thought they would, as if they were making sure we got the full experience. It was all people like me – young, white, privileged enough to be dizzy with excitement at the thought that they'd actually been arrested. Some were looking around, smirking, heaving in their breath. Others sat there, performatively grim. The flush-cheeked girl beside me on the bench was furiously tweeting.

Tamsin was sitting opposite me. Again, her eyes were closed. She seemed so calm, so sure that the right thing to do was disappear into herself, like her mind was a fortress.

I settled for a little half-smile, as if I'd been here before, as if I knew the drill. I made sure to look around at the other faces in turn, so that nobody would notice that all I really wanted to do was to stare at her.

I lost sight of her for a bit, while we were all being processed at the station. Someone started singing and everyone joined in. First 'Amazing Grace', then 'A Hard Rain's A-Gonna Fall'. I didn't know most of the words so I just mouthed along and joined in with the chorus. Then nobody seemed to be able to work out what to sing next; someone shouted, 'Anyway, here's "Wonderwall".'

We laughed like we thought it was stupid, but still we sang along. Everyone knew all those words. Then 'Rehab' by Amy Winehouse. It didn't really make sense, but it felt like it meant something when everyone started stamping their feet on the concrete floor and singing *no, no, no*.

We didn't find each other again until the singing had died away and everyone was sitting or lying on the floor. I was cross-legged, trying to sit with my spine straight, the way my teacher did in yoga. My hips hurt and my back ached. The adrenaline spike had left me feeling lifeless.

Tamsin touched my arm lightly and said, 'How are you doing now, sweetie?' As if we were just carrying on from an earlier conversation.

Her accent wasn't English. At first it sounded American, but as we talked, I started to wonder if it wasn't that international inflection that you hear when people speak English like it's their native tongue, but have no place to tie it to.

'I'm doing better,' I said.

'You looked scared when I saw you. I hope you don't mind I held your hand. I do stuff like that without thinking it through. You English don't like being touched.'

'I didn't mind.'

I didn't mind, either, when she pulled out a worn little deck of cards from her pocket and asked if I wanted to play. I didn't give my standard response – I didn't like card games, too much organised fun – I just nodded. We sat cross-legged on the floor opposite each other. She bent forward from the hips the way babies do, joints fluid, hair slipping from her shoulders and forming a curtain

7

to encompass the two of us. I couldn't work out how old she was – she could have been anything from sixteen to thirty – whether the easy way she was talking to me was a sign of naïveté or maturity.

I asked her what had brought her to the protest today.

'If we don't do something about climate change, it seems to me like there's no point in caring about anything else,' she said.

I nodded, and said that it was something similar for me. That morning I'd set off to the protests with my flatmate and some of her friends, all of us sitting on the Overground with our arms around our placards like they were something we loved.

They let us go sometime after midnight. They processed Tamsin first, and she didn't say goodbye before she left. I assumed that was that – one of those brief intimacies, like from a plane or in a queue, that never got its chance to take root. I emerged from the holding area with Hana, my flatmate, and a couple of her friends. But when I got to the waiting area of the police station there she was, sitting on one of the plastic chairs among a gaggle of people staring listlessly at their phones. One Doc Marten-clad foot resting on her knee, the way a man crosses his legs. She was reading a paperback book.

Tamsin looked up expectantly when I entered, as if she'd recognised my tread, and smiled.

'Drink?'

*

None of the bars were open. Hana and the rest of her gang quickly begged off, and it would have been obvious for me to get the last train home with them. But instead Tamsin and I found an all-night Tesco Metro. Everyone looked dull under that awful strip lighting, but not Tamsin. Her skin seemed to carry with it a patina that couldn't be scrubbed away by too much reality.

I instinctively reached for the bottle of Pinot Grigio that was on offer, but she waved her hand at me and said, 'Don't worry, I'll get this.'

She was scanning the top rack of the bottles of red wine.

'That one's on offer.' I pointed.

She shook her head. 'They're bullshitting you with these offer things, ignore them.'

She chose a bottle of Malbec, then went over to the refrigerated section and selected two different kinds of cheese. She cradled them in the crook of her arm like they were kittens, her hand clasped around the neck of the bottle.

'Okay, we just need . . .'

She walked quickly, on the balls of her feet, to the baked goods section and felt the baguettes in turn, through their cellophane wrappers.

'These are fresh,' she announced, and her face seemed to brighten, as if it was the best news anyone could have given her.

All the self-checkouts were available, but she went up to the cashier desk.

'How's your night going?' she asked the cashier, a tall, loose-limbed boy of seventeen or so, who looked like he was still waiting to grow into his own frame.

I expected him to grunt something in reply. I expected to find that she didn't really understand how London worked, how people were here. But he shrugged and said, 'Yeah, not too bad. We've had a lot of people in from the protest today.'

'That's where we've just come from.' She gestured at me, and it occurred to me that, as far as this cashier was concerned, we could be old friends. 'What did you make of it all?'

'Well, it took me a long time to get in to work.' I expected him to leave it at that, for him to brusquely twist the card holder towards her and disappear back into his role. 'But you know, I support it. I'd be out there too, if I could. It's important. I read this thing online this morning and it said "there's no Planet B".' He laughed. 'I know it's cheesy, but it stuck with me. No Planet B. Someone's got to do something.'

I'd been planning to dart forward, to tap my card on the reader, to beat her to it. But that would have felt like interrupting, so I held off until it was too late. It cost £21.89, the wine and the cheese and the baguette. She didn't even look at the reader.

The summer night was still warm. None of the parks were open. Tamsin wanted to climb over the railings into Victoria Embankment Gardens on the river. I didn't. It wasn't that

I was scared – it just felt too raw an exercise of privilege for us to trespass, knowing that if we were caught there would be no real repercussions. I said something along those lines to her.

She gave me a measured look. 'Who is it that you think that's helping?'

I didn't have an answer, so I climbed too. For a moment I felt weightless.

She somehow managed to fashion a cheeseboard out of the cardboard packaging. She poured half of the Malbec into her emptied-out steel water bottle and gave the rest to me. We clinked the two together.

'Was that your first arrest?'

'God, yeah. I'm such a rule-abiding little creep.'

'To many more, then!' She raised her bottle as if saluting not just me but the Thames, the reflection of the London Eye in its inky surface, the darting lights of the bridges as they lunged across the river. She seemed happy for the silence to remain untouched, and there was something in the quality of it that I liked too. Yet there were some obvious questions that still needed asking.

'So, you're from America?'

'Montréal,' she said, pronouncing it the French way. 'Canada. Originally. I moved to the States when I was twelve though, so you're kind of right. Connecticut. Fucking kill me.'

'Sorry. I didn't mean to assume.'

'Don't worry. Canadians are too polite to care when we get mistaken for Americans.'

'Montreal's in Quebec, right?' I couldn't have sworn to it then – it was a guess from the way she said the name.

'Right.'

'So you speak French?'

'Bien sûr.' She pronounced the words strangely, as if the vowels were dangling from her mouth. 'French and English from living in Quebec. Then my mom's Italian and my dad's Polish.'

'Like, first generation?'

'Right. Not that weird thing of saying you're Irish when no one in your family's set foot in Ireland for more than a century.'

'So you speak Polish and Italian too.'

'Sure.'

'Wow.'

'There's a lot going on there.' She took a sip of wine from her water bottle and slid down the bench so that her head was resting on the back. Staring up at the stars.

'Is Tamsin an Italian name? Or Polish? It sounds . . .' I cast about, unsure.

'It's one of those strange bastardised names. A short form that turned into a name all by itself. It's a contraction of Thomasina. That means twin.'

'Do you like your name?' A playground question.

'I've always thought it was kind of ugly. Yours is so much prettier.' Said without any smile to indicate flattery.

I didn't agree. I didn't really think Tamsin was a pretty name either. Rather, it sounded like the name of someone who didn't care if her name was pretty.

'Emily means industrious. Striving.' I sighed. 'There were seven different Emilys in my year at school.' I could still count the fleet of Emilys off in my head, ten years later. Morris, Chapman, Kim, Parker-Johns, Sullivan, Cheung.

And me.

'And are you?'

'Am I what?'

'Industrious.'

I took a sip of the wine. 'I mean, sure.'

'That's why you were at the protest. You care.'

'Everyone cares.'

'But not everyone gives up their weekend.'

I stayed quiet.

'Anyway, industrious or not, that doesn't mean it's not a pretty name. It's so classic. So English. Emily.'

She said it in an English accent – not the cod-aristocratic-slash-Cockney that I've heard Americans do, but an impressive approximation of RP, cut-glass and perfect, like Helena Bonham Carter in *A Room With A View*.

'But anyway . . .' She looked at me, popping a crumb of Stilton into her mouth. 'My god, the cheese in this country is so fucking good. I still can't get over it. Anyway. Where are you from?'

'Here,' I said, gesturing to the bench. 'I mean, London.'

'Amazing.'

'Not really. I'm not from a cool part. I'm from Wimbledon.'

I waited for her to say 'Like the tennis', as if that settled everything, but she didn't. Instead she said, 'So what's that like? Posh? Gritty?' She articulated the two ts carefully, as if she was enunciating them one at a time. 'Diverse?'

'In a sense. I mean, Wimbledon itself is quite posh.'

'I'm sensing a but. Are you posh? I find it hard to tell.'

'I'm . . .' I thought about the red-trousered croquet-playing specimens I'd met at university. 'I'm sort of medium. Not posh exactly . . . my ex was really posh.' Harry had always made it clear how gauche I was, that I'd never done a good enough job of imitating people like him. My exact social class without him was another thing that I had yet to work out. 'I went to a grammar school.'

'Is that like private school?'

'No.' Explaining myself from first principles. It was liberating to not feel stuck in the usual class shorthand. 'State school. But they did this high-pressure entrance exam, so the mood of the school is completely neurotic. All-girls.'

'My god.' She laughed. 'I don't want to be mean about it or anything.' The way she said 'about' reminded me that she was part-Canadian. A-boat. 'It's just a strange concept to most North Americans, a single-sex school. Unless you're Catholic or something. Which I actually am, and I still didn't . . . Anyway, go on.'

'So yeah . . . crazy school.'

'Crazy in what way? Is that where you learned to be a "rule-abiding little creep"?'

She repeated my words back to me in another British accent, her imitation too good a mirror to feel like mockery.

I paused. Took a sip of wine.

I didn't want to give her my spiel, the same little speech about my adolescence that I'd developed on my gap year and perfected during my first week at university. As a lawyer I was prone to the spiel, the shorthand, the potted summary. But mature people didn't talk like that.

I shook my head. 'Anyway, that's all so boring.'

'It's not boring to me. Did all that stuff affect you? I mean, I guess it must have, in that atmosphere. But did it . . .'

'. . . I'd say I got off pretty lightly. I wasn't exactly down the mines.'

'Sure.'

'Tell me about Montreal.'

I guess I was expecting a breakdown of the city's demographics. Or a quick sound bite on the politics, a survey of rent prices.

Instead, Tamsin told me about a city built on a mountain, a mountain that rose out of the vast icy river that ran all the way from Lake Ontario to the North Atlantic. I couldn't think exactly where those places were; it seemed enough to embrace the sounds of the names. She told me that sometimes, in the winter, you saw seals in the river. She said the mountain was turned into a park where people hung out and played guitar in the summer. That there was a great cross on top of that mountain that you could see from all over the city. She told me about the network of tunnels that ran underneath the city so that in the winter people could get to work, to the shops, to university, when the temperature dropped so low that you couldn't go outside.

15

'Sounds a bit like the Paris catacombs,' I said.

Her eyes lit up. 'Exactly. I'd never even thought about that before, but when I went to Paris and saw the catacombs I felt like, in a weird way – yeah, this makes sense to me. This feels like, home, even though they're nothing alike.' She laughed. 'And like, it's still Canada. It's still cars and hockey and Tim Hortons or whatever. But it's something else as well. It's this European sensibility, I guess. Truly bilingual. People flick back and forth from English to French depending on which word they like better in either language. And there's all these cultural influences. English and French obviously, but also Haitian, Lebanese, Jewish. Such beautiful food. So, when my parents moved us to this small town in Connecticut I just felt like . . . I don't know, like my soul had lost all its nutrients.'

I paused. Took note of the phrase.

'Why did you all move?'

'Dad's job. What other reason is there, for uprooting a whole family?'

'Sure. So what did you do?'

'Oh. You know. Read a bunch. Didn't talk to people much. Became a weird theatre kid in high school. The usual story. But my little sister was fine. It worked well for her, actually. That way of living.'

Her voice had become strangely flat when she said this.

'You were shy?'

'Hell yeah.'

'I find that hard to imagine.'

She shrugged.

'So what brought you to London?'

'Being a weird theatre kid.' She laughed, again. Snorted, really. 'No, I mean, if you really care about acting there are basically two places to go: London and New York.'

So she was an actress. It seemed strange to think of her being paid to pretend to be someone else, when people would probably pay her good money just to be herself, to make them feel like this.

'And LA, obviously,' she continued, an afterthought.

'You didn't fancy LA?'

'Not really my thing.'

'What's the thing?'

'I don't know. Sunshine. Fucking juicing.' She broke off the tip of the baguette and pushed it into her mouth. The crunch of it sounded buttery, resonant. 'I mean, right here, this fucking baguette, this is why I'm not LA material. That's the stereotype, anyway.'

'And not New York.'

'Right.'

'How come? It seems the obvious choice. Closer to your family.'

She paused before replying. 'It's funny.' She wiped some crumbs from around her mouth, took a swig of wine. 'Funny that you say that. To me London was the obvious choice.'

I let her keep talking.

'I mean, I guess if I were to think about it pragmatically . . .' She turned to look at me, her eyes capturing mine as her voice gained momentum. 'I'd say that it's to

17

do with the type of acting here. Like, most American acting is very much film-focused, very method. Whereas you have these British actors, these classically trained actors, and they're just on another level. They convey so much, yet they do so little.'

An indistinct image came into my mind of a certain type of old, grizzled Shakespearean actor.

'The kind of actor that can become someone else,' I said.

She didn't even reply, she just pointed straight at my chest, smiling broadly, as if words were unnecessary. I felt proud. I wasn't sure if it was because I had articulated something for her, or because I was somehow associated with the tradition she admired so much.

Or maybe it was the Malbec.

'Good call on the red,' I said, holding up the bottle.

'I hope you don't mind. You were gravitating towards the white, right? But the thing with red is you don't have to worry so much about the temperature. I love white too, for the right mood, but it's got to be fucking ice-cold. Like, right now, this is pretty tepid, but it's perfect. Red wine is always perfect.'

In the light of the street lamps and the London Eye I could see that the Malbec had stained her lips, but it didn't make her look drunk or sloppy. Just like she was tasting life.

'Anyway, that's me. An artsy stray cat. What about you?'

'I'm a lawyer,' I said automatically. 'I mean, I was. I'm in a slightly different role now, working for a charity.'

'What charity?'

'It's called the Women's Advocacy Centre.'

I paused, waiting for Tamsin to nod and then move the conversation seamlessly back onto herself. I'd met people like her before, beguiling people who were good at seeming interested but didn't really want to hear your answers to their questions. But Tamsin stayed listening, intent. Partly to fill the silence, I carried on.

'We mostly help vulnerable women who've suffered various forms of gender-based violence access legal remedies. Often it's women who can't access existing services, for whatever reason. Immigration, usually. No recourse to public funds. Language barriers. That kind of thing. So we take lots of cases on things like trafficking, female genital mutilation, sexual violence. And then we also do policy work, position papers, advising the government.' I stopped, then said quickly, 'Sorry. Massive downer.'

'Not a downer for me,' Tamsin said, leaning forward. 'I mean, you're right, those are some heavy issues. But do you think it's a downer? Does it bring you down?'

'Oh, I'm already down. Might as well put it to good use.'

Tamsin didn't laugh like I expected. She just kept looking at me, her face intent.

'Is that true? You're already down?'

'Oh no. No, I'm fine.'

'So . . . there must be a good reason why you do it. Is there a huge rush when you win?'

'We don't win very often,' I admitted. 'Usually the odds are just too stacked. But I guess . . . it's good to go to work every day and feel like there's clearly a moral value

19

to what you're doing. So it's worth carrying on, even if we don't win them all. Even if it's just to keep the idea of justice alive, until a better time comes.'

Tamsin didn't say anything, and for a few seconds I was confident that I had killed the mood entirely. But after a long pause she said, 'I like that phrase. Keeping the idea of justice alive. I'd never thought of that before.'

It was nearly three a.m. She saw me looking at my watch and leaned over to look too. She smelled of wine and something woody, like an antique cedar chest, only lighter.

'You smell lovely,' I said. Then, quickly after, 'What perfume do you wear?'

'Oh, thanks. *Féminité du Bois*, I think it's called.' She said the French words in that same strange, drawling way. 'I was just about to compliment you on your lovely ring. Is that an emerald?'

'Yeah. It was my grandmother's.' She had died a year earlier. The ring came to me in her will. 'Classiest thing about me, by some distance.'

'I'm sure that's not true. But fuck, man, it's late.'

It was.

'My place is pretty close by. If you want to crash.'

'Erm . . .' I tried to think of reasons why not. But I wanted to meet the invitation in the same spirit in which it'd been extended, so I said, 'Oh fuck it, yeah. That'd be great.'

A smile spread across her face. 'Perfect. We'll go home. I can make us some green tea. I've got this daybed in the living room and it's actually super comfy. I nap on it all the time. And in the morning we can do cardamom buns and coffee from this little Nordic bakery near my place and maybe go for a walk? If you want?'

Of course I wanted. But the mention of the bakery reminded me.

'Shit.'

'What?'

'I've got plans in the morning. Breakfast plans at nine. Back in Wimbledon, with an old friend.'

'Oh,' she said.

I felt like I might crack with disappointment, and what made it all the more potent was that she seemed like she was genuinely sorry too.

'I could bail.' Lucy wouldn't hold it against me. But it was precisely because she wasn't the kind of friend that held grudges that made me feel guilty.

'No, no, you should see your friend. I don't want to push you into bailing. Especially if she's an old friend. They're really precious.' She laughed, lightly. 'I wish I had a few more of those. You can still crash for the night though, and go off early?'

'I . . .' I knew it would have been more sensible, more efficient than getting two night buses across London. But I didn't want to just snatch a few hours' sleep in her living room and then scurry off to catch the first train. I wanted the lazy morning, the coffee, the cardamom buns. 'No. No, don't worry. It's probably best if I just get the bus back.'

We walked together as far as my bus stop in Trafalgar Square.

'I can never get over Nelson's Column,' she said. 'I know it's a cliché, it's just . . .' she kissed her fingertips, 'the essence of London. Perfect.'

'He had all these links with the slave trade,' I said, looking up to where Nelson leaned languidly on the hilt of his sword. Harry had told me once that his great-great-great-great grandfather had been one of Nelson's commanders. 'This whole city's like an awful shrine to Empire. It's gross.'

'It is gross,' she said, folding her arms and scrutinising Nelson, as if she were about to start conversing with him. 'It's gross, and it's gorgeous, and they can both be true at the same time.'

I could see my bus rounding the corner of the Strand.

'This is me,' I said. 'Are you sure you're okay getting home? Are you going to get an Uber?'

'Fuck Uber. They're neoliberal assholes. I'm gonna walk. It's a gorgeous night.'

'Are you sure it's . . .'

'Safe?' She shrugged. 'Look, man, I don't buy all that stuff about women not walking around at night. It's my city too. If a dude is going to rape me there's like an eighty per cent chance that it'll be someone I know, so . . .' she grinned, 'statistically I'm safer with strangers.'

'I've never thought about it like that before. That seems . . . healthy.'

'Or just the rationalisations of a woman who's too lazy to learn Krav Maga.'

'Well, text me when you get home.' I took my debit card out of my pocket, ready to tap.

I'd said it because it was what girls said to each other. But she said, 'Wait,' and held out her hand. 'Gimme your phone.'

She tapped out her number, and just 'Tamsin'. No surname.

'Get home safe,' I said, when I got on the bus.

'Goodnight, sweetie. Thank you for a beautiful evening.'

Chapter Two

HARRY AGAIN. THAT NAGGING feeling that I'm forgetting something important, sitting in the corner and smiling at his friends' jokes. I can't even hear the jokes but I know I'm supposed to smile. Driving home, him putting his arm around me, me knowing there's something, something not quite right.

Can't remember – easier to just keep looking at him instead.

The two of us going to bed. Me staring past his shoulder into a greyish mist and thinking over and over, *I'm forgetting something*. Was I supposed to meet someone? A Canadian girl who had seemed American?

When I woke up I remembered two things. The first was that Harry and I had been broken up for nearly a year. The second was that I *was* meeting someone – I was meeting Lucy. For coffee. In less than an hour.

Lucy had suggested the weekly meetup after things ended with Harry, when I'd said something about the specific emptiness of Sunday mornings alone.

'Let's have a standing date,' she'd said. 'Since we're so terrible at organising to get together.'

She meant me. She meant I was terrible. But she was nice enough not to say so. After all those years it meant a lot that she still bothered to be nice to me.

So now every Sunday morning we went for breakfast together at the same bakery. It was a little chain – classy, overpriced, at home on High Street Wimbledon.

She still lived there, ten minutes from her parents' house in Wimbledon Village, the house with its arms flung wide open and books everywhere. It was convenient for her job in Croydon.

I sometimes think that the only reason Lucy and I became best friends was that our names were next to each other in the register at school. We sat together in every class, friends by default.

Lucy was waiting for me when I arrived, though I was only a couple of minutes late. I had barely slept, was so tired it felt like my head had been broken open. Whatever quality Tamsin had, whatever possibilities she offered, had seemed to dissipate on the night bus home. I'd sat there, scrolling through my phone and trying to piece together why everyone was suddenly angry with a famous doughnut manufacturer. When I got into my flat at four a.m. I couldn't think about anything other than the fact that I lived so far away from the centre of things. That my Sunday mornings consisted of a standing date in a chain bakery.

Lucy was wearing exercise clothes, the Sweaty Betty leggings that she'd owned for the last six years. She'd already been for her run on Wimbledon Common, same as every week. She once said something matter-of-fact about burning off the calories from the cinnamon bun she ate with me. I'd laughed, but it pissed me off that she thought about herself that way. Like her body was a little ledger of incomings and outgoings.

Clothes never quite seemed to fit me properly. I wasn't averse, in theory, to going up or down a size. But whatever size I tried on just introduced a different way in which my body wasn't quite right. I was always on the gawky side of tall, frizzy side of curly, on the blotchy side of clear-complected. Ever since primary school, however neat I might look at the beginning of the day, with combed hair and tidy uniform, everything would seem to unravel. I should have known better than to try and work in law.

Lucy was, in her own way, sleek. Like Tamsin.

'How's your week been?' I plopped into the armchair opposite hers. She'd ordered me a black coffee and a cinnamon bun. I broke off a bit and popped it into my mouth. The texture was right, but it didn't taste of anything.

'Fine. Same as usual. You look tired.'

'Thanks.'

'You know what I mean. How was the protest?'

'Yeah, good.' I took a breath. 'A really powerful collective experience, actually. It made me feel like there's a bit of hope, that there are all these people who're ready to put themselves on the line for the environment. For something so abstract.'

I took a gulp of the coffee. There was no handle on the mug; it was a bowl, as if we were in France. You had to cradle it between your two hands. The affectation had always annoyed me, but the warmth helped with the hollowed-out feeling in my skull, the mixture of red wine on a near-empty stomach and not enough sleep.

'I'll come with you next time,' Lucy said. 'I feel bad that I didn't come this time, but it just wouldn't have worked with all the marking I had to do.'

Lucy was a secondary school teacher, like she'd always wanted. I could show up to the office, tired or hung-over, and hide behind my monitor. But she couldn't, and she took care of herself accordingly. Never out late on a school night.

'I get what you mean,' I said. 'But don't you think that it's a bit irrelevant how the kids do in their GCSE English if they've got no planet to grow up in?' I tried to say it as a joke, but I couldn't quite get the tone right.

She just shrugged. 'I can commit to it properly during the holidays,' she said, and I knew she would. When Lucy decided that she cared about something she put her money where her mouth was. It was just that sometimes she took a while to decide.

'There were some interesting people there too,' I continued. 'All kinds of people. The coverage is making it sound like it was just this white liberal elite, but that's not true at all. It was definitely a diverse crowd.'

'That seems like a good thing.' Lucy had a way of saying things that made me feel that she truly understood their

27

nature, in a way that I never could. When I got my first period it stained the back of my school skirt. Lucy lent me her science overall and stood at the sink, carefully scrubbing the blood out. She didn't seem to even care what it was she was touching.

'I got arrested, actually.'

'Oh yeah, I heard about the arrests. You really went for it, then.'

I had no idea what she meant by that, but it made me feel prickly. I was probably just tired.

'Yeah, I did. I'm glad I did. It felt like the right thing to do.'

'Do you want a glass of water?'

Before I could process the question, she stood up and went over to the station where the jugs and tiny glasses stood. I drained the glass immediately. Trace flavours of mint and cucumber.

'That's better,' I said.

I noticed, when she sat down, that she looked healthier than usual. It wasn't just the leggings. Her skin had always been clear, but now there was a pretty, delicate flush to it. Her hair was shiny, even though she'd bundled it away in a bun on top of her head. Her eyes were bright.

'You look like a vitamin advert,' I said. 'Really glowy.'

She seemed to consider the compliment for a minute before choosing to accept it. 'Thank you.'

My eyes slid down and I noticed that she was drinking herbal tea, not coffee. Lucy was a latecomer to coffee – she hadn't started drinking it until we were at university.

It was one of those changes that was so small yet seemed so jarring at the time. But normally now she always ordered a flat white. No almond milk, no soy. The full-fat classic.

Seeing the direction of my gaze she said, 'I've given up caffeine.'

Usually it was me who gave up things. Meat, dairy, soy, whatever. Lucy had always ploughed on happily through a roast dinner.

'Are you even allowed to be a teacher if you've given up caffeine?'

'I'll have to give it a go. I'm going to need to cut down sooner or later. Actually, I've got some news. Ish.'

'Ooh.' I pulled my legs up onto the armchair so I was sitting cross-legged, settling in. 'Go on then.'

'Andrew and I . . .'

Dog? Mortgage? Marriage? News-ish, she'd said. Could you go for half measures on any of those?

'We've decided to start trying.'

'Trying?'

At first my mind really did go blank. I didn't have a clue what she meant. Then my thought, prissy and adolescent as it was – *but you're not married yet.*

I'd never doubted that Lucy and Andrew would get married. They were in love, after all. Quietly, boringly, beautifully in love. They bought each other thoughtful books on birthdays, dealt stoically with each other's families and went on walks to National Trust properties. Whatever it was that they had, it seemed to make Lucy happily deal with the tedious parts of life.

'Congratulations,' I said, too quickly. Then I made my mouth smile. 'I remember what you said about the phrase "trying" when we in school. That you hated it. The image of people having really brisk, purposeful sex.'

'Yeah, well, I suppose that is what I'm having.' She looked too happy to let my jab reach her. 'I know it sounds awful, but there really isn't a much better way of saying it.'

'So when did you decide this?'

She shrugged. 'Hard to say. I mean, it's been this ongoing conversation for about a year and a half.'

A year and a half.

'You're only twenty-six,' I said. 'Don't you think that's a bit young?'

'Well, nearly twenty-seven. We're hoping that we'll complete on the flat soon, and get the keys.'

The bloody two-bedroom flat in East Croydon, which I made a point of never asking about. Harry and I had talked about buying somewhere together – he was waiting on a deposit from a rich and infirm grandmother. I kept having to remind myself that I didn't have a plan of my own for the future, that I could no longer rely on his.

'And Andrew's in a good place at work. The idea is to try and time it so I can take a full school year off, but then I think I'd still be in the running for Head of Year. I reckon I can be in a good position by the time I'm thirty, even with the baby.'

The baby. She spoke about it like it was already an entity in existence.

'Wow. Lucy Allan. Oxford graduate and mama at twenty-six.'

'I'll be twenty-seven when the baby's born. Maybe even twenty-eight. There's no guarantee, you know.'

Lucy had polycystic ovary syndrome. She didn't talk about it much, and I often forgot about how she'd suffered at school, with excruciatingly heavy periods and seemingly uncontrollable weight gain. But of course she'd got it under control in the end, through exercise and diet. Diligently considering how she might have the best chance of becoming a mother was just another part of managing her condition, I supposed.

'So old. We're getting so old.' I took a big sip of my coffee. It had cooled too quickly in that stupid bowl. 'No, but seriously, that's amazing. I'm happy for you.'

'So, you don't think I'm too young?' she said quickly.

'No, no.' I considered. Deliberated like a judge. Lucy was looking at me intently. 'I think it's great that you've thought about what you want and you're going after it.' Another pause. 'And I feel like you've always done things at your own pace.'

Lucy thought for a minute, cocking her head to one side, then gave a little noise of affirmation. 'That's true.' She nodded now, smiling wryly. 'Much later or much earlier, it depends, but I'm never quite in step.'

When they brought the bill, I made a show of paying. Her herbal tea cost less than my black Americano. 'My treat.

31

Congratulations again. I'm really happy for you. Give Andrew a big hug from me.'

'Thanks. You're still coming for dinner on the fifteenth, right?'

'Right.' My occasional forays to Lucy's place, in which she made vegetable lasagne and she and Andrew quizzed me about what they called my Tinder adventures, always left me feeling like a stray cat that they occasionally fed. It was as if Lucy and Andrew had somehow managed to bypass all the friction of life by simply landing safely in each other's arms. It left me feeling ugly, battle-bruised.

'We could go and see the new Art Rawlings film before, if you like. It's supposed to be good.'

'The one about Billie Holiday? Sounds nice. I liked his last one.'

'We'll sort it.'

'Lovely.'

A silence. Then –

'I . . .' For a second, she looked unguarded. 'I think this is the right thing. The baby thing, I mean. I think it'll make me happy.'

'We might as well be happy.' I looked out of the glass pane at the front of the cafe to the grey, pallid day. 'The world's on fire. We might as well be happy.'

Lucy didn't say anything.

'I met this American girl last night at the protest. We were arrested together, actually. She said this weird thing.' I took a sip from my coffee cup, even though it was empty but for the dregs. 'She said that she felt like "her soul had lost all its nutrients".' I did a cod-Valley Girl accent when I imitated the Tamsin that wasn't Tamsin.

Lucy looked like she was waiting for me to finish the thought.

'So painfully earnest,' I concluded.

'Yeah, well.' Lucy started to gather up her stuff – cardigan, handbag, sunglasses. 'I'm having incredibly earnest sex. Who am I to judge?'

I laughed. I always felt relieved when I remembered that our friendship could be more than a tribute act.

We hugged goodbye and I walked up the hill to my bus stop, past the end of the road where the house I'd grown up in stood. My parents had moved to Norfolk two years earlier. They had said they'd always wanted to live by the sea, and I'd felt stupid because I'd never known that before. After things ended with Harry my mum had offered for me to go and live with them, in their little flint cottage.

'You could work in a cafe,' she'd said. I'd pointed out that I was a qualified solicitor, and she'd responded, 'Yes, I know, but that doesn't mean you need to put pressure on yourself.' She'd said it like she was cross with me. I'd told her that I didn't want to leave London.

My phone rang. For a while I didn't realise it was mine. Who calls anyone these days?

The caller ID said Tamsin.

'Hey, girl,' she said, when I picked up. 'Do you eat fish?'

'What?'

33

'Come over. For dinner.'

'It's a Sunday,' I said, after hesitating. 'I've got work in the morning.'

There was a beat, and then she said, 'So what?'

Chapter Three

I BROUGHT WINE. TWO bottles clinking in my backpack. I was worried that it seemed like a lot, but the only way it made sense to me that Tamsin could possibly be living in the heart of central London was if she had some kind of eccentric rich flatmate who would need including.

I bought Malbec, same as the previous night. It made me wish I knew about wine. I downloaded a couple of podcasts about different grapes. Bought a beginner's guide on Kindle for 99p.

I arrived when dusk was just starting to fall on the gay village. Men in tight shirts with sculptural beards, bulging muscles, soft lips, were beginning to spill out of the cafes and into the street. Their glasses of rosé looked delicate and so cold in their tanned hands. They all looked at ease, as if they were with friends, as if it was too early in the evening to even think about seduction.

I pressed on a buzzer, a big old-fashioned thing that looked like it hadn't been replaced in sixty years, more at home in Berlin or Paris than London. There was no answering crackle on the intercom.

I stood there for fifteen seconds or longer, growing more convinced with each breath that there had been some kind of mistake. Maybe this was the wrong house. Maybe Tamsin hadn't meant for me to actually come over tonight. Maybe I'd hallucinated her altogether.

I was about to turn around and go home when I heard my name called from above. I looked up to see a haze of golden hair. There was a clink beside me, metal hitting the pavement.

'The intercom thing's broken. Just let yourself in with the keys. I'd come down but I need to flip the fish in like, eleven seconds.'

She sounded more foreign when it was just her voice. I heard the distant hiss of something sizzling on the stove.

I tried the two keys in turn. The second one opened the front door.

The entrance to Tamsin's building was dark. Maybe I could have found a light switch if I'd groped for it, but I went up the stairs in the blackness. The tall, heavy front door had completely blocked out the noise from the street and the air in here was cooler than the outside evening. The overstimulation of Soho was gone.

When I got to the top of the stairs, there was only one door, and through the door frame, along with the leak of light, I could hear soft guitar music and the hiss of something frying. I slid the key into the lock; the door swung open gently, like it had been waiting only for my touch.

It was hard to say what colour the walls were painted – maybe white, maybe something else. They were bathed in a rosy light that couldn't correspond to a specific paint. The guitar music was louder now, each note cascading after the other like a shower of light rain. A man singing in a strange, soft voice about a pink moon.

The overall impression was bookcases and warm brass, wooden floors so bright they looked bronze, Turkmen rugs in varying shades of crimson, a teal velvet sofa covered in fleecy blankets. French doors framed the Soho facades like a painting, and on the tiny balcony I could see an array of pots spilling herbs – mint, thyme, rosemary.

I thought about my little Sainsbury's plastic pot of basil, drooping listlessly behind the tap in the kitchen of my flat.

Tamsin was standing in the little kitchen area in front of a gas stove, the burners on full blast. The smell was butter and herbs and something sharp and fragrant. The sizzling on the stove was so loud that she didn't say anything, just turned her head to look at me and raised one eyebrow in greeting. Her feet were bare, her hair wet down her back, and she held a spatula in her left hand. She was wearing light blue jeans and a men's white linen shirt, and I realised for the first time how small and slender she was, how large her mane of hair made her face seem in relation to a delicate frame.

I had tried to dress somewhere between casual and elegant, and managed neither. I was wearing jeans and a t-shirt – both black, but faded a bit to grey. The jeans were uncomfortably tight. I'd put on some red lipstick because I had the residual idea from some magazine that it looked 'effortless'.

After she'd taken the fish off the fire, Tamsin finally spoke.

'That lipstick is fucking stunning on you.'

I put up my hand to cover my mouth. 'I just put it on to distract from how slobby the rest of me looks.'

'Welcome to the club.' She eased the two fillets off the heavy iron grill pan and onto square, white plates, then spooned a little bit of caper butter over each. 'I can't wear makeup. It makes me look like a drag queen. Not to imply that isn't an awesome look, so actually maybe not.' She bent down to take something out of the oven. 'I guess what I'm trying to say is that it makes me look like I've been playing with my mom's makeup.'

'Isn't that a bit of a problem if you're an actress?'

'Oh, acting's different. Then, I don't know, the makeup's just part of the role and it all makes sense somehow. But when I'm not playing a part . . .' She waved a hand around her face, which was framed in golden light by the steam of the potatoes. 'This is as good as it gets.'

I didn't know how to present my bottles of Malbec so I just took them out of my backpack and placed them side by side on the wooden kitchen counter. They looked like a pair of miscreants waiting to be told off, but Tamsin smiled widely when she saw them.

'You really went for it,' she said.

I waited for the sarcastic implication to follow, but there was none.

She took the bottles by their necks and slid them neatly into a built-in wooden wine rack next to the kitchen cabinets.

'We're having fish, so I got champagne, which I know is extra as hell but I just felt like it.' She picked up the two plates and carried them across the rugs, past the sofa

to the balcony. A little wrought-iron set of table and chairs
stood in the tiny space, already laid with white napkins, a
candle, a few bright leaves in a jam jar. 'That's okay with
you, isn't it?'

'Yeah, champagne's fine with me.' I was going for
sarcastic, wry, but it came out entitled, so when I spoke
again, I was trying a little too hard. 'This looks unbelievable. I can't believe you cooked this.'

'You arrived at the perfect time.' She settled in her
chair, flicking the white cloth napkin over her lap and
taking the champagne out of its ice bucket. 'You want to
do the honours?'

I shook my head.

She took the bottle, pointed it out, away from the balcony.
The pop wasn't so loud against the music and the noise
from the street, but the cork arced far away, flying across
the road and out of sight among the rooftops. I laughed,
watching the bubbles in my glass swell and then settle.

'I'm sure I'm not the first person to tell you this,' I said.
'But this place is incredible.'

She looked pleased when I said that. I felt touched, like
I'd been extraordinarily kind.

'It's my little mouse hole,' she said. 'I love it so much.
It's tiny and it's noisy and the buzzer doesn't work, but
I just love it.'

The fish was delicious. She'd served it with samphire, which
I'd never had before, and new potatoes roasted with garlic
and rosemary, served straight from the oven in a sky-blue

dish. A basket filled with hunks of deep-coloured sour-dough sat on the table alongside a little dish of golden olive oil, flecked generously with crystals of salt.

'I just get whatever my fish guy tells me is good that day,' she said. 'As long as you can basically sauté a piece of fish you can just wing it and it's fine. It's my go-to.'

'I don't think I have a go-to. Maybe pasta and pesto.'

'That's good though. That means you've got better stuff to do.'

'I think it means I need to learn to cook.'

'People talk about being a good cook like it's some virtue. I'm just gluttonous, dude. It doesn't make me a good person.'

Her slender wrist, holding the champagne flute, seemed to suggest otherwise. But the fish didn't taste indulgent at all, it was light and fresh. I felt satisfied without being bloated.

'Anyway, I'll cook for you any time. Seriously. I love to cook for people, it's my favourite thing in the whole world.'

I wondered if that meant that she cooked for people every night, that maybe I was just Girl Friday and tomorrow there would be another lucky recipient of the Tamsin Experience.

'So anti-feminist, right?' she was saying. 'Our ances-tresses fought for our right to get out of the kitchen and I'm in there all the damn time anyway. All I want to do is feed people. I can't help it, I'm Polish and Italian. We're feeders. We're sad, we eat. We're happy, we eat. I never had a chance.'

The guitar music had stopped and now it was Nina Simone singing, her voice winding out through the open French windows like a silken rope. She sang that she was feeling good, and I sang along. Tamsin sang too, her voice fluting an octave above Nina's, mine indeterminate and off-tune. But I didn't feel self-conscious.

I mopped the scented butter off my plate with a piece of bread and washed it down with more champagne.

I'd only drunk champagne for toasts before, never in any real quantity. I only noticed then that it wasn't sweet like Prosecco or slightly bitter like cava. It was buttery and biscuity and the bubbles seemed to swell in my mouth and fill me up.

'I think I can see what all the fuss is about,' I said, holding my flute up so that it shone softly in the light of the street. 'I'm a champagne convert.'

'You think it's gonna catch on, huh?'

'It's going to be huge.' I grinned stupidly. 'You heard it here first.' Then I felt a bubble popping inside me. 'But it must have cost you an absolute fortune, this and the fish. Will you let me give you some money for it?'

Tamsin finished chewing a mouthful of sourdough crust and then gave me a severe look.

'My mother always said that it's rude to spoil a host's pleasure by offering to pay. And admittedly my mom said a lot of shit, but I took that one to heart. Don't you dare offend me by making this about money.'

I felt chastened, and I must have looked it too, because she softened.

41

'I invited you over, I picked out the food and drink. That's on me, got it?'

'But you got the stuff last night . . .'

She waved it away. 'Babe, it just truly isn't a big deal. It's only money.'

We washed the dishes together quickly, quietly, so easily that it didn't feel like a chore at all. A song I hadn't heard before. *Won't you stay? We'll put on the day, and we'll talk in present tenses . . .* Then we opened one of the bottles of Malbec and Tamsin got out a little box of dark chocolates filled with salted caramel. They were so bitter and so sweet that you only wanted one.

'That was the most gorgeous meal I've had in a long time,' I said, putting one foot over the rail of the balcony and crossing the other ankle on top. Tamsin did the same, closing her eyes and smiling dreamily.

Without looking at me, she reached out her glass to clink mine.

'Perfection,' she said. 'But it's so easy to get good food in London. Easier than New York, even.'

'I thought New York was supposed to be some sort of foodie paradise.' I'd never been.

'Sure. It is. But it's really more about the restaurant scene, or ordering in. People aren't so into good ingredients and cooking at home.'

I couldn't remember the last time I'd selected good ingredients and cooked them at home, but I liked the idea of it. Maybe I could become the sort of person who did that.

'Which is what I learned from my mom, of course,' she continued.

'Right. Italian. How long did you live in New York?'

'Too long, baby.' She rolled her eyes. 'Sorry, that's basically what every New Yorker says. But then they never leave.'

'Yeah, London's like that. People complain about it all the time, but then couldn't imagine living anywhere else. I know I'm guilty of that.' I looked over at her. Her skin had that golden cast again, in the street lamps. 'But *you* left New York.' I said it uncertainly.

'I can definitely see the similarity between the two cities.' She held her wine glass up to the light. 'It's an energy, I guess. An urgency. And in some ways the more chill cities like Montreal are preferable for me because when it's so frantic, you forget how to slow down. But here I am, so I guess that probably says something about what I want, deep down.'

'Which is?'

'To act, to the best of my ability. To get good at my craft.'

'That's all?'

'That's plenty.'

I wanted to ask her how far along she'd got with that. I wanted to ask her whether she thought she really was good, but you couldn't ask someone how accomplished an actress they were. Only how much money they made.

'Do you think you'll stay here?'

She considered it carefully, toying with the silk tissue paper from the chocolate box.

'There's a lot here for me right now, artistically.'

'I guess this is where a lot of the good parts are,' I said tentatively. I was inferring, from what she was saying, that she wanted to do theatre rather than film. I couldn't imagine anyone moving from America to London to make movies.

'It's not so much the parts. Like I said the other night, it's the whole philosophy.' She didn't expand, and I didn't ask.

I was busy biting back the instinctive question – how much did she pay in rent for a place like this? There was no space for any flatmates. What had looked like a bookcase along one wall turned out to be the underside of a set of wooden stairs, which led up to a mezzanine, where I assumed she slept. It was somewhere between a studio and a one-bedroom.

I wondered again if she had many visitors.

With all my other friends the story was predictable. They earned too little and paid too much in rent and got by with overdrafts and credit cards or handouts from their parents, same as I did. Clearly Tamsin's story was different. I didn't want to hear about a trust fund or a windfall from a dead grandparent, or parents who'd bought the flat for the investment. I was like an audience member in a drag show. I wanted the illusion.

I knew that mixing champagne and red wine would give me a nauseous hangover, but that didn't stop me from accepting when Tamsin brought out a bottle of Japanese whisky.

'This stuff's incredible. So smooth, like drinking silk.' She took the smallest sip and then let her head fall back on the sofa, eyes closed. 'Oh my god.'

I'd never had whisky before, let alone this stuff. 'This is gorgeous,' I said, even though I had nothing to compare it to and to me it tasted of rubbing alcohol.

'So good, right? God, I'm pissed.' She laughed. 'British pissed, I mean, not North American pissed.'

'I'm pissed too,' I said. I liked the way that the words sounded authentic in my accent, though I was probably slurring. 'What time is it?'

'One a.m.' As if to agree with her, a grandfather clock that lurked in the shadows under the staircase struck once. She waved a hand at it. 'That's my buddy Earl. Naming a grandfather clock is this whole thing for me. The neighbours hate him cuz he's so loud, but he keeps me company.'

'I love it.' Then: 'Fuck, that means I've missed the last train. I'll have to get a bus.'

'Dude.' Tamsin looked impatient. 'You're crashing here. I'm serious. That daybed is super comfy. Where do you work, anyway?'

'Vauxhall.' One of the tattered charity buildings that sagged gloomily on the other side of the river.

'Perfect. You leave here tomorrow at like, eight thirty, you have a beautiful walk, there you go.'

'People at the office will think I'm doing the walk of shame.'

'Oh, like you care what people at the office think. Anyway, aren't you supposed to work for a feminist organisation?'

'Sure, but—'

'Are you seriously telling me that you're going to get two night buses back to wherever it is you live . . .'

'Streatham.'

'I don't even know where that is. It sounds far away.'

'It is.'

'I mean, it's up to you. Don't let me pressure you or anything. The offer's open, that's all I want to say.'

I stood up and crossed the room to the little daybed. There were a few Berber blankets and a couple of silk cushions. I drew one of the blankets around my shoulders and curled up like a cat.

'This might be the comfiest I've ever been.'

'I fucking knew it.'

Tamsin had a spare toothbrush that she lent me, along with an unctuous creamy cleanser that smelled of roses and some cool, light moisturiser. I had a poke around in the bathroom cupboard and found several unopened boxes of condoms sitting alongside a spartan edit of luxurious body products. Then I had a long wee before I brushed my teeth and stared at the back of the toilet door. There was a framed cross-stitch hanging next to the towel rack.

I rise with my red hair
And I eat men like air.

A little embroidered rose underneath.

'Nice Plath reference,' I said, when I came out of the bathroom.

'You got it? Of *course* you'd get it.'

She produced a huge nightshirt that made me look like Wee Willie Winkie. It hung past my knees and I didn't feel self-conscious about wearing neither knickers nor bra underneath.

She herself had changed into a pink silk kimono, which rustled gently along the floorboards as she moved around, taking tiny steps like a geisha, finding me a towel, pouring a pint of ice-cold water from a jug in her fridge and setting it next to me as I snuggled down among the blankets.

'Goodnight, sweetie,' she said. In the gloom, with the lights out, I could sense that she was smiling at me. 'I don't know if I'll be up to say goodbye in the morning. I'll try, obviously, but I've got crazy insomnia so I just kinda grab sleep whenever I can.'

'No worries.' I was suddenly exhausted, and so comfortable. More than comfortable. Relaxed. 'Sleep well, lovely.'

'You too.'

A swish of her kimono going up the stairs. The soft click of her reading lamp being switched on. The steady ticking of the grandfather clock. Outside, behind the seal of the heavy velvet curtains, life throbbed on deeper into the night.

Even though I was so tired, I slept the light, uneasy sleep that comes with being drunk and in a different bed. I'm not sure what made me realise I was awake. It might have been the sound of her coming down the stairs. The luxurious rustle as she pushed aside the curtains and stepped out

47

onto the balcony. The slice of light from the street lamp cutting across my face.

'Look,' I heard her saying into the phone, her voice tighter and denser than I'd heard it before. 'Yes, I'm calling you back, but I'm just calling back to say don't call me again, okay?'

A pause. A police siren. People, out late and drunk.

Tamsin's voice scraping harsh against the sounds of their laughter. 'I'm done. This thing has been my life for too long, and I'm past it now, all right?'

Another pause. A laugh from the street that could have been a scream.

'I'm not going back there.'

At various points in the night I rolled over, unsure if I could hear Tamsin's regular breathing from above, or if she was still outside, her voice wound as tight as a springing trap.

Chapter Four

I DECIDED TO BUY coffee on the way to work, rather than clatter about in the unfamiliar kitchen and risk waking Tamsin. I didn't have any paper so I tore a blank page out of the Elena Ferrante novel in my bag.

Thank you for a gorgeous evening.

I considered putting kisses, but I remembered that North Americans didn't usually use them. I liked the unadorned elegance of the note without them, the way it didn't rely on the neediness of an exclamation mark.

The coffee from the shop turned out to be the kind that cost four pounds fifty; the sign promised to 'build' me a coffee instead of just making it. The bearded barista squatted down so that the water was pouring at eye level, as if he could control the molecules with his stare. I shuffled from foot to foot. By the time he actually handed it over it was lukewarm and I was running late. I didn't get my leisurely walk across the river. Instead I half jogged it, sweating through the clothes that I'd worn yesterday. Not that anyone at work would really care what I looked like.

I'd been working at the Women's Advocacy Centre for more than six months by then. The role was listed as paralegal, but I think Renee had wanted someone a bit more general. An all-round right-hand woman. A lieutenant, an ally against Mo the office manager, who raised her eyebrows whenever anyone said the word 'feminist', and Jim, the curmudgeonly sixty-something man who came in once a week to do the bookkeeping.

'Morning, Emily.'

Mo was looking quizzically at the coffee in my hand and then at the clock. Five past nine.

I ignored her, addressing my boss instead, who was standing with her own cup of coffee in one hand and a brown card file in the other.

'Sorry, Renee. Train problems.' Then, even though she hadn't said anything in reply, 'I'll stay a bit later tonight.'

'No need,' Renee said briskly.

I felt, as usual, like I'd let her down. Renee always got to the office at seven in the morning and left late at night. She just wanted to be there.

When I was applying for the job, I'd learned that the Women's Advocacy Centre had been set up by a QC called Renee Walcott. From her name and the tone of her *Guardian* opinion pieces I developed an image of her as iron-pressed and glamorous, but that wasn't the truth at all. She was tiny, dumpy, always untidy, her clothes covered in a fine layer of hairs from her golden retriever, Molly, who spent most of her time under Renee's desk. She was there now, and as I passed by the office door she raised her head, looking pleased to see me.

Not everyone in the legal field knew who Renee was, but those who did congratulated themselves on their good taste, as if she were a cult film. When I was applying for the job I waded through a few profiles about how inspiring she was: how she'd been raised by a Jamaican mother (a Windrush nurse), and left unraised by her absentee white British father. How she'd been the only Black woman to be called to the bar that year, one of the first ever. How she'd turned down a Damehood because she didn't want the association with the British Empire.

'You were at the protest on Saturday, Emily?'

Even though she'd grown up in Tottenham, Renee's voice was resonantly, musically, aristocratic. Her mother had taken her to elocution lessons to give her the best chance in life (I learned that one from her *Desert Island Discs* episode). Despite her best efforts, the polished veneer in her voice couldn't be chipped away.

I nodded eagerly in answer to her question, and her eyes returned to the file in her hand.

'Good.'

My story was the usual one for someone who had ended up in the charity sector – I'd swung out of university and into a law conversion course, then immediately into a traineeship at a corporate firm. Not Magic Circle, but the highly profitable rung just below.

I'd crashed out. I hadn't exactly been asked to leave, not in a way that would have left the firm open to any duty-of-care questions. A series of tiny pushes that had added up to a big shove, all done too subtly to ever allow me to know whether Harry had anything to do with it.

When I'd told Renee what had happened in the interview for the Women's Advocacy Centre, she'd told me I had been brave to walk away. I didn't think I had been brave enough to stay, but there was relief in seeing things her way. All the things that I'd assumed made me unprofessional were, according to Renee, good qualities.

I sat down in my usual chair and Renee slid a slender file across the desk.

'Sexual harassment case,' she said briskly. 'Amina, Senegalese woman. Was working on a zero-hours contract as an office cleaner when the boss of the office assaulted her. Bastard's a Tory MP.'

'Oh my . . .'

'Yes.' She shook her head as if my horror was wasting precious time. 'No one to complain to at the time. He had her sign an NDA. She doesn't bloody speak English.'

'God.'

'Now that's what you call covering your arse. My instinct is that he's done this before and run into trouble. Now he knows how to *protect* himself.'

I glanced at the non-disclosure agreement in my hand. In my first job I'd filed dozens of NDAs for corporate clients and even signed a handful myself. This one ran to several pages – longer than the ones I'd encountered doing grunt work on behalf of Gulf royalty. I flipped to the back.

'She didn't know what she was signing,' Renee said. 'My understanding is that she thought he was giving her an employment contract.'

'Reasonable assumption, I guess.'

'No space for reasonable assumptions with these fuckers. She told her husband about the whole episode, he kicked up a stink at the MP's office.'

'Oh god.'

She shook her head again. 'Now the husband's been remanded in custody – and the MP is suing *her* for violating the terms of the NDA.'

'For telling her *husband?*'

'Read it.' She jerked her head at the document in my hand. 'Specific stipulation against telling her spouse. It says she can't tell her *therapist*. As if she's got time or money for therapy.' She gave a tight smile. 'All very American. I suppose it's the newest cultural import.'

I tried to picture Amina in my mind. I could visualise nothing more than a bundle of sighs and sadness.

'Great,' I said, and Renee frowned a little. 'I mean, not great. I mean, let's get to it. Can I make you a coffee, Renee?'

'Nope.' She brandished the mug in her hand before shoving an even bigger sheaf of papers into her bulging old leather handbag. 'I'm off to see Amina. I want you to do a bit of digging. See if there are any rumours floating around about this fucker.'

'Rumours?'

'You know the sort of thing.' She hitched her bag up on her shoulder. 'Do people call him a ladies' man? Do they say he's been *scandalous? Indiscreet?* Any photogenic young aide who might have left his employ suddenly? We'll never get anywhere if we're just talking about . . . about Amina.'

I took the file from her and in the attached photo caught a glimpse of a long neck, almond-shaped eyes, Debbie Harry cheekbones.

It was so easy, so tempting, to imagine myself coaxing a statement out of her, urging her to share her story with the world. Amina in front of the camera, those cheekbones made devastating by the photographer's flash. Me behind the camera, with my gentle encouraging eyes. A front-page news story.

Chapter Five

On Wednesday I decided I needed more friends in London. I texted a couple of people who'd been initiated with me in my corporate law days, saying we needed to catch up. One suggested meeting at a cocktail bar near Gray's Inn.

I spent £45 on cocktails just to be told that nothing had changed at the firm, that I'd done the right thing getting out.

She called me brave. I managed not to ask about Harry all evening.

I downloaded Tinder on the train home. I made my plans for Friday night while I was brushing my teeth for bed, trying to work out the source of the mouldy smell in the bathroom.

Stu, 29, worked in recruitment. Big beard and three-piece suits that I could immediately tell were a substitute for a personality. They were nothing like Harry's navy City boy uniform. No ab shots, no big cats, no children. I flicked back and forth between his three photos and wondered when I'd last changed my bed sheets.

He suggested we meet at Gordon's Wine Bar. I'd always liked it there; the indoor decor made it feel like the cabin of a ship. But Stu had said to meet outside because he was a smoker.

*

The terrace was just next to the Victoria Embankment Gardens, where I'd spent that first evening with Tamsin. It felt like the orientation had been flipped around and everything was facing the wrong way.

I arrived first. I'd realised that if I was going to be drinking with a guy I didn't know, I needed to eat something, so I sat with my handbag on my lap and stole mouthfuls of the Tesco Meal Deal that I'd bought on my way from work. I'd had the same pasta salad for lunch.

On the other side of the gardens the Thames slunk along just out of sight; though the evening was warm there was a chilly breeze sliding along the river.

I could tell Stu wasn't impressed by me the moment he arrived. Yet he still edged closer with each passing drink. He smelled good and the three-piece suits fitted in a way that I kept noticing. I wanted him to fancy me. He opened the date with a lengthy monologue about his boss. I didn't feel bad about doing the same thing back to him, hearing myself casually distorting Renee into a caricature that I wouldn't feel guilty lampooning.

He got up to get another bottle of wine – our third – and I was scrolling through Twitter, watching a captioned extract from some MP's smackdown in the Commons, when my phone buzzed.

Hey!!! How's your week been? I've been in this super intense workshop the whole time but I'm done early today. Are you around? Like right now?

I tapped back hastily. *Hey! Week was okay but I'm currently on a shit Tinder date. Wish I could do something now though.*

A wait, a wiggly line.

I could see Stu walking back towards me with an ice bucket in one hand and two packets of crisps in the other. I turned my phone face down.

'All right?' Stu's face was red from drinking, which made me realise mine probably was too. He clattered the ice bucket and glasses onto the table and sat down heavily. 'Just bear with me a second,' he said, reaching into the pocket of his waistcoat. 'Just need to check on something for work.'

I thought he was going to have a quick look at his email, but he made a call. His whole posture changed to one of ebullience as he squared his shoulders with a bigger smile than the one he'd used to greet me.

'Tariq! Mate! How's it going?' He turned his back on me.

I turned my phone over and opened one of the bags of crisps.

I'm gonna come jailbreak you.

Then.

Send me your location.

I looked at Stu. Considered him. He'd mentioned that he owned his place. Somewhere out in Kent.

'Just a quick train from Charing Cross,' he'd said, nodding at the railway lines over my shoulder. 'You can get there in the time it takes to cross London, easy. And you're in the countryside. Lovely.'

I'd worked my way through exactly half of the first bag of crisps and was eyeing the second.

I could guess almost exactly what I'd be letting myself in for. Probably he'd have some Kiehl's soap in a shower with a rain head, and a dressing gown that he'd let me borrow. He would inevitably have a fancy coffee machine and in the morning he'd ask me if I wanted the beans from Venezuela or Ethiopia. Once we'd silently agreed to never meet again, the coffee together, maybe still naked, might be cosy.

I'd had a bottle of wine to drink, maybe a bit less. A bottle was my hard limit for giving consent.

I looked at his big hands that held the phone to his ear. His fingers were long. Maybe he'd want to wrap them around my throat.

I tapped my phone, and the map blossomed onto the screen.

She appeared within minutes. I saw her from a distance, wearing a little floral slip and brown leather sandals, her hair tied loosely away from her face. When she came closer, I could see that it was the tiniest bit greasy.

When she saw me there was nothing in her face to betray that she'd been seeking me out. It was a tiny master-piece of a performance, played to Stu's back – the slight frown, then the way her face lit up.

'Emily! Oh my god!'

Stu's gaze fell on her like gravity and a boozy smile started to pull at the corners of his mouth.

'I was supposed to be meeting a friend here, but she just bailed.' A little anger tugged at the edge of her voice. 'Fuck this city, man. People are so flaky.'

'Aww, that sucks,' Stu intoned sombrely, though Tamsin's body was angled only towards me. Then, brightly, stowing his phone back in his pocket, he added, 'No worries, you can join us. I'll get you a glass.'

He lurched off along the path, his wavy gait ridiculous in its sense of purpose.

'That there is the walk of a man who genuinely thinks he's going to have a threesome tonight,' Tamsin said. There was something professional in her appraisal.

'One hundred per cent.' I reached for her hand. 'He is so boring.' I pretended to weep histrionically. 'Save me.'

'Girl, why do you think I came?'

'You were here in a flash.'

'I Boris-biked it.'

'You didn't need to do that.'

'No time to lose.' She glanced over her shoulder. 'Let's blow this taco stand before he gets back.'

I sighed. 'I can't.'

'He's an asshole. He probably voted Leave.'

I glanced from side to side. Wondering if the group of paunchy bald men sitting to our left had overheard us. The huddle of women to our right laughed noisily.

'We can't. I've got to make up some excuse, at least. We can't just leave him.'

'Emily, I did not just Boris-bike flat out in a dress to save his feelings. I did it to bust you out. Let's *go*.' She gestured at the exit to the terrace. The gate seemed to edge a little closer.

59

'Excuse me.' I leaned over to the group of suited men, who immediately fell silent, all of them looking at Tamsin. 'My friend's just in the bar and we have to go. Could you keep an eye on his stuff until he gets back?'

We left the table with Stu's leather shoulder bag shoved underneath. Tamsin took the mostly full bottle of wine from the cooler, tucking it neatly under her elbow.

We ran. Unnecessary, but it felt wonderful. We ran across Trafalgar Square. The dress I was wearing required a strapless bra so I held my boobs down with one hand. Tamsin loped ahead, laughing, bronze-limbed and gazelle-like, her sandals slapping the hot pavement. We ran to the rhythm of my phone as it rang, howling from my handbag until the sound of the traffic and the roar of the fountains drowned it out.

We stopped to sit on the graceful marble steps outside the National Gallery without saying anything.

My phone buzzed.

Fuck you bitch

I passed it to Tamsin.

'Well,' she said, typing something quickly in reply and then swiftly blocking his number, 'it's like Ms Maya Angelou says. When someone shows you who they are, believe them.'

'To be fair, I'm the one who ran out on him.'

'Right. And does he say "Hey, where did you go?" Or "Was there something wrong?" or "Did I do something to upset you?"'

I stared at the fountains.

She shook her head. 'No. He goes straight for bitch.'

'Very original.'

'Fuck him.'

'I was planning not to.'

'Smart girl.'

She grinned. I did too, but it was just an automatic movement, mirroring hers.

'Look, you don't need to feel bad.'

I said nothing.

'Did you see the way he was staring at my tits?'

'It was still kind of a dick move to run away. And we took the wine that he paid for.'

'Okay.' She sighed. 'So you didn't handle the situation like the most saintly person in the whole fucking world.'

I waited.

'How are you feeling right now?'

'A bit guilty.'

'*And?*'

'And . . . and a bit free.'

'Right. You pulled a dick move tonight. Now you're a person who sometimes acts like a dick. You're not a saint, you're a free agent. Welcome to the rest of your life.' She paused, and gave a little laugh. 'Take it from me. I was raised Catholic.'

I took my phone back and opened Tinder.

'Oh, wow.' I showed her. 'He's already blocked me.' I shut off the screen. 'That was quick.'

'Shit.' She reached over and very gently took my phone and returned it to my bag. She caught my gaze and carried it away until I was no longer looking at the phone but at her, at the square, at the city lights as the day faded away. 'Now you'll never find a husband.'

'And there was me,' I buried my face in my hands, 'hoping to be wed by Michaelmas.'

'It's a stone-cold tragedy.'

After a few minutes, Tamsin remembered that she still had the bottle of wine pressed to her side and took a long swig. Then she said, 'Here's what we're gonna do. You're gonna have yourself a little sip of wine, then we're going to go back to my place. I'm going full Nora Ephron and making you a carbonara, okay?'

At that moment Tamsin's phone screen lit up and started to vibrate. She frowned, withdrawing it from my sight and switching it off. When she carried on speaking, her tone hadn't changed.

'We're doing carbonara and Beyoncé tonight, and then a hangover cure in the morning, which I suspect you will be needing.' She leaned forward to look into my eyes. 'Does that work for you, ma'am?'

'That sounds perfect.'

With the arm that was holding the wine bottle she reached out and pulled me in for a tight hug. 'I'm so glad I met you,' she said.

I smiled back at her, and was suddenly reminded of how she'd caught sight of me at the bar. How startled she'd seemed, how for a second even I'd believed she was surprised to see me.

'Come on.' She stood up without using her hands, her body moving all as one piece. 'We need to swing by the deli so I can pick up some guanciale. I'm starving. Have you eaten?'

'I had a meal deal at six.'

'So the answer is no.'

We finished the wine in water glasses, ice cubes clinking defiantly. Tamsin put a deep pan of salted water on to boil. I started blasting 'Sorry' by Beyoncé on my phone, and she switched it to Bluetooth so that it came out over a hidden speaker as she started to fry the seasoned meat.

I took the lead vocal, the refrain of *sorry*, while she chimed in, puckish, with the backing line, *I ain't sorry.* I started dancing, twirling my wrists above my head in a way that felt balletic, soothing. I closed my eyes. *I ain't sorry.*

We snacked on little crumbs of Pecorino Romano while the egg yolks and cheese alchemised into sauce. She asked about my work, how I'd got into it.

'My first job – my training contract – was at Radner and Wise.'

'I think I've heard of them. Have I heard of them?'

'Maybe. I mean, probably. Big American law firm. I guess it shows how terrified I was of unemployment that I somehow managed to seem genuinely enthusiastic about working on a merger between two pharmaceutical companies.'

'Bleak.'

'What's bleak is I gave everything I had to that merger. Went back on antidepressants, put on a stone, let my university friendships slide away until there was only Lucy left and only because she doesn't take offence if I never text her back. And then the night it came off, no one bothered to tell me. I wasn't considered important enough. I had to hear it through the intern, Rafe, this kid freshly hatched from Cambridge. Everyone agreed he was very *impressive*. Then I found out I got paid three thousand a year less than a male counterpart – he was my ex, actually – so I quit.'

'Good for you.'

'Easy to pass off humiliation as activism, I guess. If I'd had the balls, I'd have stayed. Gone through the whole tribunal thing.'

'You'd have been wrung out by it, and they'd have won.'

'Sure. Probably should have done it anyway.'

A pause.

'But you didn't.'

For the rest of the evening we listened to pissed-off women. Patti Smith, Janis Joplin, Sinead O'Connor. As we got drunker, I got less embarrassed about my music taste and we played Alanis Morissette, bawling along.

'I know it's naff, but when I was a teenager this spoke to me,' I said.

'It's not naff. Not totally sure what naff means, but it sounds bad.'

'It's not great.'

'The point is . . .' she waved her wine glass around as if she was conducting our conversation, 'I have a personal policy about not being ashamed for liking the things I like.'

'I guess one of the main reasons we're told not to like certain things is because they're by women, right? The feminine is treated as inherently humiliating.'

I thought it was a fairly run-of-the-mill observation, but Tamsin looked glowingly at me.

'You've got a way of putting things,' she said. 'So concise. It took me years to figure out that I felt that way and you just summarised it in one sentence.'

She reached out with her fork and scraped a couple of scraps of carbonara off the plate balanced on the arm of her chair. Her grandmother's recipe, she said. The trick was to add an extra egg yolk.

'It makes dating impossible,' I said to the ceiling. 'Like tonight.' With the last glass of wine Stu had stopped receding from my mind and now seemed to appear at the corners of my peripheral vision, smirking, Harrylike, in a way that left me gulping down my drink nervously. 'There was no way I could have behaved with that guy that would have been honest without being labelled a bitch. And even when they're not like him – even when they seem nice, I'm just waiting for them to trip up. To let on that they actually hate women, deep down.'

'I feel you.'

'It doesn't help, the work I do,' I carried on, the cadence of my speech a little faster even though the words felt sluggish in my mouth. 'Every single day I see all these awful things. Every single bloody day, all these abuses of power, and you start to look at dating and relationships and see that the guy just *always* has the power.'

'Mostly, I guess.'

'Mostly, always . . . Anyway, it's humiliating.'

'Right.'

'So how do you do it?' I shifted on the sofa to look at her, where she was curled up in an armchair. I couldn't imagine her ever letting guys get away with treating her like shit.

'Oh, there's a simple way to do it.'

'Go on.'

'I just don't date, honey.'

I thought I must have misheard her over the furious squalling of the music. 'Sorry?'

She took a sip of her wine, holding eye contact.

'Are you serious?'

'Deadly serious.' She leaned forward to pour herself some more wine. 'I decided a few years back that I wanted to heal my relationship with . . . I guess with the daily pain in the ass that is being a woman. So I made this decision to just not date men for a while.' She took another sip and then said, 'That made it sound like . . . I mean, I don't date anyone right now. Anyone at all.'

'When you say you don't *date* . . . do you also mean . . .'

'Sex?' She said the word as if it signified just another transaction.

'But how do you . . .'

'Vibrators are a thing.'

'Right.'

A long silence. I wanted to phrase myself intelligently. To be clear that I saw her choice as one among many.

'Do you mind me asking . . .'

'Why?' She seemed to have been waiting for this. Her tanned, slender legs were stretched out in front of her, resting on the coffee table, and as she thought about the question she lightly stroked her right calf with her left foot. On someone else it would have looked seductive, but she did it like it didn't matter if anyone was watching. 'It was in response to a bunch of things that happened when I was younger, I guess.'

'Something in particular?' My voice was casual, but I could feel myself growing greedy for the details of her life.

'Kind of. I mean, nothing so big that most people would think that it was worth changing your entire life over. But you know, it mattered. To me.'

'Go on.'

'So . . . I was once on a plane with a bunch of people I was working with. This guy – he was the big cheese, you know? – he followed me when I went to the bathroom and said he wanted to squeeze my tits. To see if they were real.' She looked down at her own chest and flung her arms wide. 'I mean, as if I'd ask for these little golf balls if I was getting plastic surgery.'

Her breasts didn't look like golf balls. In the little slip dress, unsupported, they looked neat, shapely, firm. Beautiful. Not my assessment, really. Just a fact. I knew what beautiful breasts were supposed to look like, and they didn't look like mine. Big but half-deflated, stretchmarked and spilling out to the sides. So unlike Tamsin's that you could hardly say they were the same body part.

'That's disgusting.'

'Foul, right?' She pulled one of the woolly blankets off the back of her chair and wrapped it around herself. 'It wasn't like it was this gigantic thing to me, it was that I'd already met so many men like that. Too many men. I couldn't take it any more.'

'So you just . . . stopped having sex?'

I must have sounded judgemental. Her eyes, which had been lazily half-closed, snapped open. She pulled herself up into a cross-legged position and started speaking in a voice that was different to the one I'd heard before. Urgent, and rhythmic in its urgency.

'People talk all the fucking time about female sexual liberation, right? And what do they mean by that? They mean you can fuck any way you like. Fuck guys. Fuck girls. Fuck in an open relationship, fuck in the ass, fucking let him come on your face, whatever. But you'd better *be* fucking. And fucking had better be the thing that defines you.'

'Yeah,' I said. I wanted to say it with all the courage of my convictions, but it just sounded like I was providing punctuation for her speech. Soft, crackly notes bent through the room. *I'm a fool to want you . . .*

'But what about liberation from having to have sex at all?' she continued. 'When a woman makes art that's about sex it's supposedly this big subversive thing. Oh! She wants to fuck all these guys. So *empowering*, right? Well, I'm bored talking about female sexuality. I'm done with it.' She waved her hand through the air, as if to capture a little bit of Billie's voice. 'What about female existential terror? Female world-weariness? Female craving for power? Why is the only thing that's interesting about a woman the way she wants to fuck? Why do we have to be so *up for it* all the goddamn time?'

I didn't say anything for a while. Tamsin wasn't making any noise, but her breastbone was moving slowly, heavily, as if she was trying to control her breathing.

'It was like that with my ex,' I said.

Tamsin looked up at me sharply.

'It wasn't that . . .' I hurried to clarify. 'I don't know. Maybe this is totally unrelated . . . But when you were talking I just . . .' She was still listening intently. 'It was just sometimes . . . there were things . . . like you said. Things that if you said them out loud, they wouldn't seem worth changing your entire life over. But they mattered. To me.'

Tamsin said nothing.

'And . . . and I wish I thought about it less than I do. I wish I was more over it than I am. Because so many women have it so much worse and . . . and, well . . . he was nice most of the time,' I finished.

'Do you want to tell me what it was he did?'

'I would if I could put it into words,' I said, very quietly. 'But that just feels . . .'

'Impossible,' Tamsin finished softly. 'It's okay. I get it. This is the ex who's a lawyer?'

'Yeah.'

'You could tell someone. You know. At the law firm. When you're ready. One day.'

'No one would believe me.' The words were out of my mouth before I could process them. 'I mean to say . . . No, no, it wasn't that serious. It wasn't . . . you know. It was just, I don't know. Him being a bit selfish, me being a bit naïve.'

For a time, neither of us spoke.

Finally I said, 'I'm glad I didn't go home with that guy tonight.'

'I am too. I'm glad you're here.' She picked up the wine bottle and made to pour me more, but it was empty. 'Okay, I guess that's our cue to go to bed. Billie agrees.' That voice seeping from the speaker, like silk and shrapnel.

'I'm seeing the new film about her next week. *Baltimore Holiday.*'

'The Rawlings one? Yeah. He'll do her justice.' She sighed softly.

'She deserves justice.'

She reached her glass forward to clink with mine.

'One more for the road, okay?'

'Cheers.'

'I prefer this to the Sinatra version, don't you?'

'I do.'

I drained my glass. My vision was blurred and all that registered was the brass squall of the trumpet, the labyrinth of Billie's voice. Tamsin's face luminous in the yellow light.

We didn't even discuss whether I was going to stay over; I found the same nightshirt as before, brushed my teeth, and drifted off into a heavy sleep.

Chapter Six

THE REST OF THE apartment seemed blurred out; the only thing that I could see in focus was a pint-sized mason jar of sparkling water, radiant with ice and an iridescent slice of lime. A wedge of light parted the heavy curtains and cut through the glass, and all the bubbles fizzed up, diamond-bright. A blister pack of paracetamol sat next to the glass, within reach but still too far away to contemplate trying.

Out of the upper frame of vision there was a slow cascade of old gold, and Tamsin's face floated into view. She was bending over me, her cheeks tight to hide her overflowing grin.

'Feeling a little off, huh?'

I grunted.

'If you drink that water I'll let you have a coffee.'

'Coffee.'

'You've got to rehydrate first.'

'Hm.'

'I'm not feeling so hot myself. Luckily for you, I'm up to fixing us a couple of bagels, and then we'll be feeling a ton better.'

It took me a few minutes to sit up; when I did I found that the pain in my head wasn't as bad as expected.

After I'd drunk the water and soothed my parched throat, I started to find the faint nausea almost pleasant.

Tamsin was moving unhurriedly around the kitchen, geisha-like in her pink kimono, Radio 4 leaking out of a little box on the kitchen shelf. I could hear eggs frying, the smell of the yolks equally appealing and repelling.

'I can help,' I mumbled ineffectually.

Tamsin turned to me and laughed, bending at the waist.

'Sorry . . . I don't mean to be mean . . . you just look like the most hung-over person who's ever lived. Here.' She picked up a silver coffee pot and held it out to me. 'Take this out to the balcony. There's spare sunglasses out there for you too. I figured you'd need them.'

It reassured me, when she had placed the two plates on the table and put her bare feet up on the rail, hugging the fabric of her kimono to her stomach, that she looked worse for wear too. The greasy sheen to her hair had deepened, and her golden complexion had dropped and sallowed. She saw me looking and let a little laugh escape.

'I know, I look like shit.'

'I wish my version of looking like shit looked like that,' I mumbled, then glanced back at my plate. 'This looks amazing.'

'I get them delivered from those little twenty-four-hour places in Brick Lane. You know them? Closest thing I've found to a New York bagel. They're like, half the size, but whatever. And for the record, a New York bagel isn't as good as a Montreal bagel, but we'll let that slide for now.'

She'd filled the poppyseed-dusted bagels with sliced avocado, a fried egg, a little drizzle of searing-hot sauce, little pickles glowing magenta. The first bite was difficult and made me gulp, but the second bite seemed necessary, and by the time I'd finished it my stomach was settled. I washed it down with a great swig of black coffee and felt like I'd been made anew. Even the thin shaft of pain running through my skull wasn't objectionable: just a sharpening, a heightening.

Below us, Soho was waking up. A young Mediterranean man was sitting on the steps of the jazz club across the street, the neck of his white shirt open wide, a mug of coffee in one hand and a cigarette in the other. Opposite, an Italian cafe owner strode back and forth, irritated, it seemed, that the weather wasn't to his liking. An old man with a long white beard and a morning suit in blue and gold Liberty print was walking a toy poodle. A rubbish truck was rattling down the street, spraying out its foul smell and the screech of its brakes. Birds sang.

We drank the pot of coffee, saying very little, focusing instead on letting the sun fall onto our faces and warm our blood. I held my forearms out, pale undersides up, in the hope that the near-translucent skin would soak up a little more sunshine.

'As far as hangovers go, this isn't bad.'

'Pretty perfect, right? Enjoy it while it lasts.' Tamsin pushed her sunglasses an inch down her nose so she could give me a severe look. 'Once I've finished my coffee I'm gonna cure that hangover completely.'

'You make that sound ominous.'

'I bet you want to lie around eating mac and cheese and watching Netflix today, right?'

'Those serial killer documentaries aren't going to watch themselves.'

'We're getting out. I have my tried-and-tested hangover cure. I'm pretty evangelical about it.'

'Hair of the dog?' I was looking at the opposite balcony. I could see a hairy middle-aged man with a prominent gold earring cracking open a can of beer, taking a long slug and then balancing it on his over-tanned belly.

'British people think that's the solution to everything.'

'Are we wrong?'

Tamsin shrugged, drained her cup and stood up.

I was still wearing my dress from the previous night. In the jaundiced light of the Northern Line I realised how bad I must smell. I felt my bare legs scratching and sticking to the harsh velveteen on the seat covers.

A man a few seats down and across from us was wearing an unseasonable parka. He was staring at Tamsin. The raging clatter of the train, close in my ears, was inextricable from the aggression of his gaze, and I felt a strong urge to seize Tamsin's hand and get off the train, to get away from him, all the while pretending not to notice the cold, stony look on his face.

But Tamsin caught his eye and gave an exaggerated smile, waving. He looked away quickly.

'If some dude's staring at me I like to remind him that I'm a fucking human being,' she said to me once we'd alighted onto the platform. 'It freaks 'em out.'

'He looked like a psycho. But I always feel like I'm the one being rude. Assuming they're staring,' I said. 'I feel like I ought to give them the benefit of the doubt.'

Tamsin shrugged. 'That's how they get you,' she said.

Walking through the streets between the tube station and Hampstead Heath the sun felt too harsh.

I started muttering at intervals, 'We drank too much last night. We drank too much.'

Tamsin took up the chorus, and in her mouth the words morphed from self-reproach into celebration, the secret joy of getting away with something.

I heard the pond before I saw it.

'See? Hangover cure.' Tamsin arced her arm out in front of her, as if she were giving me my own city as a gift. 'You've been here before, right?'

I felt a failure. I shook my head.

'But you're from London?'

'Wimbledon.'

'Wimbledon has a heath, right?'

'A common. Anyway, it's a different . . .'

'Part of town? System of values? Set of possibilities?'

'It's right at the other end of the Northern Line,' I finished. Then, 'Tamsin, you realise that I don't have a swimsuit, right?'

'Aha!' She gestured at her capacious tote bag. 'Luckily for you, I have a spare.'

'I can't . . .' I wanted to say that I couldn't possibly invade her like that, or else be invaded, by the idea of wearing something of hers – a second skin. 'I can't fit into your swimsuit. I'm twice your size.'

She gave me a severe look.

'That just, quite simply, isn't going to be a problem,' she said.

And it wasn't. The plain black garment – the kind that could only be described with the Victorian-sounding 'swimming costume' – fitted fine. It didn't pinch at the shoulders or crotch. It didn't flatter me; it didn't need to. It held me, without holding me in or back.

I wasn't expecting Tamsin to get undressed in front of me. I didn't look at her for long, but enough to confirm that, naked, Tamsin had the kind of body that meant she was allowed to like herself. It wasn't that she was so skinny – she wasn't, you couldn't see a trace of slicing hip bone, no echo of ribcage. But she seemed to be made of something sleek and firm that confined her body into taut, sinewy lines. My body was undisciplined compared to hers. I was distantly disappointed to see that she'd had a Brazilian wax. I held a towel in front of me so that my unkempt pubic haircut was covered.

There were several old ladies walking around and chatting, completely naked but for their neoprene socks.

Tamsin saw me looking at them and smiled, saying quietly, 'I love it here. It took me a while to get used to it. People are such prudes in North America. I've been trying to be more European about nudity.'

'Europeans can be prudes too.'

'German. They like to get naked, right? Whatever. It's helped me a lot, seeing all these buck-naked sisters grabbing life by the balls.'

I laughed, though a small, gnarled part of my mind wanted, for the first time, to snap at her, to wonder what it was about living in a perfect body that she needed so much help with.

But any spiked thoughts disappeared when I stepped into the water. Though it promised to be a warm day, the sun still wasn't high in the sky, and when I put a foot in I gasped at the chill.

'You'll get used to it,' Tamsin said. She was already immersed up to the neck, her old-gold hair gleaming through a fine layer of dark silt. 'It's just cold relative to the air. It's not going to kill you.'

She held out her arms to me, swaying slightly as she trod the dark water. Instinctively I held my own arms back, like we were a mother–baby pair learning to swim together. There was a strangely coloured bruise, about the size of a walnut, on the inside of her bicep. She saw me looking.

'Where did you get that?'

'No idea. I bruise like a peach,' she said. The cliché was incongruous in her mouth.

I immersed myself to the shoulders, forced long, slow breaths. She was right, of course: the water was cold. But it was pleasant, not cruel. It seemed thicker than other water, and velvet-dark. It moved gently and independently;

I was sure there must be some great dark fish sliding along the bottom. The thought didn't disturb me.

I tilted my head back so that the water reached my hairline. Only my face remained above the surface. I bent my legs behind me and arched my back, hanging suspended, like a wheel. I ran my hands lightly across my stomach and hips. I seemed to have taken on some of that sleek, otter-like quality. When I pulled in a breath the air seemed to flow to my lungs more easily than usual. If I swam here every day, I thought, I might grow muscular, like a salmon swimming upstream.

'Isn't it perfect?' Tamsin twisted her body, floating, her hair billowing like Ophelia.

I'd never tried floating before but I found that I could. I lay back in the water like a bed and listened. To the birds, to the soft wave of chatter from the meadow beyond the pond, to the rustle of leaves, the lap of water against Tamsin's body. Then I rolled over and began to swim, the water parting to welcome me, a silky veil to cover me and hold me close. Through the noises of splashing, rustling, talking, there was a great and generous quiet.

Then something happened.

With my ears still underneath the water, flattening out the world, I heard the distant *fuck off*.

I felt so dreamy that it seemed part of the landscape. But then I heard it again.

Fuck off.

One of those brayingly posh voices like some mouldering antique, rich and fruity and fermented. *Fuck off.*

I rolled in the water to see a shower-capped woman standing on the wooden deck, feet planted firmly, hands on the hips that must have been somewhere beneath the acres of swimming costume and sagging flesh.

'You've no fucking right to be here! Get out! Now!' she bawled.

My first thought was that she was talking to me. But then I flipped in the water, no longer otter-sleek but clumsy, splashing myself and Tamsin, and heard a sound that seemed to exist apart from the soft hum of the clearing.

A click.

A camera shutter.

The shouting woman was pointing theatrically, gesticulating with the other hand at the yellow t-shirt-clad lifeguard. They formed a council of war, faces hardening against the intruder.

My first impulse was to laugh. But then I heard Tamsin give a little cry. That sound was made distant by the splash of half a dozen swim-capped women as they darted through the water to form a ring around us. They'd taken up the chant of the first posh woman and they too were yelling, 'Fuck off, fuck off,' in the direction of the camera lens.

For a few seconds Tamsin's head dipped below the surface; then she re-emerged, a distinct cast of olive green in her bright hair, her face white against the dark water.

'He's gone, I think,' one woman said after a few minutes. She sounded out of breath. 'I suppose he was perving after you girls. We don't get men trespassing here for us old bags.'

79

I gave a shaky little laugh. Tamsin was already striking out for the wooden deck.

'Ghastly,' the woman said grimly.

'Wanking off, no doubt,' an old lady of at least eighty added sagely. 'They used to climb the trees to do it in my day. I haven't seen one of those pervs for a few years. Disgraceful.' She looked at me and added, 'Look after your friend, dear. She's upset.'

I started, splashing up water. When I turned, I saw that Tamsin had climbed the ladder out of the pond and was talking to the lifeguard, her arms wrapped around her body. She looked skimpy, her sexless black swimming costume hanging baggily off her frame.

As I swam closer I heard the lifeguard – all tanned, muscle-corded limbs and bright blue eyes – say briskly, 'It's not a regular thing, you know. It's the first time I've ever had something like that happen, and I've been doing this six years.'

'I know,' Tamsin said quietly. 'Don't worry, Jan, it takes more than an asshole like that to scare me off.'

Jan gave a tight, sympathetic smile and patted Tamsin on the shoulder. The slap of dry skin on wet was harsh. 'Towel,' she instructed. 'No shower. You're shivering.'

I climbed the metal ladder to the deck and stood behind Tamsin. At first she didn't notice I was there; when she turned, I realised that for a moment she didn't recognise me. Perhaps the moment when she had disappeared under-water had washed away the surface friendship, and reminded her that we didn't really know each other at all.

'Bloody men,' I heard Jan mutter as I followed Tamsin back to the changing rooms.

But to me he wasn't just a man. To me, in that brief moment when I caught sight of him, the fragment of recognition, made him more than a rustle of leaves, a click, a swift reminder that the pond was too deep for my feet to touch the bottom. I had recognised the face, the coat, the eyes, and then slipped beneath the surface, water filling my mouth like a gag.

Chapter Seven

'That guy.'

I had to lean in close to whisper. Tamsin's eyes were huge.

'That guy, Tamsin.'

'What about him?'

'He was the same guy who was staring at us on the tube.'

I had waited until we were both dressed again to say it. The only thing that could have made me feel more frightened and exposed was if I'd spoken the words aloud when I was still half-naked, my skin sticky from the water.

For a second her great cat's eyes seemed to dilate, but then she shook her head.

'I don't think so, Emily.'

'Tamsin, I'm sure. I saw his face. I saw that ridiculous jacket. It was the same guy.'

'So you're saying he followed us.'

'He must have done.' I leaned even closer to her, my eyes darting from side to side. 'I mean, that's fucking *weird*, right? He must have got off the tube after us and . . .'

But she was shaking her head slowly. 'Emily, I really don't think it was the same guy. It doesn't make sense.' She seemed, in a moment, to iron out all the creases in her face. 'I guess there are just a lot of perverts in parkas in London. Hey, maybe they all shop at the same stores?'

'Tamsin, I—'

'Come on,' she said firmly. 'Whoever he was, let's just forget him. Fuck that asshole, okay?'

I remembered how she'd looked standing on the wooden deck, hugging herself, suddenly little girl-ish. So I just nodded and said no more.

The tree-lined path from the pond to the rest of the Heath didn't feel inviting, secluded, the way it had when we'd walked down it an hour earlier.

We walked into Highgate, trying to claw back the day, paying special attention to pretty houses, dogs and window boxes. We didn't head for anywhere in particular but snaked our way through the streets. Bit by bit, the colour started to seep back into the flowers and the sky.

We went into an overpriced bakery, away from the exposure of the streets. Inside, the queue pressed close. My skull felt paper-thin, as if it might collapse just from the sound of the coffee machine. I wasn't hungry, but I ordered a pot of Earl Grey and scones anyway.

'Clotted cream was one of the great revelations of moving to London,' Tamsin said. 'I need to find more ways to use it.'

'When I'm an old lady,' I said, spreading clotted cream and jam with Jackson Pollock abandon, 'I plan to get heavily into jam-making.'

'With a whole shelf of jams.'

'All different colours. Like jewels.'

'Live like a witch somewhere in the woods. Going out at midnight to pick berries for your jammy potions.'

'Eating scones every day.'

'Your clotted cream bill will be through the roof.' Tamsin poured my tea. 'Can I come?'

'Sure. We can be celibate, jam-making witches together.'

'The patriarchy's gonna be so fucking scared of us.'

I only insisted that we go back to the Heath because it felt like something Tamsin would have done. That I needed to wear her mantle for a while, until she was able to take it back.

We raided the supermarket with buccaneering spirit. Ciabatta and Boursin and garlic-stuffed olives, baba ghanoush and hummus, chilli squid, salt and vinegar crisps. A ball of burrata, cherry tomatoes on the vine. A tiny packet of smoked salt. A bag of ice cubes, a pack of disposable cups. Two bottles of crémant.

I paid, feeling magnanimous, not looking at the price on the card reader.

While we were walking back to the Heath, Lucy called. In fact, she called twice. The first time, I didn't pick up, assuming it was a butt dial. Lucy never called me.

'Hi,' I said when I answered the second time, casual to hide my confusion.

'Hi.' Her voice was small. Or maybe it was the same as it'd always been. I wasn't used to talking to her on the phone.

'What's up? Are you all right?'

'Yeah.' There was a soft crackling sound and then her voice seemed to break through something. 'Yeah, I'm fine, how're you?'

She was calling to cancel our standing date, which I'd forgotten about. I reassured her that it was fine, all fine. She didn't seem to want to give the reason, and I figured we'd been friends for too long for me to ask. Mostly I was just wondering why she hadn't just texted.

I hung up and transferred the double load of plastic carrier bags back into balance. 'Sorry, that was my friend Lucy. The one I see on Sunday mornings. She cancelled for tomorrow, so I'm freed up.' I shrugged as best as the weighty carrier bags would allow.

'Why?'

I considered, then it came to me. 'Probably ovulating.'

'What?'

'Yeah.' I nodded grimly. 'She told me last week. She and her boyfriend have decided they want a baby like, *now*. She probably cancelled so she could stay home and *try*.'

Tamsin looked grave. 'My god.'

'I . . .' I opened my mouth and closed it again, as though I were reconsidering what I was about to say. 'I mean, she's my friend. I love her and everything.'

'But?'

'But . . . she's made some weird choices over the last few years.'

'Like, societally weird?'

'No, no . . .' We were re-entering the Heath now. 'The opposite, in fact. She's just turned out so *conventional*. I mean, I suppose most people are conventional. By definition.'

'Maybe she's the kind of person who needs to feel safe.'

'But she was always so . . . so smart and thoughtful and quiet. And when she was a teenager, you always had this sense that she was a dark horse, that she was going to blow all our minds one day by doing something amazing. But then something happened and . . . Oh, it was all very weird, I won't go on about it.'

Tamsin gave me a careful look. 'So what does she do now?'

'She's an English teacher at a secondary school. Her big ambition is to be made Head of Year.' I wrinkled my nose. 'In *Croydon*.'

'What's Croydon?'

'Exactly.'

The early blue promise of the day had dissipated and now the sky was blanketed in a layer of anaemic white cloud. A few people didn't seem to have realised, still sunbathing with their skirts pulled to their hips and their white stomachs out, mirroring the sky.

'And now she wants to have a baby, and she and Andrew want to buy this flat and it's a new build and it's got good transport links and schools nearby, and it'll get them on the ladder and it's all so sensible and safe.'

'But?'

'But . . . oh, I don't know. The world's burning. And they want to add another person into it.'

When Tamsin opened one of the bottles of crémant, the cork arced out of the neck and disappeared off into the panorama, seeming to alight somewhere between the thorny upcroppings of the Barbican. I took two plastic glasses from the packet and held them out while she poured. We brushed them together; of course there was no clink. 'To day drinking,' she said.

'In defiance of hideous men everywhere.' I raised my cup, toasting the skyline. 'This is ours, and no fuckface with a camera can take it away from us.'

She leaned her head on my shoulder. 'I'm glad I'm here, with you.'

'Me too. I love it here.'

'The Heath's special. And the Ladies' Pond. When I moved to London, it was September. I was doing this acting workshop in Highgate and I started coming here every day, first thing in the morning.'

'Bloody cold. September. Oof.'

'Yeah. It was cold.' She said it almost reverently. 'There were all these ladies here, ladies like you saw in the changing room, and they just embraced me. Not in a big gesture. Just in that way that women of a certain age have. I was so scared to swim. I thought that if I was cold, if I was uncomfortable, I'd . . . I don't know.' She cracked a cherry tomato between her teeth. 'I guess I thought I'd die.'

'I think *I'd* die if I went outdoor swimming in September.' I wished, as soon as I'd said it, that I wasn't always so flippant.

'There's this thing,' she continued, 'about cold water. It makes you realise, when you get in, that there's no use for your panic. You've got to keep moving forward.'

'Like a shark.'

'It's impossible to think about anything else. You can lie awake all night tangled up in a thought, but when you get into that water, it cuts straight through all that mess. You're cold – you're really fucking cold – but that thought can't get to you any more.'

'I could use a bit of that. Wish I lived nearer to here.'

'I swam all the way through the winter. I swam on Christmas morning. And you see all these other women swimming around you and you realise you're all there for a reason.'

'Right. All been through some shit. All dealing with fucking perverts. Like that guy this morning. You know, I'm really sure it was the same—'

'I know what you mean,' Tamsin interrupted. 'That sense that they all kind of merge into one predator.'

That hadn't been what I meant at all, but I nodded anyway. 'Everyone's got that history, I guess. Everyone's got a story. I remember one time when we were teenagers, this guy followed Lucy and me around town for hours. He was saying the most awful things, pornographic things. And all these people around us could hear. And nobody said anything.'

'Was that the thing that happened?'

I smeared a piece of bread with Boursin. 'What do you mean?'

'Earlier. You said that something happened to Lucy. Was that the thing?'

'Oh no, that was . . .' I chewed my bread. I couldn't say 'Oh no, that was normal'. I swallowed and shrugged. 'That was just, I suppose, one of those little traumas that every teenage girl goes through.'

Tamsin's face darkened. 'Sure.'

'So, yeah. No, the thing that happened with Lucy wasn't really a *trauma*. It was just so weird. And she was so weird *about* it.'

'And what was "it"?' She poured me more crémant. 'I mean, you don't have to tell me. I know she's your oldest friend and everything. I don't want to push you into spilling her secrets.'

'Oh, it wasn't a secret,' I said quickly. 'I mean, half our year knew. It was just one of those weird things, one of those mortifying teenage mistakes. I guess she must have been really embarrassed because she just lost her edge afterwards, like I said.'

'So something big must have happened?'

'Something . . .' I started, then stopped. 'So, there was this teacher.' I paused. Really just to make it seem like I was reconsidering, that I wasn't just going to tell it all to a woman I'd known a week. I remembered Lucy's voice on the phone: how small it sounded, and how unlike her it was to call me. Out of the blue.

89

Chapter Eight

'SO YOU KNOW I told you about my school?'

'The hothouse?' Tamsin nodded. 'Sure.'

'The all-girls neurosis factory, manufacturing doctors and lawyers on demand for the edification of middle-class parents who lived in the right catchment area. Right. You'd take some young guy – maybe twenty-three or twenty-four, in a River Island suit with an ego problem – and set him loose among all this . . . this burgeoning female flesh. And at first he'd obviously like all the attention and feel like he was this real . . . god, I don't know. A stud. That's a cliché, but that was what it was. A pure fucking cliché.'

'Wow.'

'You know that wild, uncontainable adoration that you can feel for another person when you're a teenager? That obsession that you'll probably never feel again? I think that for most of the girls in that school that whole rite of passage was directed at the male teachers. But never Lucy. She was always a bit more far-sighted than the rest of us. More mature.'

There had been lust in that school, plenty of it. Our class noticeboard had been decorated with the objects of our affection – American actors, Korean pop stars. Obama, who'd just been elected. Mufasa, from *The Lion King*. Everyone agreed that even if he was just a cartoon lion, he was a hot lion.

I thought back to the way I'd felt at the time, like I needed to show that I had crushes too, to prove to myself that I felt something. But Lucy never seemed caught up in that. I remember seeing Lucy getting changed for PE, being faintly amazed to see the front of her white cotton knickers swelled by a sponge of pubic hair.

'So that was why it was so incongruous, what ended up happening.'

Tamsin filled my glass again.

'We had this one teacher. He was the fun teacher. Strict. Not just in the sense of getting us to count beans. He wanted us to understand things. He was our English teacher—'

'Of course.'

'. . . Of course. But he was interested in all sorts of things. He loved politics. Physics. He started this jazz ensemble in the school. He played the piano.'

I looked over at Tamsin. She was listening intently, staring out across the cityscape with a little crease in her brow.

'There were rumours about him.'

'There always are,' Tamsin said. 'About any fun teacher.'

'Nothing too extreme,' I said quickly. 'Just little things. You know – the kind of thing that might actually be true. That he told some of his favourite students to call him by his first name. That he invited his sixth-form classes over for dinner parties at his house so they could talk about poetry.'

'Of course he did.'

'No one thought it was such a big deal. He had a wife, whatever. I remember, she was a surgeon. He talked about her a lot. This gorgeous, aspirational woman. They used to turn up together at school functions and it was like a spotlight fell on them. They were beautiful.'

'When you're a kid, people like that have this glow around them.'

'Exactly.'

I looked over at Tamsin. Even in the flat white lighting of this half-blown summer's day, she seemed to have a burnish of her own.

'Anyway, his big passion was getting young people involved in politics. He used to berate us – in this really funny way – for not understanding how parliamentary democracy worked. He'd wave a whiteboard pen around and yell that if we didn't understand how the system worked, then there was no hope. It made us feel important. Like there was a purpose to knowledge. Beyond passing exams, I mean.'

'That must have been . . .' Tamsin stared off across the city. 'Seductive. For a little hothouse plant. To receive what you'd lacked for so long.'

I nodded.

'It was our GCSE year. We were all so caught up, we went completely mad. Apart from Lucy – I think she knew it was just a means to an end. Anyway. There was a general election. I remember Mr Hawkins decided that we should hold a hustings for local MP candidates. None of us could vote yet. That wasn't the point. He said that we needed to take responsibility for growing up. He got a team of us together – about fifteen girls, including me. And Lucy. We set up this event. Most of the school came – loads of parents. He got promoted to deputy head off the back of it.'

He'd MC'd the whole thing. I remembered looking at the shape of his shoulders, the drape of his tie, and thinking how much more real he looked, how much more right, than the clutch of politicians and would-bes up on the stage. How comfortable he'd seemed, how he'd held them to account.

'And then, afterwards, there was – I guess, an after-party. At his house.'

He'd made it sound like such an obvious thing for us to do. We'd all got the train to his house together, tracing out the commute that he took every day. We'd all known that he took the train to school; there had been excited reports from a girl who got on at the same station as him, how sometimes they chatted on the platform, that he always bought a Diet Coke from the vending machine in the mornings.

Tamsin gave me a long look. 'So you were all at a party. At your teacher's house. Totally fucking normal.'

'We were sixth-formers – nearly. His wife was there. A couple of other teachers. There was food and music – jazz, like he loved.'

93

I could hear it even now. It had been the first time I'd heard *Kind of Blue*. Those first uneasy chords, then the way they resolved themselves. I remember thinking, *I get this*.

'He'd invited all these local youth activists and the sitting MP.' Who'd been drunker than anyone and looked down all our tops. Gross, we'd all agreed. A gross old man. 'And . . . I know, we should have been out at house parties with guys our own age, shagging. But we weren't. And we were the kind of insufferable teenagers who pretended to look down on that stuff anyway. And people had brought wine and his wife had chilled all these bottles of Prosecco for us.' The glass in my hand, the unfamiliar feeling of holding a flute lightly.

I remembered looking at Mr Hawkins, learning to make eye contact as I raised the glass to my lips. Standing outside his back door, talking to him about where I wanted to go to university, talking about poetry. I'd just read 'The Love Song of J. Alfred Prufrock' for the first time. I think I recited a little bit of it to him. The memory made my insides shrivel.

'And I guess at some point we were all too pissed and we trooped home, vomiting all the way, and that was that.'

'And Lucy?'

Someone had asked where Lucy was once we were all on the train together, and we'd all giggled guiltily at each other, amazed that we'd gone this far, that we had been drunk enough to leave one of our number behind. There had been reports from someone that Lucy had gone home early, and I'd said, 'That sounds like her.'

And no one thought any more of it.

'I honestly don't remember her disappearing. That's scary, isn't it? She could have been anywhere.'

'You were – what?'

'Sixteen.'

'And drunk.'

'I guess so.'

'So he took her upstairs and fucked her.' Tamsin's voice was flat. Worn-sounding.

I reached to pour myself more crémant. There was no sense in eking it out. I divided the rest of the bottle between our plastic cups.

'Yeah. I guess.' I wanted to sound as world-weary as Tamsin. I sighed. 'I mean, the thing is, we actually *were* surprised. He was married.'

That had seemed like such a strange thing for a person to be, at the time. A real person, not just a parent.

'She said that it was all above board, that he'd told her he and his wife were in this open marriage – this was way before any of us had heard the term open marriage or open relationship. He . . . Yeah. They had sex.'

It had come out a couple of weeks later, at someone's sixteenth birthday party. All of us teasing Lucy, trying to drag it out of her, until eventually she muttered, 'He had sex with me.'

A moment of stunned silence. Then a clutch of delighted whoops. A collapsing sensation in my chest, like my friend was a citizen of a new country, that I was a stranger to her now.

'Huh.'

'This . . . whatever it was, it dragged on for a while. The whole time we were in sixth form. She sometimes didn't mention it for months at a time. He used to come and see her, when we went off to Oxford.'

He'd prepared us both for the interview. Or rather, he prepared her, and she passed on the book lists and practice interview questions to me. Sometimes he stopped me in the corridor and asked me to pass on a message for her, only ever some variation on 'see me'. I'd tell Lucy, and try to draw her into speculating on exactly what it was that he might want. There would be looks between them in class, a strong golden thread binding them together that some- times, tenuously, seemed as if it might also include me.

'It petered out eventually, I guess. And I don't think it was like, this damaging thing, because really soon after she met Andrew, and now he's her . . . I don't know. Future baby daddy. Partner. He's her person.'

'And she was how old again when this started?'

'Sixteen.' A long pause. 'Legal, in this country.'

'Legal. Sure.' Tamsin opened the second bottle of crémant. This time the cork didn't fly off but simply slipped away with a dull thud. 'My little sister's sixteen.'

I said nothing.

'So Lucy is off doing her teacher thing now,' Tamsin said, as if continuing the story for me. 'Doing well. No harm done, you think. And he's where?'

I shrugged and held out my cup, indicating for her to top me up.

'I hope to god he's not still a teacher,' she continued.

I could see Mr Hawkins so clearly in my mind's eye. I wanted to show him to her, to make her understand him fully. To see that there was no question: this man was born to teach. I could still remember every word he'd said about every poem that had ever mattered to me.

'Well, he had this meteoric rise. Like I said, he became deputy head off the back of doing all these extracurricular activities with the girls.' I paused. If I'd been with my school friends, we might have cackled over the double entendre, but Tamsin didn't react at all. 'Then head of another school a year later. I think he got divorced. He became this sort of super-head, got this reputation for turning schools around. He advises the government on educational policy now. He goes on the radio quite a lot. Getting kids involved in politics, stuff like that. As far as I know, that's what he's still doing.'

'He still works with *kids*?'

'Mostly sixth-formers, I think,' I said. 'Or . . . I'm not sure. Maybe he's totally on the policy side now.' Tamsin was looking very closely at me. 'I'm pretty sure he's not in frontline teaching. I'm pretty sure.'

Tamsin was still looking at me.

I leaned over to pick up the bottle so I could break eye contact, and waved it at her. 'Anyway. More tea, vicar?'

'I'm just gonna go pee,' Tamsin said. Perhaps her tone was a bit abrupt. Perhaps I was imagining it.

'There's a pub about ten minutes away.'

'I'll just go in the bushes.'

97

'Bold move.' I grinned at her, wanting to reinstate our sisterhood. But her smile was a little distant.

Watching Tamsin walk away, I noticed how close the air was sitting, how the spaces between the trees seemed to crackle with the promise of a storm. My mind fell into the excruciating episode when Mr Hawkins had come to a festival with a group of us. It was towards the end of our first year at university. One of those experiences that I often lay rehearsing and relitigating in those hours when I couldn't sleep.

A disaster, from start to finish. I think we all assumed that Mr Hawkins would pick us up to go to Sussex together, since he was the only one who could drive. But then Lucy rang the day before to let us know that he'd taken her to a hotel near the campsite ('One last night in a decent bed') and he wouldn't be able to give us a lift. We had to buy last-minute train tickets and used up all the money we'd been planning to spend on food. The booze budget wasn't likewise reduced.

On the first night, after I'd struggled to pitch my tent – while Mr Hawkins watched dispassionately from a camping chair, occasionally reaching out to caress Lucy's bum – I drank a bottle of vodka on an empty stomach. It was the closest thing I've ever had to alcohol poisoning.

Lucy held my hair back, dithering around the question of whether to get St John's Ambulance. I remember thinking after vomiting, when my head felt artificially clear, that when she was around Mr Hawkins she deferred all decisions to him.

'Leave Emily in her tent, she'll be all right,' he'd said. 'She's just hammered.'

'She's really bad.'

'Then she'll learn not to do it again.'

'I'm just going to put a bottle of water and some paracetamol next to her sleeping bag.'

She checked on me several times that night. I felt her there. That blended too freely into the sex noises coming from her and Mr Hawkins' tent. Her high-pitched sighs, his guttural moans. I heard a male voice say in a low, rough tone, 'You've been a bad girl,' and heard her gasping as he spanked her. It seemed to me in that moment that Lucy and I were more on a level than we had been at any point in our friendship. Like she'd joined me, grubbing about in the dirt.

I couldn't look at Mr Hawkins for the rest of the festival, even though he seemed to warm to me again after a few cans of beer. He went into teacher mode at a poetry reading, explaining metre and rhyme in sound bites that I recalled from his A level English lessons.

There was no dramatic SOS when he and Lucy split. I didn't receive a sobbing phone call, the request to come over with wine and frozen pizzas. I just saw Lucy for coffee several months later (she'd started drinking coffee at this point, skipping the milk phase and going straight to black and strong) and she mentioned in passing that she and Chris – Mr Hawkins – weren't seeing each other any more. I remember how different she looked then, how sharply defined her jaw had been, how limp her hair. The compulsive motion of her stirring her coffee, even though she hadn't added any sugar. Her glamorous secret, her coming-of-age, bohemian love affair. Over now.

'It's run its course,' she'd said, after a long, slow sip. 'He still emails me sometimes. Poems and things. But that's it.'

I'd considered asking her, at the time, whether she wanted to still be in touch with him. But I knew she'd just say that she still cared about him, that she didn't want to be childish by cutting him off altogether.

Eventually she met Andrew. I was sure that the communications from Mr Hawkins had stopped then, though I'd never asked.

Chapter Nine

WE ATE THE PICNIC and stayed on the Heath until the stormy horizon was at a rolling boil. I tried to string it out, insisting on buying another bottle of wine.

Tamsin was quiet, pensive, and I found myself trying too hard to make her laugh.

'Sorry, dude,' she said softly, when we'd drunk another glass each from the third bottle. 'I guess that creep bummed me out a little more than I realised. I'm feeling a little off.'

So we left, me swinging the half-drunk, flattening bottle of bubbles in my hand.

We got on the tube and I expected all the while that Tamsin would want me to go back to hers, maybe for a light dinner. But when we got to Leicester Square she raised her eyebrows in a clear goodbye.

'Enjoy the rest of your weekend,' she said.

I squinted as she walked along the platform, trying to see if there was a man in a parka in the throng of people pushing towards the exit. There were too many bodies to differentiate.

Once the train was out in the open air I felt seized by guilt for my failures as a friend. I texted Lucy, a long message telling her that I was so happy for her and Andrew, that I couldn't wait to meet their baby. I spellchecked it carefully before sending, struggling to focus on the screen. She didn't reply.

I wouldn't have cried on the tube if I hadn't been drunk. Then, with the fuzz of the alcohol draining away, I felt like an idiot.

I bought a meal deal in the Sainsbury's local by my flat. A haggard-looking egg sandwich, a packet of steak-flavoured crisps, a Diet Coke. The storm had broken all over London by that point and I was soaked by the time I got in my front door. The violence of the change in the weather was disturbing, as if the bright morning had mutated. I remembered, lying in the dark and staring up at the bruised sky, how I'd woken that morning, how the shaft of sunlight had burst through the glass of fizzing water.

I told myself that a Saturday evening in was exactly what I needed. It would be good for me to be alone. That I'd cook myself something light and delicious. I'd have a bath and do a full-body exfoliation, then I'd put on my best set of pyjamas and get into something good on Netflix, something hearty yet substantial.

I managed the bath. There was only enough hot water to cover me up to my hips, and the bathroom was chilly so I kept my jumper on. I lit candles, but they didn't burn away the lingering smell of damp. I drained the bath and lay in it, emptied out, for a long time. I was cold, but I didn't want to rub the damp towel against my body.

I drank the rest of the flat crémant at room temperature and watched half a series of *Scrubs*, my laptop left playing to let me drift off to sleep on top of the duvet, still wrapped in my towel. It had stopped raining outside but the air felt waterlogged.

I woke with a sugar rush at three in the morning, convinced that it was a work day and I'd forgotten to set my alarm. I couldn't ease off back to sleep, so I scrolled through Twitter for a bit. I read an article about soil depletion and how there would soon be nowhere left for crops to grow. I watched a few more episodes of *Scrubs* in the background and dropped off again around five.

I'd woken in a half-panic again, sure this time that I'd overslept and I was supposed to be meeting Lucy in an hour. But of course, she'd cancelled.

I got up at eleven to make coffee. In the six months we'd lived together I'd never known whether to talk to my flatmate. Her name was Hana, which she always insisted was pronounced differently to Hannah, though I could never quite figure out how. She was an agonisingly thin girl who worked in fashion marketing and always made elaborate dishes involving rocket leaves, tiny cubes of avocado, a theatrical sprinkling of salt.

When I went into the kitchen she had clearly already been for a run and was sitting in the one chair, eating one of those overnight chia seed puddings that she'd make with vegan yoghurt and leave in the fridge, studded with a few blueberries.

'What are your plans for today?' Hana was the type of person who could ask a question like that in a way that felt like a reprimand.

I muttered something about going to a museum, maybe reading my book in the park.

I put a couple of pieces of bread in the toaster and rummaged among the various half-empty jars of peanut butter.

'You're not going to the climate protest?'

There was another one. I'd forgotten.

'Not judging you or anything,' she said hastily. 'I'm not going either.' She hunched around her yoghurt pudding, chewing each mouthful thirty times. I imagined the purple pulp filling her mouth, spilling from between her gums like garish baby food. She stared steadily at her locked phone, which was lying on the table.

I spent the rest of that day lying on my bed, rewatching more *Scrubs* and listening to the early albums of Taylor Swift on repeat. I remembered the stacks of old copies of *The New Yorker* that Tamsin had dotted around her flat, and considered paying far more than I could afford for the online-only subscription. I tried a long article about an American mayor who had been born a Sudanese refugee, but I found myself getting bored and skimming it.

A slice of sunshine made its way across my bed over the course of the day. I moved myself around it.

In the evening I ordered a pizza. I wanted to want it, but when it arrived it was so greasy and cold that the fat from the pepperoni had hardened into little grey slabs. I ate less than half of it and left the rest by my bed as I fell asleep again.

*

It was a relief to get into the office on Monday morning. I found a woman sitting at my desk with tears running down her cheeks.

'This is Amina,' Renee said, gesturing at the woman. She was covering her eyes with long, slender fingers.

'Hi Amina,' I said, sitting down at the next desk. 'It's lovely to meet you.' It was like meeting a celebrity.

'He's dropping the case against her,' Renee said in a low voice after following me to the kitchen with Molly, her golden retriever, at her heels.

I was making coffee for the three of us. I knew they spoke French in Senegal, and I'd managed just enough to gather that Amina wanted tea. I had no idea whether I was supposed to use *tu* or *vous*, so I'd just muttered the names of different drinks at her until she'd nodded.

'That's good, isn't it?' I paused, then glanced back towards my desk. 'Why's she crying, then? Shouldn't she be feeling better?'

'No idea.' Renee was staring determinedly at the kettle. 'Relief, maybe. Or guilt. Or maybe she's worried about what her husband thinks. Maybe she's feeling ashamed. Maybe she's just exhausted.' Renee wrapped her arms around herself. 'But if you want to know, you'd have to ask her.'

I said nothing.

Renee continued abruptly, 'She's decided she doesn't want to take any action against fuckface.'

That was her habitual way of referring to defendants.

'No further action?'

'She's convinced that if she kicks up a stink they'll deport her. She says she just wants her job back.'

'Working for *him*?'

Renee shrugged.

'So what now?'

'No case.' She sat down at the little kitchen table and stared into Molly's devoted eyes. 'Not unless someone else comes forward.'

The rest of the week was unremarkable. I turned up at work and spent most of the day trawling through Twitter, riding out waves of anger. A famous comedian had been overheard using slurs against Asians.

In the evenings I looked on meetup sites and signed up to three different book clubs, but didn't buy the book for any of them. One day, I even suggested to Hana that we make dinner together, but although she seemed keen on the idea I decided not to mention it again.

I spent the hour before meeting Lucy at the cinema thinking about ways I might be able to cancel, and when she appeared, with her tired smile and canvas tote full of exercise books, I felt like the last of my energy had drained away.

But from the opening sequence, as the strange, knotted voice began to twist around the auditorium like mangrove branches, I was drawn in.

The biopic of Billie Holiday made me ache in exactly the right way. It was built around several important performances of 'Strange Fruit', and bounced around her life. The rape at eleven, prostitution at thirteen, singing in nightclubs. I loved her – the fictional Billie and the real one – for the uncertain way that she stood onstage until she began to sing. Then archive footage was expertly blended in so that it felt more real than reality.

We talked about the film on the walk back to Lucy's. I liked it when we talked about books and films; it reminded me that there was a present to Lucy, not just a past.

'The way that her success was so inextricably linked to singing about lynching. The way she felt she had to keep singing about it, even though she was so traumatised by it.'

'Yeah.' Lucy said. 'It was very sad.'

'But I thought it was really clever, the way Rawlings seemed to kind of interrogate the idea of female genius – like, why do we have to make it about biographical detail in a way we'd never do for a man? The way he kind of moved the camera away at pivotal moments of her life.'

'That's true.'

'But he didn't do that with the rape scene, did you notice? He kept a steady eye on the whole thing, like he was bearing witness. And then when she was singing "Strange Fruit", it was the same thing. That whole idea of testimony.'

'It was very sad.'

'But clever with the whole idea of sadness, right? The way he flips it and deconstructs it, trauma as artistic inspiration and the myths surrounding that.'

'Yeah.' Lucy fell quiet and took out her phone. After tapping for a few minutes she said, 'Just texting Andrew. Letting him know he can put in the lasagne.'

I made a small, respectful noise, feeling irritated and rebuffed.

I always felt at home at Lucy's place. It wasn't the flat itself – she'd moved as many times as anyone. This flat wasn't particularly inviting – the air was a bit chilly, the walls slightly dingy and the fake-leather sofa uncomfortable. But it felt like home in the sense that anything could happen here – not the broad, expansive sense of anything, but common-or-garden anything. Rows and sex, birthday celebrations and duvet days.

Andrew was standing in the little galley kitchen, spatula in hand.

I had never had a huge amount to say to Andrew, though I'd always thought he was a good person. I'd never been quite sure what he and Lucy talked about when they were alone, but they seemed to slip into a quality of silence when they were around each other that felt sweet and comfortable. I'd have said he was a pleasant, kind, non-abusive man. What more could you want for your friend?

While Lucy messed about getting plates and forks and assembling a green salad, I explained the structure of the film to Andrew. Andrew's big hobby was watching films, and he blogged about them. I was glad that it usually provided something to talk about when I saw him, but privately I didn't think his reviews were much cop.

'Sounds like Oscar bait,' he said.

'I wouldn't say that,' I replied. 'I feel like a proper film that does justice to Billie Holiday has been a long time coming.'

'Sure.' He poured me tap water and a glass of wine. 'Still think it's probably Oscar bait. It's Art Rawlings, right? He knows what game he's playing. But don't get me wrong, I would have come along too if I hadn't been working late. I think *she's* brilliant.'

'Ijeawele Nwadike?' I said her name quickly, nonchalantly, as if I hadn't practised it several times. 'Yeah, she is. Not that the Oscars mean much, but if she doesn't get the Best Actress award then there's no justice.' I paused. 'Which, you know, there probably isn't.'

'She's got the Rawlings stamp of approval now. If she doesn't get it for this, she'll get it for something else.'

Andrew said it with breezy confidence; a person who lived in a world where everyone got their dues if they were patient.

'Hopefully.' I picked up my wine glass and took a big sip to smooth the spike out of my voice. 'There aren't too many meaty roles like that for black women in big-budget films.'

'True.' Andrew picked up my plate and served me a piece of lasagne. 'Maybe that's changing.'

'Hope so. People like your boy Quentin can't dominate forever. Except, you know, they do.'

It was a running joke – or feud – between us. Andrew loved Tarantino. I had once given him a tipsy monologue, insisting that aping classics and gratuitous violence against women did not a genius make. Andrew said I was probably right, but he enjoyed the films anyway. It was very hard to have a conversation with someone like that.

'I heard that this Billie Holiday film was pretty violent.'

'It's *about* violence.' I took another big gulp of red wine. 'But that's different to just *using* violence.'

Andrew looked at me politely, waiting for me to expound, and I grasped to find something to say.

'Billie Holiday spent a massive chunk of her career fighting for her right to sing about the lynching of black men, right?'

'Ye-es . . .' Andrew said slowly.

'That's the whole point of the title, that even though she left Baltimore she could never leave her *roots*, discrimination followed her *everywhere*. That there's no taking a holiday from that.' I snorted and took a big bite of lasagne, signalling my mic drop.

Andrew always listened to my opinions very carefully and intently, always making eye contact. It had made me think several times, in passing, that if I'd gone on a date with him I'd probably fancy him for that reason alone.

But he was Lucy's.

'That sounds completely worthy, and I don't mean for that to sound dismissive.' He paused. 'I guess . . . I just struggle with those films . . . if I'm honest with myself, what I really want is to be entertained.'

A cold sort of energy filled my muscles.

'And Tarantino-style sexualised violence is entertaining?'

'He showed the rape.' Lucy spoke up very suddenly before Andrew could reply. 'It was exploitative, the way Rawlings showed the rape. Billie was eleven. A kid had to act that scene. And he showed it.'

'It was unflinching.'

'It was fucked up,' Lucy said softly, like she was offering a sombre eulogy. 'It was. I've been thinking about it ever since. It was fucked up.'

Andrew seemed to spot something that I didn't. He leaned towards Lucy, put his arm around her and pressed a kiss into her hair. I looked away.

Chapter Ten

THAT FRIDAY EVENING, I went to an event I'd seen
advertised on one of those social media sites for people
who didn't have enough friends – that was the subtext,
anyway. Like Tinder without the sex part. This one was
for people who claimed to 'enjoy intelligent conversation'.
It was taking place in a bar in Soho. I only stayed for half
an hour. A young, nervous-looking Hungarian guy hesi-
tantly offered a series of topics – futurism, Black Lives
Matter, carbon capture technologies – out for general
consumption. No one took him up on it. The only time
the conversation got going was when someone passed
around a meme based on one of Trump's tweets. I stood
up in a way that implied I was going to the loo, and left.

Tamsin opened the door like she had been expecting me,
wrapped in her pink kimono. Her hair was bundled away
from her face, apart from a few framing tendrils. There
were traces of dark eye makeup and bright lipstick. It
would have made most people look wan, but it gave Tamsin
a vaudeville look, a theatrical little enhancement.

'I love this,' she said when she saw me. 'No one does
this in London. I love it.'

She stood aside and, after hovering for a few moments, I stepped into the flat. I had been ready to give my story, to exaggerate the awfulness of my evening to make my turning up like this seem, if not appropriate, then at least understandable. But it didn't seem necessary.

There was a film projected on her wall – *When Harry Met Sally*.

'I needed Nora,' she said, gesturing. 'Comfort viewing.'

'I've never seen it all the way through.'

Meg Ryan was wearing a crimson sweater. It would have looked bulky and sloppy on anyone less slender. But with Meg and her sculpted lips, her golden hair like a toddler, it hung off her tiny frame as if she were prettily drowning.

'How's your week been?' I asked.

Tamsin had accepted my presence so unquestioningly that I realised I couldn't count on any of the usual conversational rituals. For a moment she didn't seem to hear me, but then her eyes snapped back to my face and all at once she was attentive.

'Fucking intense, man,' she said. 'I was doing this clowning workshop in Hackney.'

'Clowning?' I laughed out of reflex, but then tried to pull the sound back as I realised Tamsin was serious. If my laughter had the capacity to hurt her, she didn't show it.

'Yeah. I always wanted to study clowning. When you look into it, you realise that so many wonderful actors have done it. It just seemed like an obvious next step for me.'

At that moment I was struck by the differentness of her accent, that every sound she formed bore no similarity to mine. Her voice was gentle and mellifluous; mine was jagged, brittle, faintly ridiculous. No one like me could ever admit to studying clowning, or even that they might want to.

'Unbelievably intense. Wearing your vulnerability on your sleeve,' she was saying, speaking rapidly, eyes bright. 'Not just the hours. All the mechanisms for giving feedback. I haven't even been looking at my phone.'

'Self-care,' I supplied.

'Sure.' She gestured at the flickering image of the film on the wall. 'Audre Lorde would be so proud of me right now.' She said it without self-reproach. Her wide smile made me feel blank, an empty space.

Tamsin's phone buzzed, and her hand darted out immediately to pick it up. It made me realise for the first time how rarely I had seen her looking at it.

I was startled to see dozens of notifications, and more metastasising on the screen even as I watched. Her agent, perhaps? I didn't even know if she had one – she'd never mentioned it.

She looked at the screen for a long moment. If it had been Lucy I would have asked what it said.

After a long pause she threw her phone down, and it seemed to disappear into the blend of silk, wool, the plush rich colours of her sofa.

'Hey . . .' she said.

Another long pause.

Then she seemed to start the sentence again in her mind. 'Hey . . . do you feel like . . . basically just wreaking havoc?'

I was wearing one of her dresses – a little wisp of silk that had seemed like it would never contain me, no matter how many miles I ran or meals I missed. But, just as her swimsuit had, it turned out to fit perfectly. I'd nearly choked when I'd seen the designer label. I'd told her not to let me wear it. But she insisted.

'I thrifted that dress. It cost me, like, ten bucks. Honestly, don't worry.'

We stood together in her bathroom, doing our faces. I painted my nails with her Chanel Rouge Noir and for once my grandmother's emerald ring didn't look out of place on my hand. Her foundation wasn't the right shade but it didn't matter. I didn't look orange, even in the bathroom light. If anything, I looked pale, my eyes large and smoky and a little sad. She kept adding layers of mascara, even when I was sure it was enough.

'Come on. You said you'd wreak havoc with me. *Commit.*'

She wasn't even wearing foundation, just a squirt of her woody perfume and a layer of red, creamy lipstick. It seemed to cast her beauty into a whole new aspect, exposing a different way for her features to become timeless, iconic. She wore a little black sheath dress, like Holly Golightly recast in gold.

As we stepped out of the cab and through the lobby into the bar, I felt as though the world were flickering between its normal self and a version in black and white, pearled in Old Hollywood glamour. There was a mirror behind the bar and rows of spirit bottles, and perhaps it was the light, but I felt that the two of us together formed a picture that was greater than the sum of its parts, framed in the rich damask and soft carpets of our surroundings.

It wasn't a big bar, nothing ostentatious. They asked us if we had a reservation in a way that implied that that kind of thing would normally matter.

The bald barman in the pale jacket moved like a dancer when he brought the cart to our table. Vodka martinis; it has to be vodka, Tamsin said.

'You need the clean flavour. A martini is all about being clean.'

I hadn't had a vodka martini before, but it tasted bright and brittle, and after a few sips I announced that this had to become my signature drink.

'Signature drink,' Tamsin said, flapping her hand lightly at me. 'Capsule wardrobe, Instagram colour scheme, Pinterest kitchen. Fuck it all. It doesn't need to become your identity, honey. Just enjoy this, right now.'

I told her about the Billie Holiday film, and she listened intently, and asked the kind of questions that made me appreciate anew how much Andrew had missed the point. She remarked on Ijeawele Nwadike's technique, told me about her first few films, murmured that she was glad she'd 'gotten her break' in a way that made it sound like she knew what she was talking about.

'This is how I thought being a grown-up and living in London would be,' I said quietly after a while. The martini was already starting to go to my head. 'Sitting in a beautiful bar, talking about interesting things.'

'Well, tonight, this is exactly what being a grown-up in London is,' Tamsin said, clinking her glass against mine. 'Cheers.'

I was struck with a memory of the games I used to play with my best friend (not Lucy, the best friend before that) in school, the games that we spent more time plotting out than actually playing. They always had the same climax – the moment that we two girls found out we were long-lost sisters.

We were less than halfway through the second martini when a man came over. I would guess that he was only in his early twenties, despite the superbly cut suit, the heavy scent of oud, the beautifully styled black beard.

'I just came over to pay you ladies my compliments,' he said. 'And to ask if you might care to join my friends and I?'

He rolled the r in 'care' in a way that made me think he might be Middle Eastern. From one of the Emirates.

I started a deferential sentence that might have ended up being either an acceptance or an apology, but before I could implicate us too much Tamsin stepped in.

'And why would we want to do that?' Her face had frozen strangely.

He turned to Tamsin and frowned slightly. 'Do I recognise you?'

Tamsin's face was still calcified. She barely moved her lips when she replied, 'Why would you recognise me?'

I wondered if she got that a lot. She exuded the air of someone who ought to be famous.

He was looking at her in a way that seemed to take in her whole body. After a long pause, he said, 'Perhaps not.'

'Perhaps not.' Tamsin was barely speaking above a whisper but articulating each sound so fiercely that it would have been impossible not to hear her clearly. 'And perhaps, since we don't know each other, you could leave me and my friend in peace.'

'I just thought . . .' He took a step backwards, his posture deferential.

'Thought that because we put on our favourite clothes and came out for a drink we must just be here as a bit of set dressing for you?' Her tone, though still quiet, was fierce and contemptuous. 'You thought wrong.'

The man took another step back and gave another pacifying smile, aimed at Tamsin. 'I can see that I've caused offence.'

'Yes.'

I looked over at Tamsin. Her voice had risen now, and a couple of people in the bar were looking over towards our table. Tamsin's expression had tipped beyond firm and was challenging, even sullen.

I shifted as though my seat were uncomfortable, though the leather was so fine that it could have been silk.

'Believe me, that wasn't my intention.' He gave Tamsin another look, that look that seemed to take in every inch of her. 'Perhaps we'll meet again, under other circumstances. But for now, I'll leave you ladies to your drinks.'

I muttered 'thank you' to fill the silence. Tamsin didn't say a word, didn't take her eyes off him until he'd returned to his table and put on a good show of resuming his conversation.

'*Have* you met that guy before?' It was the only reason I could think of to explain the hostility of her reaction, but Tamsin turned bemused eyes on me.

'That guy? Never seen him before in my life.'

'Oh.' A sip of my martini, and then hastily, 'Perhaps he's seen you before. Acting in something. Maybe that was why he thought he recognised you.'

'Oh . . .' Tamsin swatted the idea away with her hand. 'I doubt that. No one's ever seen me in anything.'

I realised I had no idea to what extent that was false modesty (or otherwise). It had never seemed polite to ask how much of an acting career Tamsin really had. I didn't want to be the tedious person who asked what I might have seen her in or if she was really famous. I'd just made my assumptions based on the Soho apartment.

The interlude with the man seemed not just to have annoyed Tamsin, but disturbed her in some deeper way. Her eyes kept darting around the bar restlessly, and since a few people were looking at us oddly, I couldn't blame her for looking a little uncomfortable. I tried to resume the conversation, but she mumbled something and disappeared off to the loo.

For those two or three minutes I felt cold, scared, convinced that she wouldn't come back, that she would have finally changed her mind about me, or else seen me for what I was – slight and inconsequential. I looked around the bar and caught sight of myself in the mirror. My face didn't seem my own. The face of the woman in the black silk dress looked too calm. Even if she was frightened, it was with distant elegance. Where were my flushed cheeks? Where was my unravelling hair, my sweat patches, my leaking ugliness?

But then Tamsin came back. She didn't even sit down.

'Come on,' she said. 'Let's get out of here.'

'To where? Home again?'

'No . . .' She narrowed her eyes, which were wandering around the room again. 'Just somewhere else.'

I couldn't finish my second martini, so she knocked it back in one gulp.

I was bracing myself to pay for the cocktails. I knew that Tamsin was probably going to discreetly take care of the bill, but when it came to it, it turned out that the man with the beard had already paid.

We swayed out of that bar, just two cocktails each but already staggering. I didn't have a clue where we were, but after rounding a couple of bends we burst out into Trafalgar Square as if surfacing for air. The square was lit like a stage, the sound of the fountains filling our ears like applause.

Overwhelmed, I sat down at the foot of the stone lion statues. Tamsin said she was going into Tesco.

'You need some water, honey.'

She came back with a big bottle, and told me to drink it all. She didn't take any water for herself. She just stood with her back to me, staring at the glowing fountains, stepping lightly from one foot to another, her pencil heels twisting beneath her without ever giving out.

Across the square, through the rainbow-shot spray of the fountains and the smudgy lines of a flock of pigeons taking off, I could see a man in a parka watching Tamsin.

I gripped her arm and pointed. 'Tamsin.'

'Aren't the fountains gorgeous?'

'Over there.'

'Later,' she said, still staring up at the illuminated rush. 'Whatever it is, I'll worry about it later.'

We ended up in the American Bar of the Savoy. More cocktails. Gimlets this time.

Tamsin insisted that I needed to eat something and ordered me a burger, somehow managing to talk the waiting staff into bringing it straight to me in the bar. I managed to focus long enough to eat half of it, but I kept forgetting about my food and getting lost in staring around the room.

There was a jazz band playing. As I ate Tamsin went to stand in front of them, smiling dreamily. A beautifully dressed old man of about eighty tapped her on the shoulder and, without either of them saying anything, they started to dance. His wrinkled hand on her waist could have seemed disgusting, but instead there was an elegiac feeling

121

about it, a wry quality in his smile, something humane in the light way her hand rested on the fine tailoring of his suit jacket.

I watched the two of them dancing, struggling to stay fully awake, and it occurred to me that there was no point in feeling bad about the great gulf between Tamsin and me. That if I just accepted that she was beautiful, and I was not, then that would leave both of us liberated.

'Your friend's quite a character,' said the barman.

'She's amazing,' I said, feeling myself getting just a little bit tearful. He poured me a glass of tap water and slid it across the bar. 'And you know what else?'

The barman didn't reply, but he tilted his head politely.

'She's relaxed,' I carried on, 'and that's really a revolutionary thing for a woman to be.'

There was no telling, from the barman's smile, whether he thought I'd said something insightful, or if that was just the smile he gave to all the drunk women who sat and watched their beautiful friends dance.

Tamsin's dance partner didn't join us, didn't even suggest it. He kissed her hand in courtly fashion and a few minutes later a bottle of champagne appeared in front of us. We looked over towards his table, and he gave a little bow.

Tamsin poured me a glass and leaned towards me.

'What do you think?'

'What?' I could only taste the champagne very distantly. I felt I was wasting it, so I held the flute up in front of my face to better appreciate the bubbles.

'What do you say the two of us give that old guy the night of his life?'

I giggled, then held out my glass to the barman. 'More tap water, please.'

'He's staying in the hotel,' Tamsin continued. 'He says he's got a suite.'

'Poor old boy doesn't look like he'd survive it,' I said, looking over at the shrunken figure, still upright in his beautiful suit.

'Exactly.' Tamsin drained her flute. 'I bet he's got all sorts of stuff lying around. We could show him a good time, he kicks the bucket, we strip it for valuables and go on the run.'

'As if you need the money. Anyway, Tamsin, I'm a lawyer. So, I feel qualified to tell you that that would be murder.'

'Manslaughter, surely? At the very worst. And a hell of a way to go.' She poured me still more champagne. 'And there's theft, I guess. We could steal a car too. In for a penny, in for a pound, as you guys say. Thelma and Louise it.'

'I've got work on Monday.'

'Oh, live a little.' She actually stood up and took a few steps towards the old man's table. 'Follow my lead.'

'Tamsin, I'm far too drunk.' I was almost certain that we were still joking, but I wasn't in complete control of my voice, so it came out sounding more serious than I intended.

Tamsin stopped abruptly, and turned to look at me. Her eyes seemed to refocus.

'You're right.' She signalled to the barman for more water and pushed my plate towards me again. 'Come on, baby, eat your chips.'

I ate the thick-cut chips, which seemed enormous and cumbersome – very slowly, one at a time. As I concentrated on chewing, Tamsin's eyes resumed their swivelling around the room, checking every dark corner. Her hands were restless, picking up her champagne flute, then putting it back down again.

'You don't have to stop drinking on my account,' I said. I started to feel slightly tearful again. 'I know I'm a lightweight. A goody-fucking-two-shoes. I know I'm no fun.'

'You're plenty of fun, honey. You're just the right amount of fun.' She put an arm around me and kissed me firmly on the cheek, like a mother offering brisk comfort.

'I'm a sanctimonious little bitch,' I mumbled. 'That's what Harry said.'

There was a pause. I looked around the bar, unable to focus properly on anything. Then Tamsin gave me another squeeze. 'You're just a person who worries a lot about doing the right thing. Okay, you're hard on other people. You're even harder on yourself.'

I nodded, half asleep on her shoulder.

'Fuck Harry,' she finished.

'Yeah.' I snuggled closer. 'Fuck'm'all.'

We sat on a wall near the Savoy for a while, until I'd convinced Tamsin that I wasn't going to be sick.

Another black cab. Tamsin talked the driver into meandering around until we could decide where it was that we wanted to be. She asked him what his favourite spot in London was and he took us to the middle of Waterloo Bridge. I was glad to get out of the cab, worried that I might be sick after all and ruin the kind cabby's day.

The skyline was like a mural picked out in stars. Each swoop of new skyscrapers and discreet church spire seemed placed especially for us. We put our arms around each other's waists and leaned together, heads on shoulders.

'It's so beautiful,' Tamsin said.

'But I never thought that it was mine, not the way it feels tonight.'

'You don't think that you deserve something like this?'

'Armchair psychology.'

'Am I right?'

'Of course you are.'

'The secret thing to remember is . . . it's not that you deserve it, it's that no one does. Life isn't about what you deserve. The thing that matters is what you take for yourself.'

If I hadn't been drunk I would have probably rolled my eyes, dismissing what she said as either too obvious or too esoteric to be true. But my body and my heart were full, and she seemed to have poured into me precisely the right measure of truth.

The cab driver came back and we clambered into the back seat.

'Where can I take you ladies next?'

Tamsin opened her mouth, and I had a feeling that if she spoke she'd tell him to take us wherever he wanted to go, and my heart froze as I remembered John Worboys. More than a hundred women, they thought he might have raped.

'Could you just take us back to Soho?' I interjected quickly. Turning to Tamsin in apology, I added, 'It's late.'

Tamsin sighed and looked at her phone screen as if she was checking the time. Her eyes seemed to dull. I could see a mess of text messages on the screen, but I felt too sick to look at them and had to turn my face out the window. 'It is late,' she agreed. 'It's getting really late.'

She directed the cabby to her flat, but when she saw a group of drag queens sitting outside Bar Italia like a flock of peacocks she changed her mind.

'Stop right here,' she said. 'We'll get out.'

She tipped him a wild amount. I didn't feel so bad when I realised it was the first time that night either of us had spent anything.

'I had to stop the car,' she said to the group outside the bar, her voice fluting out. I remembered again that she was a trained actress. 'Just to let you ladies know how stunning you look.'

One of the drag queens had some sort of glitter effect enhancing her full red lips, which were currently pursed around a cigarette. She exhaled. Smoke framed her face in the greenish light of the bar sign. She blinked slowly, sensuously, as if enjoying the touch of her false lashes as they fell sleepily across her cheeks.

'Thank you, darling,' she said, her voice low and cigarette-torn, but sharing some quality with Tamsin's. 'That means a lot coming from you.'

A white-haired man came to take our order. In the scraping of metal on the pavement I understood that we were there to stay, that we were part of the grand tableau.

Tamsin ordered in rapid Italian. The drag queens seemed charmed by that, and raised their Aperol Spritzes in appreciation when the bar owner brought out not only two espressos for Tamsin and me, but slices of pizza and hunks of bread drizzled with olive oil. He presented them to Tamsin, but all of us ate.

I got into a long conversation with one of the drag queens about Dante. She was planning her new act around the seven circles of hell. She would be journeying through them in the persona of Taylor Swift, with Madonna as her guide.

'I love that,' I said. I couldn't really visualise it, but I was happy that someone could.

I have no idea what time it was when we finally staggered back to Tamsin's flat.

Nothing needed to be said, I'd established a routine – I helped myself to the nightshirt, the cleanser, the glass of ice-cold fizzy water. I drifted off to sleep in a bed that was distinguishable from the reassurance of my own only in that it was softer, more comfortable. Better quality, I suppose. I fell asleep to rhythmic creaks from the mezzanine over-head. I didn't question them at the time, too fuzzy to focus, but I suppose they must have been Tamsin pacing, up and down, up and down.

Chapter Eleven

I woke first. It was well past noon. I sat up and immediately had to run to the bathroom to vomit.

I lay on the sofa for a while, sipping water, and eventually went up the steps of the mezzanine to see if Tamsin was awake, to ask if she wanted coffee.

The floorboards of the mezzanine were painted white, studded with the faded covers of colourful old paperbacks. The little lamp was on. Next to it lay a baseball bat.

Tamsin was asleep. Deeply so. Her phone lay on the pillow beside her, and as I looked down at the screen it flared with another message from an unknown number. I bent to see it, telling myself that it made sense to check, that if it was Tamsin's agent it might be time-sensitive. An audition, perhaps.

We understand. We're going live at midnight. Can't push it back any further.

I had no idea what it meant but concluded that whatever it was, there was plenty of time for Tamsin to deal with it without me waking her up. I decided to let her sleep in and made my own coffee, helping myself to one of the old copies of *The New Yorker* from the stack by the sofa.

When she woke up a while later, she didn't mention anything about an audition. I asked if she was free for the day and she said, 'Of course.'

We spent the day hung-over, but after I'd been sick, I no longer felt particularly headachy or nauseous. Just heavy, languid. There was something even faintly pleasant about it, as if there simply wasn't room in my head for too many different thoughts at once.

I asked tentatively if Tamsin wanted her hangover cure, her dip in the Ladies' Pond. She said no.

Instead we had breakfast in a little Italian-owned greasy spoon. The cook greeted Tamsin tenderly, bringing glasses of freshly squeezed orange juice with our fry-ups and black coffee. I generally liked that Tamsin ate meat, that she didn't want almond milk in her coffee or egg white-only omelettes. One of those people, like Lucy, who didn't need to turn every aspect of her life into a neurosis, a stick to beat herself with.

But Tamsin didn't eat much of her full English – I thought she must have been more hung-over than she was letting on.

We didn't speak very much – I supposed there was no need. Tamsin stared out the window, her eyes narrowed against the morning sun.

We bought the *Observer* and read the weekend supplements on Tamsin's sofa, then watched *Bringing Up Baby* on her projector, drinking cup after cup of Earl Grey, pausing the film occasionally to replenish the pot. We started off slow and sluggish, but Tamsin grew increasingly fidgety as the film went on. I wondered if she was starting to want her space back.

I left just after five. I wanted to go on my own terms, before there was any need for Tamsin to suggest that I should leave.

She started making noises about sorting out something for dinner. 'Something easy,' she said.

'No, no, I think I'd better head back to mine.' I said it with a firmness that I didn't feel. I didn't want my need to leak out of me and onto her.

I was taken aback to see a look of childlike distress flicker across her face. But then it was gone, and her eyes returned to their usual catlike composure.

'I feel like I need a proper Sunday to myself,' I said, but I'd already seen the hurt. I couldn't begin to grapple with the idea that Tamsin might need me.

It would have been too embarrassing to tell her that I had plans, but in the depths of the week, before our Friday-night adventure, I'd swiped right on James, 28. He had a friendly face and there was nothing too try-hard in his bio; it hadn't seemed like the worst idea to arrange to meet up. But I had no memory of anything I might have actively liked about him. By the time I started getting ready, each of his suggestions for our meeting, from the venue (a pub by the river) and the time (Sunday, early evening) irritated me.

When Art Rawlings started trending on Twitter, I immediately worked out that he was either dead, a rapist or a racist. Sitting on the train on the way to meet James, I couldn't be bothered to find out which it was. If the news story was going to stick, people would still be talking about it on Monday. If not, I could write it off, place it on the ever-mounting pile of half-reckonings and allegations against whichever Hollywood man had been a mainstay of my teenage years.

When I walked into the pub garden I recognised James immediately and saw that he'd found us an undeniably nice table in a glowing patch of sunshine. I was about ten minutes late and hadn't texted to explain. Standing at a distance, I saw him glance at his phone. The motion gave his face and the lines of his body a vulnerable look.

I hurried forward, smiling more than I'd intended. My earphones were still in my ears, so I didn't catch the first part of what he said. I jerked them out.

'She's already been round to order, but I didn't know what you wanted so I just got some tap water and said to come back soon,' he said. It was as if we were picking up mid-conversation.

'No problem.' Impulsively I leaned down to kiss his cheek. He wasn't to know that I didn't always greet people that way. I saw a flash of something across his face that I was sure he hadn't intended. A sense of being surprised but pleased by the surprise, or at least not leaping to a snap judgement.

'I should probably have gone Don Draper and ordered you an Old Fashioned or something without asking,' he said. 'But it seemed like a high-risk strategy.'

131

'The risk being?'

'Strong possibility that you don't like them. Even stronger possibility that you do like them but would think I'm a dickhead for ordering for you without asking.'

'I see you're well-versed in the tactics of the fuckboy.'

'It's like Sun Tzu says: know your enemy.'

'You're a Sun Tzu fan?'

'Massive. Primary hobby. Was that not in my bio?'

'I'm going to have a gin and tonic. What do you want?' I took my purse out of my handbag and draped my coat over the chair opposite him.

'I'll get it.'

'No. I was late. Tell me what you want or I'll just assume you want an Old Fashioned.'

'I've never had one, but from what I know, they sound a bit . . . advanced for me.'

'Beer then?'

A pause. Not awkward. Leisurely.

'No. Now you mention it, I think I fancy a gin and tonic too.'

When I went to the bar to order, the barman reeled off a list of gins that I'd never heard of. I paused for half a second, then chose one that I knew I liked already.

The glow in the bar was friendly, like the sun outside but concentrated. It caught the slices of lime in the gin bowls and lit them from within. Even though there was soft music playing, I could hear the tiny bubbles fizzing and bursting, or thought I could. I caught sight of the back of a man's head with curly hair, like Harry's, but I focused again on the play of light on the spirit bottles, refusing to let the image take over.

I don't remember what we talked about. It wasn't the adversarial, modular tour of the major topics of the day that I'd come to associate with intelligent conversation with boys, or rather with boys who wanted to show me they were intelligent. It was quiet and friendly and sometimes we lapsed into silence, or looped back to refer to some little joke or aside from earlier. We talked about childhood pets. About what subjects we hadn't paid attention to in school and whether we regretted it now. The talents we'd want to have, if we could have any talent in the world.

We realised we were getting a bit drunk and ordered cheesy chips, then decided it wasn't enough and ordered burgers. They came with more chips and garlic aioli. Our breath must have smelled as we leaned closer. When he ate I saw the juices from the burger running down his chin, and almost made some judgement about it until I realised that my face was just as covered, if not more.

'I'm worried you won't think I'm weighty enough,' he said, bringing over my third gin and tonic. 'I can do politics, if you like. A tight five minutes on Israel and Palestine.'

'Go on then.'

He took a deep breath in, and then let it out again. 'I just know enough to know it's complicated and my opinion probably doesn't matter that much.' He smiled. 'I know I'm disappointing. You can leave now, I swear I'll understand.'

I laughed and tinkled the ice cubes in my drink. 'Luckily I've still got most of this left. Anyway, what makes you think I want political discourse?'

'Well, you work for a charity, don't you? I assume you're very well informed.'

'Only about sexual abuse, mostly.' My instinct was to immediately apologise for the downer, but I managed to stop myself.

He nodded sombrely. 'Right. I guess all the stuff about Art Rawlings this week is in your wheelhouse, right? Do you think there'll be any consequences?'

I still hadn't put much together about whatever the Rawlings scandal was, other than that a French actress was involved, so I shrugged and said, 'There usually aren't. I'm not hopeful.'

'Yeah.' He looked at me considering. 'I imagine in your line of work it's probably the hope that kills you. They're going ahead with that lifetime achievement award thing next week at the BFI, did you see? Rolling out the red carpet for him.'

I nodded. I'd seen something about how the president of BAFTA should resign. It was all starting to fit into place.

'So I guess you can answer your own question about whether there'll be consequences.'

I didn't kiss him goodbye; I wasn't sure if I liked him enough to brave such a garlicky encounter. His friendly smile and intent look weren't enough to convince me that he liked me, either. Maybe that was just his manner. Maybe

134

he looked at everyone like that. Maybe the careful listening was a new pickup artist tactic.

But I liked him enough to look him in the eye when I said, 'Let's do this again.'

And something about the way he nodded and brushed my hair back from my face briefly as we hugged made me think that he probably meant it, too.

Chapter Twelve

JAMES TEXTED BEFORE I'D even got to the tube station. It was just a silly text, but it made me smile as I stood on the escalator. I wondered later if it was that little smile that was to blame, if that set in motion what happened next.

I could hear the roar of the approaching train and thought about running for it, but I was too lethargic. I couldn't tell whether I heard the laughter first, or felt the hand grabbing my bum, seizing a fistful of my flesh, the mechanical imprecision like a metal claw.

Two seconds later, in exactly the same spot, dampened by my jeans, a sharp slap.

I jolted to one side, grabbing the handrail to stop myself falling. A muscle in my neck seized at the sudden jerk and pain shot to my head and down along my arm.

I cried out. A sound not strong enough for a yell and not plaintive enough for a scream, largely drowned out by the sounds of, well . . . of my attackers.

Two long, spindly beings, like daddy-long-legs with outsized clumpy trainers, scuttling down the escalator, two steps at a time. Their tread was so heavy that it felt like the escalator, the tunnel, the subterranean world, were rocking from side to side. Their laughter yelped from their guts and bounced violently around the tunnel.

A white-faced woman was rising out of the gloom, peering up at me from the ascending escalator, upturned face traced with surprise. Instinctively, I smiled at her. She turned her face away.

I could feel the hands on me still. They had seized a chunk of my viscera, of my fat; it felt as though it had failed to return to its original shape, as if I was permanently distorted.

I heard the train rushing out of the platform where the two men had disappeared. They had made their tube. They were gone.

I got the tube after theirs. I stayed on past my stop and had to double back.

My anger took a while to come, and when it did, I wasn't sure where it was rooted. In indignation, perhaps. To them, what they did to me had all been part of the fun.

I went to the police station in Streatham. Opposite me on the plastic seats, there sat a young black boy of maybe thirteen. There was a rusty stain on his jeans. When he wiped his hands impatiently along his thighs, more blood flaked away. His face was scrunched up, set in a way that was perhaps meant to be stoical but just made him look even younger than he was. Then his mum appeared and snatched him out of the chair, hugging him so hard that it was as if she wanted to pull him back into her body. He squirmed out of her embrace. I looked away.

I hadn't really come to the police station of my own volition. I came because I felt it was what Tamsin would have done. That, by emanating her confidence, I too might make my mark on the world, hold injustice in my hands. Not for myself – but for some other girl.

I knew that even in the unlikely event that my attackers were caught, they would laugh off the reprimand. But if they weren't, some transport officers would be required to look at the CCTV footage and see what had happened to me. And that the sight of my humiliation might forge some tiny neural connection, force some near-imperceptible shift in the way they saw the world.

I didn't have to wait that long. The officers took my statement quite quickly, before the little boy in the blood-stained jeans. He was now texting in an impressive approximation of boredom.

I told the officer on duty what had happened. The legal training kicked in. I couched the experience – the assault – in blood-drained terminology. I could see the officer pursing her lips slightly. Perhaps I needed to be more upset, to justify the police time spent. I described the two or three seconds in exquisite detail and then realised that I'd stretched out those moments into a statement that lasted thirty seconds or more. I immediately felt embarrassed.

'I felt I had to come and report it,' I said. 'I know there's probably not much chance of you actually catching the guys, but I just thought . . .'

'Why didn't you notify the transport police stationed at Victoria, where the incident took place?'

I stopped short.

Why hadn't I?

The problem wasn't that she posed the question in a barbed way. It was just that she asked it like it had an answer.

I didn't respond quickly enough. She moved on.

'Did these men have any recognisable features?'

I stared at her. It was like I'd opened the booklet for an exam and realised I hadn't done the right reading.

'They had . . .'

Limbs that unfolded with the casual menace of spiders. Stamping trainers that filled the whole of the tube station with their noise. Yelping laughter, like young wolves.

'They were wearing jeans and trainers.'

'And their physiques?'

Those long spindly legs that crossed the tunnel in a single bouncing stride.

'Tall. Slim.'

'Ethnicity?'

'White, I think.'

I thought of the boy in the waiting area, his lapful of dried blood.

'Look,' I said, 'I don't want to take up too much of your time. It's not like I'm expecting you to . . . to catch them or anything. It's just I figured . . .' The police officer was looking at me, waiting. Some reassurance that I wasn't wasting her time clearly wasn't forthcoming. 'I thought there could have been similar attacks – I mean, incidents – and I just thought ...'

'We appreciate you coming forward.'

I started to rise. She quickly followed suit.

'Well, we've got your details. And we'll notify you if anything comes of it. The CCTV will be reviewed and hopefully there'll be a lead from that.'

Her eyes were already drifting away from me, towards the door of the interview room where the bloodstained boy and his mother were walking past.

'Thank you for your time,' I said quickly, making eye contact, wincing at how earnest I must seem.

'Take care of yourself.'

There was an uncharitable way of taking that, I thought as I went through the sliding doors and the humidity of the street hit me in the face. But it was probably just what she said to everyone.

Walking home, I wanted something to do with my hands, some little buzz. I took a picture of my feet standing on the pavement and wrote a long caption about what had happened. I preambled by acknowledging my privilege and noting that I could only speak for myself.

But this has to stop, I wrote. *I have notified the police, and I found myself blaming myself even as I did it. But this can't go on. Women's lived experience is too often defined by their trauma and lack of safety in navigating public spaces. I speak out not because I'm special, but because I'm not. My experience is only the tip of the iceberg.*

I added a few hashtags and posted the thing, reverting to my profile to see the image settle my grid.

It got more likes than anything I'd posted recently. I checked them before I got into the shower, and again straight afterwards. Lucy had texted me.

I saw on Insta what happened. Just to let you know I'm thinking of you x

I imagined Lucy settling down, clearing her space, clearing her mind, so that she could think of me and nothing else. I quickly ricocheted back to her. *Ah I'm all right, thanks though. How's your weekend been?*

She sent back a long reply. I left it unread, planning to give it my full attention later. My phone was fizzing with comments, likes, notes of affirmation and agreement from strangers. When I clicked on their profiles, I could see that several of them had written about things that had happened to them, too. They all seemed much worse than anything I'd experienced.

A second text from Lucy. *Let's speak soon. I've got news.*

Chapter Thirteen

THERE WERE NO MESSAGES on my phone when I woke up on Monday morning, so I lay in bed scrolling through Twitter. Everyone was talking about Larissa Larroque now. I still wasn't sure who she was, but had the vague idea that it was something to do with Brexit.

Walking through the station that morning and looking at the news boards, I worked out that Rawlings was in real trouble, not just Twitter trouble. I hadn't got up to speed yet, though my conversation with James had cleared up the question of whether the Twitterstorm was triggered by death, racism or rape.

I clicked on the magazine article that seemed to be at the centre of it all while I was walking to the office.

If movies were the dominant entertainment form of the twentieth century, then Art Rawlings has been the dominant among the dominant. He is known for his combination of artistic vision and a knack for securing the money to make that vision a reality, with Oscar winners including Emma's Game, End of the Line, OthXllo, Riding Home, Here's To You *and* Swann's Cry. *Further afield, he has wielded his cultural capital to endorse a slew of Democratic politicians, including White House incumbents and Democratic nominees.*

Rawlings possesses a nose for great material, smart crews and fresh acting talent. He also has a notoriously strong arm in his business dealings, creating a potent mixture of allegiance and fear among those who deal with him. Rawlings' work has garnered more than fifty Oscar nominations, and he has more films in the IMDb top 100 than any other living director.

He also possesses a reputation as a ladies' man, and over the years, there have been swirling rumours of improper behaviour. Attempts to uncover the truth have been . . .

To enjoy unlimited access to all our articles, please subscribe or login

I never paid much attention to any news story that was behind a paywall. I just waited until it trickled and eventually roared into the river rush of the Twitter feed.

I didn't think I'd seen many of Rawlings' films apart from *Baltimore Holiday*. But reading the litany of his achievements reminded me of how I'd fallen for the lithe elegance of Raina Gupta in *Swann's Cry* when I was in my teens. It had been one of the first films that I'd properly appreciated. I realised the same director who'd given me the louche, post-war elegance of *Swann's Cry* was also behind the gritty urgency of *OthXello*. That the same hand had been behind the biopic of Anaïs Nin, the poster of which had adorned the bedroom wall of every arty girl at my university.

I'd never have guessed it for myself, and yet, I thought as I put the kettle on in the office, it made perfect sense.

And he'd made *Emma's Game*. A film so exquisitely, achingly precise in its rendering of what it was like to be a young, scared woman that it had never even occurred to me that a man could have made it.

I made coffee for me and Renee and mentioned the Rawlings scandal as casually as I could. She barely took her eyes off the screen as she said, 'His films are still doing well, aren't they?'

I thought of Ijeawele Nwadike, her eyes squeezed shut as she sang, *Southern trees . . . bear strange fruit.*

'Prime Oscar bait,' I said.

'Then it'll blow over. A lot of powerful people are shitting themselves this morning. They'll do whatever it takes to protect each other. They're still giving him that lifetime achievement award next week. I cycled past the hotel where he's holed up.' She snorted. 'Fucking bristling with security.' Swearing always sounded so funny in her plummy tones. 'Thanks for the coffee.'

I understood myself to be dismissed.

'What's happening with Amina's case this week?'

Her eyes popped up over the top of her screen briefly before she resumed typing.

'I've just been sent a new case this morning. Up to my fucking ears. Trafficking ring in Whitechapel. A load of Bulgarian women. Ten. Their passports have been confiscated, Home Office involved. Fucking mess. You're picking up with Amina.'

'Renee, I don't know if—'

'There's not much to pick up,' she interrupted. 'She says she doesn't want to speak out, we have to respect that. You just need to tie up the loose ends, make sure that she understands exactly what she's signing.'

She stopped typing for a moment.

'You *can* do it, Emily,' she said. And it wasn't encouragement.

I worked till lunchtime. Busywork. Every so often, I checked Twitter, where the name of Larissa Larroque was still blossoming, her head superimposed onto the body of Daenerys from *Game of Thrones* or Beyoncé. I still couldn't place the name. I googled her. Nothing to do with Brexit – that must have been someone else. She was the head of a charity. FCVM – *Les Femmes Contre la Violence Masculine*. In her photo she looked unearthly, beautiful and determined, her short hair slicked back as if wet, her tattooed shoulders exposed. Good for her, I thought.

I tried the number I had for Amina. No answer.

The French translator I'd contacted had emailed me the translated draft settlement that Renee had hammered out with the MP's lawyer for Amina to look over. It stretched to several pages, and took me a while to decipher. To get myself through, I made a deal with myself that for every page I read, I was allowed to check Twitter for one minute.

By late afternoon, a new wind had blown in. According to the internet, Larissa Larroque was a pathological liar. I followed her on Instagram. Her most recent post was a selfie, in black and white, her face stark and beautiful.

The caption just said, *Je parle parce que je dois*. I speak because I must.

On Tuesday, the internet said that Art Rawlings was problematic, because of the way he filmed women.

On Wednesday, the internet said that Larissa Larroque was problematic, because she had directed a short film that glorified the French colonial project in Algeria.

I finished the lousy final season of *Scrubs* that evening. I started the latest David Attenborough series but paused it after five minutes and started scrolling through Twitter, reading a thread about Larissa Larroque and why it was problematic to treat her as an archetypal victim of sexual assault. When I saw my phone bob and buzz, my heart flung itself up my throat. But I did a good job of keeping the disappointment out of my voice when I saw it was Lucy calling, not Tamsin.

'Hey, sweetie,' I said. 'How are you?'

'It's been a weird week,' Lucy said, her voice measured.

I fumbled. 'The Rawlings stuff?'

'Rawlings? I . . . no, what do you mean?'

'Oh.' I took my phone away from my ear and put it on speakerphone, starting to scroll through Twitter. 'Just – I guess it really shocked me, is all. After the Billie Holiday film.'

'Oh. I see.'

'Anyway, why's it been weird?'

'Oh . . .' She paused.

I tried to make my silence sound encouraging.

'Nothing.'

'Nothing?' I stopped scrolling. 'Are you sure?'

'Yeah . . . It's this funny thing, I . . . Year Eleven are on their last week before study leave.'

'Oh.' I had nothing to say to that.

'They're all trying to play it cool, but I can tell they're anxious.' Her voice trailed off. 'Why did you think it was the Rawlings thing?' she carried on, her voice clearer now. I thought I could hear an edge to it. If it had been ten years ago, I would have been sure, but I couldn't read Lucy these days. If there was something wrong, I thought . . . well, that was what she had Andrew for.

'I don't know.' I felt lassoed. 'I feel like pretty much every woman is doing some kind of personal soul-searching.'

'Sure.'

My fingers lingered over an article. *Why all the malicious takes on Larissa Larroque aren't it.* I opened it in a tab to read later.

'I mean, it would be nice if some of the analysis had been directed inwards, instead of at Larissa Larroque.' I was still scrolling, Larroque's face appearing every few moments between pictures of kittens and tracts of deforested Brazilian landscape. 'You know she's been pulled to pieces online.'

'Everyone gets pulled to pieces online. But yes, I did see that. Even by feminists.'

'It's brutal,' I said, scrolling greedily through the mentions. 'Death threats, too. I mean, sure, I don't like her that much myself, she seems a bit—'

147

'I don't really know whether I like her or not,' Lucy said slowly, cutting off my increasingly hurried speech. 'I hadn't really thought about it. I believe her, though.'

'Oh god, yeah, me too. Obviously.' I paused, then reached for one of the gobbets of information that I'd absorbed about the case. 'It's awful, what's happened. The way he bought her silence.'

'Two million dollars is a lot of money.'

There was something metallic in her voice. Something that seemed to belong less to the semi-suburban Lucy, the calorie-logging, ovulation-tracking Lucy, and more to that odd, uncontainable girl who had been my best friend. The pre-Chris Hawkins Lucy.

'You could do a lot with two million dollars. You could have your dream life.'

'It's so complex,' I said, unhelpfully.

'I suppose it is.'

It seemed too early to end the conversation. I asked her about her Year Elevens.

'They're getting ready to go off on study leave,' she said. Her voice was muffled for a few moments, then cracked back into life.

'Yeah?'

'It's weird, watching them get ready to go. They feel like they've finished something big, I guess. But seeing them . . . They all got dressed up for their prom the other day. All the girls in their heels, wobbling around like baby deer. Made me realise how young they were.'

There was something in her tone that I didn't recognise, and I almost asked the question at the back of my mind – got as far as drawing in the breath. But then instead I pretended that I needed to go, that I'd just been heading out for a run when she called. We said goodbye without mentioning whether we'd do the usual Sunday-morning coffee.

On Thursday, a truce was reached. The internet had decided that everyone was problematic. The case was closed.

And though I kept trying, Amina did not pick up.

When I left work on Thursday night, I texted Tamsin *Crazy day*, wondering if she'd have a take on it all.

I was cooking my pasta for dinner when a female newsreader tweeted, *It is becoming painfully clear that a lot of people are content to have an opinion on the Rawlings/ Larroque situation without actually having read the article.* I'd adored that newsreader since I was at school, her throaty voice, her gorgeous hair, her gorgeous opinions.

I clicked on the article again, as if in hope that the paywall would have gone away. I dithered around the idea of getting the free trial but couldn't find my debit card. In the end, I found a forum thread where someone had posted screenshots of the article from her phone. Not the whole thing, which apparently stretched to some seven thousand words, but the bits that mattered, the OP said. She'd gone through and highlighted the most egregious details.

At first I skipped to the end, just scanning for Larroque's name. But there was something I kept missing, numerous highlighted mentions of private jets and non-disclosure agreements. I went back to the beginning.

My eye caught on *twelve women*, and the part of me that worked at the Women's Advocacy Centre gave a grim little nod. Twelve grim apostles. A full complement of witnesses.

. . . a pattern of work encounters that amounted to poorly disguised pretexts for sexual advances on young actresses and models . . . the problem was commonly known within both Flat Iron Productions, Rawlings' production company . . . owned by WalWorld . . . many employees at his companies operating in full knowledge of his conduct . . . A female executive with the company described how Rawlings' assistants and others served as a 'honeypot' . . .

A GIF of an enraged bee.

Flat Iron Productions issued the following statement: 'These allegations have come as a complete shock to the Board. Any insinuation that the Board was aware of this behaviour a lie.'

An angry emoji underneath.

I was skimming the screenshots. There was a part of me that didn't work for the Women's Advocacy Centre, a part of me that needed screams and violence and a knife to the throat for rape to matter. That part needed to smell blood to stay engaged.

But then names started to appear. Names I recognised. Luminous, spangled names.

. . . forcibly penetrating them with his fingers . . . coercing them into manually stimulating him . . . forcing vaginal sex.

And words from a world I didn't recognise. Blacklistings, glittering careers ended, media smear campaigns.

Rawlings seemed to make attempts to salvage his reputation by conceding that his behaviour in the past had been 'below par'. 'We are all plagued by our demons, which is a theme I've always tried to explore in my work, and I'm sorry to say that I'm not perfect either. I have always felt that I must balance my responsibility towards others and their feelings, particularly those who hold less power than I do, and my responsibility to my art. It is possible, and seems evident, that in the past I have gotten that balance wrong.'

He also called attention to his body of work, which includes critically acclaimed adaptations of the work of Toni Morrison and Anaïs Nin, as well as Baltimore Holiday*, his biopic of the troubled jazz star Billie Holiday, which was tipped to sweep the board at this year's Academy Awards.*

There was already a campaign on Twitter to ban *Baltimore Holiday* from the Oscars.

His publicist commented, 'Mr Rawlings has entered into therapy, has taken note of the feedback that he has received, and his resolve is stronger than ever to be a better man going forward.'

There was a story about a young actress called Lila Carter. That sounded like the sort of name, I thought, that could have belonged to someone famous. A Fifties screen siren.

But Lila had never become famous, had barely acted after leaving Juilliard and meeting Art Rawlings. Instead, Rawlings had lured her to a 'meeting' on a private jet, then sexually assaulted her in the bathroom. Now she was a teacher in the Midwest. She had panic attacks and couldn't travel. She'd only told her husband about it all when he'd booked a trip to Paris for their wedding anniversary, and she had to explain why she couldn't go.

Then there was the story of Gabriela Ortiz, the breathtakingly beautiful Mexican actress who'd starred in Rawlings' film *American Flight* – about migrants crossing the border – before fading into obscurity. It had been fairly well known, at the time, that they'd been having some sort of affair. Paparazzi photos of passionate kisses on set. Long-lens pictures of the two of them in bathrobes on the balcony of his hotel room.

But again, the article indicated, there had been the meeting on the private jet, a job offer that was all but signed

... He asked me if my breasts were real ... tried to grab me ... I was wearing a skirt, like an idiot, and he molested me.

And then.

... mental breakdown ...

... refusing to get out of her childhood bed ...

... not talking to anyone for several weeks ...

And I skimmed until my eye caught on another name. *Raina Gupta ...*

God. Raina Gupta. I googled her and stared for a while at her face, puffed and shiny from botched plastic surgery, exaggerated as a pantomime dame, hamming it up on *Dancing with the Stars*. When I was about thirteen I'd thought she was the most beautiful woman in the world.

... who became famous for her collaborations with Rawlings in the late Nineties, told me that he routinely sexually harassed her and insinuated that there would be further opportunities for her in Hollywood if she would supply him with sexual favours.

I hated that phrase. It made the whole thing sound fun, silly, like a Carry On film.

Several of the women I spoke to cited Rawlings' reputation as an auteur as a key part of the tangled web of coercion that he wove around the women in his vicinity. 'As a director, he's scintillating,' Gupta says. 'Every film is a masterpiece in itself, and even the ones that have less commercial success are a building block for this body of work, this whole new way of doing cinema. It's breathtaking, and in the moment it just feels like an honour to be part of it. In the moment, you think, okay yeah, I wasn't comfortable with this and that, but isn't that kind of the point of being a genius? That you don't act like everyone else? Isn't that just the price we pay?'

At least one actress seemed to have decided, even at the time, that she was categorically not prepared to pay that price. The French-Russian actress Larissa Larroque was only nineteen when she met Rawlings, when he was considering casting her as Natasha in a new adaptation of Tolstoy's War and Peace, *which he was developing.*

Larissa Larroque. I googled her again, just to feel the ache of her beauty – the cut-glass cheekbones, the pointed chin, the cat eyes.

'He kept pointing at me and saying, "Yes, that's it, that's what I'm talking about, it's all about the innocence,"' Larroque tells me. 'I was nineteen, I wasn't a virgin, I was so mad at the idea of this old man telling me that I was innocent! But I smiled and went along with it. My eye was just on the part. I ran into him again in the first-class lounge of an airport, waiting to get a flight to Paris which was delayed, so I was there alone in the middle of the night. He started saying all this ridiculous shit, chasing me around, grabbing me . . .

A vomiting emoji.

He apologised, he told me that he was flying to Paris too, that I could come on the jet with him, that it would be so much nicer, that I'd be able to sleep on the plane. I laughed in his face,' she says. 'I was only nineteen, but I grew up in a bad part of Paris and I saw the way the older men, the gangsters, groomed and exploited schoolgirls who were too young and stupid to know any better. I could see Rawlings for what he was, and I know that scared him.'

Someone had commented underneath, 'OK LARISSA, WE GET IT, YOU'RE NOT LIKE OTHER GIRLS'.

As soon as Larroque landed back in her native France, she called a reporter at Le Figaro *and told him that she wanted to give an interview detailing her encounter with Rawlings. The reporter was interested but told Larroque that it didn't sound like a crime had been committed, and that without evidence, the newspaper would be charged with libel.*

Angered, Larroque tried getting in touch with the French police. Likewise, officers were sympathetic but stated that since the attack had not taken place on French soil, there was nothing that they could do.

'At that point I was really mad,' Larroque says. 'The reporter at Le Figaro *had made it very clear that he wasn't surprised by what I was saying, and I realised that the way Art was behaving was an open secret. That he was considered a great man, a genius, so people just let him get away with it.'*

Several tears fall down Larroque's cheeks, but she brushes them away as if angered by their presence. 'I'm not sad,' she insists. 'I'm angry. I'm angry that this happens and no one stops it. If someone is being treated in this way, is being violated, the world should stop to protect them. But we don't. We look away. We say it is not so convenient for us.'

She went to the NYPD. They made it sound like they'd heard similar stuff before. She told her agent, who warned her that nothing ever seemed to stick when it came to Rawlings.

But she believed that this time would be different.

Larroque's communications with the NYPD, which in the beginning of the investigation were frequent and reassuring, began to peter out. A month after the incident with Rawlings, Larroque called the precinct to ask how the investigation was progressing, and was told that the case had been closed.

'And I realised, Ah, okay, there is something different going on. Something that I had not understood before.'

The police dropped the investigation. Larroque was black-listed and fell into a depression.

And the man won.

I kept eating my pasta long after I was full. Then I set my alarm and got into bed, taking off my work trousers but leaving on the day's bra, knickers and t-shirt. I curled up into a ball and scrolled through my phone, reading about carbon emission targets until my eyes started to itch.

It was only when I was dropping off to sleep that something darted back into my mind and I sat upright, feeling like a hand had closed around my throat.

'It was in response to a bunch of things that happened in my early twenties, I guess.'

'Something in particular?'

'Kind of. I mean, nothing so big that most people would think that it was worth changing your entire life over, but it mattered to me . . . I was once on a plane with a bunch of people I was working with, and this guy – he was the big cheese, you know? – he followed me when I went to the bathroom and said he wanted to squeeze my tits to see if they were real.'

156

Part Two

Chapter Fourteen

WHEN I WOKE AT one, and then again at half four, it seemed obvious beyond question. The man who had touched Tamsin was Art Rawlings. It was only a matter of where. How. What. A game of Cluedo: the movie director, in the private jet bathroom, with the filthy, grabbing hands.

There was no why. There never was.

The thought gave me a feeling of being close to truth, to the things that mattered.

I lay there and rehashed everything Tamsin had ever said to me, handling all those words and looks and quiet moments carefully, as if I were the archaeologist and they the artefacts.

At two fifteen, at twenty past three, it was just as obvious that Tamsin had nothing to do with the whole thing. There were plenty of actresses and creepy rich men, an abundance of planes and bathrooms, more moments of transgression and distress than could ever be counted. Tamsin's experience was just one of the many, the mundane. Art Rawlings had nothing to do with it. Hadn't I mentioned his films in passing to her? Hadn't she praised them? There had been no flinch, no clouding of the eyes, no sign of distress.

And if it had been Rawlings who had hurt her, in the way that was described in the article, she would have been distressed, surely. Clearly none of the women he had assaulted had got away with their well-being intact, and Tamsin was . . . Tamsin was more than well. She was an example of what it meant to seize life. She was written on the world more clearly than I could ever be, whereas the women in this article were little more than ghosts.

Around five I woke from a dream. I'd misread the article. Tamsin *had* appeared, *had* spoken out. I got up and found my wallet to sign up for the trial subscription, then searched the page of the original article for Tamsin's name.

I realised I didn't know her surname.

I reread the article. None of the pen portraits could have been a disguised Tamsin. I had a strange, sudden, sleepy feeling, as if a fever had broken.

When my alarm went off at seven, I texted Tamsin, *Maybe see you this evening.* There was a long line of texts from me that never received any reply. Yet I was her friend. Of that, at least, there could be no doubt.

I arrived at my desk and made my second coffee. I felt splinteringly tired, and nauseous with it.

An email popped up from Renee, just a line in the subject heading, *Any word from A?*

I started to type out a verbose apology, listing all the times I'd tried to reach her. But, with the email written and unsent, I picked up the phone with my pounding head in my hands.

She answered after two rings with a weary 'Yes?' As if she'd been expecting me.

'Amina.' The sound of her voice left me slightly taken aback, as if I'd unexpectedly got through to a celebrity. 'It's Emily. From the Women's Advocacy Centre. *Ça va?*'

She ignored my attempt, perhaps in indication that it was too feeble to be worth bothering with, and said again, 'Yes?'

'I just wanted to check,' I said, speaking slowly, 'if you had received my email with the translated draft settlement attached.'

A silence, and I tried again.

'*Avez-vous reçu mon* . . . er . . . email . . .'

'I receive.'

'Er . . . right. And have you, er . . . comprehended all of it?'

'I understand,' she said, and her voice seemed to sink lower still under its burden of weariness.

'Oh.' My voice absurdly bright. 'Oh, that's wonderful. In that case, it's now just a question of signing so that we can get the funds sent to you. Then you can book your flight home. To, er, to Senegal.'

'Yes.'

'Great. I'll await your signed copy then. Er . . . *Merci*, Amina. *Au revoir.*'

Putting the phone down, I deleted my message to Renee and typed out instead: *Yup, spoken to her and awaiting her signature, then we're good to go.*

It was the hottest day of the year. I didn't even let myself consider the yawning void of the weekend ahead. It was obvious what I'd do. I'd turn off my computer, leave the office a little bit early, walk across the bridge in the golden light and make my way to Tamsin's.

I stopped off to buy a chilled bottle of rosé from an expensive wine shop in Soho. I felt like I'd finally worked out how to *do* London. The flower-coloured wine wouldn't have the chance to warm before the two of us poured it into graceful-stemmed glasses and toasted another weekend together. Time outside regular time, outside the tug and flow of the emails and the dog videos and the plastic in the skeletons of seabirds and the Post-it on my computer screen that simply read 'Amina'. Time that switched into something more significant.

I rang Tamsin's doorbell. For over a minute, there was no reply.

As the bottle of wine warmed, I felt the glow in my chest start to cool. I remembered Tamsin as I'd last seen her. Her wide, defenceless eyes when I told her that I was going home, that I was leaving her. The memory of feeling wanted lifted me.

I tried her phone. No answer.

My elbow nudged the neck of the wine bottle and I felt something humiliating in the cool touch of the glass, in my own presumption. I was too hot, too tired. It was the end of the week – and it had been an emotional week.

I checked the app on my phone. My period was due at the weekend.

I tapped out a message to Tamsin. I decided I'd send it and wait five minutes, to see if anything happened, and then I'd head home. I even set a timer on my phone.

It occurred to me that I didn't have a clue what it was that Tamsin got up to on weekdays. She alluded to workshops and training courses, and I assumed that an agent was somewhere in the mix, though she never seemed to have the jittery anxiety about auditions that I associated with actors.

I heard the window above me open, and the familiar voice calling out, 'Emily?' It was a different timbre to the rest of the street noise; even though she spoke softly, I could hear her as though she were murmuring in my ear.

'I'm here!' I was reaching up towards the window like Romeo, my shoulder weighed down by the heavy glass bottle in my bag.

Tamsin's face appeared above. It looked white and strange, as though all of its negative spaces had been arranged differently. Maybe that was just the angle, me looking up at her.

When she dropped the keys, I barely realised they were falling before I caught them on reflex.

'Shut the front door behind you,' Tamsin said. Her voice was different, still low and distinct but rougher.

I shut the heavy door carefully. Walking up the stairs seemed to take a long time; when the timer on my phone beeped I leapt and almost lost my footing, grasping the banister so tightly that I felt a splinter lodge in the palm of my hand. When I got to Tamsin's door it was closed. Normally she'd have left it slightly ajar for me. Normally she'd have been standing in the kitchen, mixing up some aperitif, putting together something delicious to eat.

I knocked. 'Hey, darling,' I started to say, but before I could even finish the greeting, Tamsin pulled me inside and shut the door behind me. I was struck silent for a moment.

The sepia-tinted girl in the Savoy bar was gone.

She looked like she'd lost weight in the space of the week. It made me see how quickly her healthy slender figure could give way to gauntness. She was wearing her pink kimono, but stains distorted the shoulders of the lovely antique silk, as if she'd been walking around with wet hair. There were a couple of other stains that looked like black coffee.

'Hey . . .' she said. I could smell a trace of halitosis on her breath. Careful not to move away too fast, I took a step back.

Looking around, I saw that there was just enough warmth and cosiness left in the flat to make stark how the feeling of a pleasure palace had drained away. There were still the same soft furnishings – the books, the rugs and bright pans. But the lighting was all wrong. It looked like raw film footage before post-production stepped in to smooth away the hard edges.

'Are you all right, darling?' I spoke quickly, gently, like I'd seen nurses do. 'You don't look too well.'

'I'm totally fine, I just . . .' Her hand trailed uselessly through the air; her gestures were normally so clean-cut. A sheen of sweat lay on her brow.

'One of those days?' I finished off.

She nodded, grateful.

'I don't have to stay long.'

'Stay.'

She looked at me with a need that divided me clean down the middle. Tamsin needed me. But there was an impulse, strong enough that I almost couldn't push it down. An instinct to bolt.

'I brought wine,' I said, brandishing the bottle. It had warmed to the same temperature as the rest of the airless apartment – for once, on this hottest of days, the French doors on to the balcony were closed.

'Thanks so much,' she said, taking it. She didn't even look at the label but placed it on the kitchen counter, where it sat, sweating.

'Maybe it's a tea kind of evening, rather than wine? If you're sure you want me to stay?' I went over to the fridge to put the rosé away. The fridge was almost empty.

'I'm certain I want you to stay,' she said.

'Why don't you go have a shower, brush your teeth, get dressed?' I coaxed.

She blinked.

'I don't mean . . . Sorry to be bossy, just maybe put on some clean pyjamas?' She was still looking at me uncomprehendingly, so I added, 'You'll feel better?'

Tamsin nodded slowly and shuffled off to the bathroom, clasping her robe tight around her. Her movements were so careful that it was as if she were newly fragile, as if she wanted to stop pieces of herself from falling off.

I put the kettle on and used its white noise to drown out the alarm ringing in my head. I looked around and saw the baseball bat, which I'd previously glimpsed lying beside Tamsin's bed, propped against the doorpost. Could she be having some sort of manic episode?

When she returned from the shower, her hair in rats' tails around her thin face, still with the same slow, dragging step, it seemed too obvious to point out that something was weighing her down. She was wearing jogging bottoms and a baggy sweatshirt, even though it was such a warm day. They engulfed her. She looked the way she had when we had been swimming, when something seemed to be pulling her under.

'Tea or wine?'

She shrugged.

'What's going on? You're not yourself.'

'When we're least like ourselves we reveal the most,' she said flatly.

'What? Is that a quote from something?'

'Don't worry. I guess it's just the mean reds.'

'Is something worrying you?'

'Something.'

'What?'

She stayed silent.

'Tamsin.' I could feel the need to know growing, physical and shameful in its insistence, as if it might cause my hands to reach out and yank the words from Tamsin's unwilling tongue. 'Something's happened.'

'Nothing's happened.'

I gestured to the baseball bat by the door. 'This isn't normal.'

'No.' Her eyes drifted from mine.

'Tell me.'

She gave a little ironic smile. 'I'm amazed you haven't figured it out. You read *The New Yorker*, right?'

Her eyes gleamed for a second. There was Tamsin, the Tamsin I recognised. Bold, smacking down the gauntlet, stepping back to admire her handiwork.

I felt a leap of excitement in my chest and forced myself to be still. 'Sometimes.'

'So what's to tell?' She was swaying slightly, as if she felt gravity more strongly than usual.

I swallowed. 'Your story.' The room seemed to grow, my little words echoing within it.

She shook her head. 'Stories have a beginning, a middle, an end. This is just a thing that happened.'

'Okay, maybe story's the wrong word. It's . . . it's your lived experience.'

'It's not my lived experience.' She dropped onto the sofa and gathered her knees up. 'It's just my life. It's so fucking mundane.'

'I'm not here to be entertained.'

'Aren't you?'

'Tamsin.'

A pause.

Then I said, 'There's a value to talking about stuff.'

'You believe that?'

I realised that I didn't know if I did, really. It was an article of faith.

'I do,' I said, making my voice firm.

Tamsin was looking at me closely.

'You don't talk about *your* stuff.'

I drew in a breath, then shook my head quickly. 'You mean . . . Harry? Oh, Tamsin, that's just some silly . . . It's nothing like this. This is really important.'

'I guess if victims don't speak up, you're kind of out of a job,' she said. I might have been offended if I hadn't felt her edging closer, hadn't known she only needed one last push. She was vibrating with a magnetism that repelled and attracted me in equal measure.

'Tell me.'

I realised she needed me to say it aloud.

'Tell me about Art Rawlings.'

Triumph darted briefly across her face, then faded away to be replaced by a haggard look. Then she unfolded her long legs onto the couch. Crossed them at the ankle.

'All right. Pour the wine then.'

Chapter Fifteen

'I MET ART RAWLINGS when I was eighteen years old,'
she began, then stopped. Sighed. 'Eighteen years old. Two
years older than my sister is now.' She glanced down at
her phone. 'I should call her. I worry about her.'

I waited for a second, and then prompted. 'Art
Rawlings?'

'Right. He came to a screening of my movie – my only
movie.' A little self-deprecating smile. 'This French movie
I did when I was sixteen. They screened it at Cannes. I
played this little ingénue, it was all black hair with curls
like Ava Gardener. Very cute.'

I'd never considered her with black hair. But immediately I could see that it worked.

'*He* comes up to me afterwards and starts praising my
performance. Pours all this flattery onto me. He told me
my performance had "erotic intelligence", whatever the
fuck that's supposed to mean.'

'That's so creepy.'

'It was Cannes. And not Cannes now. Seven years ago.'

'Sorry.' I twisted my fingers in my lap. I thought about
going to get a wine glass for myself, but I didn't want her
to stop talking. 'Go on.'

'Yeah. Art . . .' She stared off into space, as if she'd lost the will to speak.

'Art?' I prompted gently, and she snapped back into the room.

'So we were at this after-party and he brought me a glass of champagne and I was like, I guess I have to hang out with this dude while I drink this. He started talking about what he was working on, this biopic of Anaïs Nin. How she used to fuck her patients on her psychoanalyst couch, how *transgressive* her life had been.' She rolled her eyes. 'And he started talking about my *fabulous* screen presence, how I'd been *made* for period pieces. My face. My *figure*.' She looked down dismissively at her own body, as if impatient with it. 'And I was young, and stupid, and even though it probably made me feel weird I basically took it as a compliment.' She snorted. 'I'm assuming you remember that Anaïs Nin movie?'

I had seen it with a group of university friends just before we graduated. We'd spent a drunken evening arguing about whether anything was okay as long as it was consensual. The lead actress had since become a household name. That movie was the making of her.

'I remember it.'

'Anyway, Rawlings tells me he's borrowing a private jet to get back to the States. It was from that financier – you know, the one who's in jail for child pornography now. His jet.'

My mind stuck on her words. The girl I knew seemed to be falling away, slipping through a newspaper page and into a world I didn't understand at all.

'Contrary to what all those women in *The New Yorker* made it sound like – Ortiz and Gupta and the rest – I wasn't completely dumb. I knew what he was like. I *must* have known.'

Her hand gripped the fabric of her oversized sweatshirt, as if she were gathering herself in.

'So he says he wants me to fly with him on the jet, that I can read for him. Read for the part. Young Anaïs. He'd adapted the screenplay from her diaries, you know.'

I did know. He won the Oscar for Best Adapted Screenplay that year. It had been a big deal at the time, that a French-language film had got the Oscar. That an American had engaged with the source material in the original language.

'He didn't write that shit, by the way. He had this French assistant, Marianne. Twenty-four years old, brilliant. She left her job not long after. I'm guessing she got sick of having her ass groped. She'll be NDA'd now, I figure. So there you go. Secret's out.'

'That's . . . that's unbelievable. That's her intellectual property. Couldn't she sue him?'

'I'm no lawyer,' Tamsin said, her eyes boring into me, 'but I can see a few problems with trying to sue Art Rawlings.'

I looked at my hands.

'Anyway,' she continued. 'There was only one thing Art liked more than fucking young girls who were scared of him. And that was people telling him how smart he was. He managed to build a life for himself where he got

171

both. And, because he was Art, he could make stuff that other people – people who weren't household names like him – would never have got the chance to make. Living the dream. You've got to admire it, in a way.'

'No, you don't.'

Tamsin shrugged. 'Okay, you don't. But I digress.'

She seemed to be getting into her story now. I'd noticed her beauty creeping back into her pale features, her upright carriage, the timbre of her voice deepening.

'So I'm on the plane with Art, and I'm reading this part, and the words are leaping off the page. There's this monologue that's taken straight from Nin's diaries and it's genius, it's *undeniable*. Even looking back on it now it makes my heart race, the way I felt when I was reading those lines. Like that was the moment I finally became an artist, like this was what I'd wanted my whole life and I hadn't even realised it until now.'

She was half smiling, eyes closed.

'He offers me the part on the spot. I'm so overwhelmed that I know I'm going to start crying, so I get up and say I'm just going to go to the bathroom. I figure I'll come back, we'll toast the project, this'll be the beginning of our collaboration. Like Woody Allen and Diane Keaton, Tarantino and Uma Thurman. Hitchcock and Grace Kelly. I figure it's going to be *beautiful*.'

Her eyes were open now, focused distantly on the ceiling above.

'I take the script with me to the bathroom. I think – I've just got to capture this feeling. I take my phone out. I

172

press record.' She held an invisible phone in her hands, touching it gently with an index finger. 'I start reading the monologue out loud again. I pretended to myself that I just wanted to check that I was doing it right, to listen back to myself. That sounds like it was humility. But it wasn't humility at all.'

A wide smile across her face. She looked dazed, a little ill.

'In that moment, I just felt like, fuck yeah, I am *nailing* this. I have something that other people don't have. I have talent. I can do this shit justice, and I just wanted to take a little moment to put that down for posterity. Hubris, am I right? Pride comes before the fall.'

Her voice was soaked through with irony.

'So anyway, I'm in this bathroom – it's not like a bathroom on a normal plane. The sink is marble, there're all these vases of flowers. It's like nothing I'd ever seen before. I'm standing there looking at myself in the mirror and I just think – I'm dreaming, I'm drunk, I'm high. There is no earthly way that I can actually be *here*, that I could actually have got this lucky off the back of one little indie film – a French-language film – and suddenly I'm on a private jet with one of the biggest directors in the world.'

She looked around the room as if she could still see it, a smile distorting her mouth.

'I actually start laughing a little and I hear this voice behind me going, "What's so funny?" And I turn around and there he is.'

She swallowed; the smile now gone.

'And I think, dear god. That is the corniest thing I've ever heard in my life.'

A tiny shade of contempt entered her face. I wondered if it had been there when she was on the jet, if Rawlings had seen it too.

'He was so old ... he kind of smelled musty, like a grandfather. It was the least sexy situation I've ever been in my whole life, so I just kind of laughed and said, "Hey, have you checked out this bathroom, isn't it crazy?"' She laughed, the sound jarring. 'And he ... he ignored me. And stepped closer. And locked the door behind him.'

Her whole body had changed now. She had become a stranger, slipping further away from me and into the smudgy silhouettes of the women from *The New Yorker* article.

'Even then, I wasn't really scared. Or I told myself I wasn't, anyway. I don't remember what I actually felt. I figure he's testing me somehow. He starts quoting Anaïs Nin, in French, from memory, and I think, okay, it's all part of the film thing, nothing to freak out about. I'm just thinking over and over, Don't lose your cool.' She paused.

'Then he asks if my tits are real, and the spell is broken. I'm like, oh okay. I get it. He's just a man doing what men do.'

Her face flattened out. She looked old.

'He comes closer and closer and he's just saying you've got to be *authentic*, you've got to be real with me, I need to know everything, I need to know if you're fake, there's no space for lies between us.' Her eyes flicked to mine. 'It was so intense, but also so *ridiculous*. Like he was a teenager. I mean, I was young, but even I had heard that script before. My heart was pounding but there was this part of me that was still so detached, that was still going who is this guy, why's he saying all this crap?

'And then he grabs my tits.' She said it with so little ceremony that I might have missed it. 'And . . .' She paused, sighed, looking still more tired. 'And at first I say, "What the hell, dude, don't do that." And then . . . then he turns me around so we're both looking in the bathroom mirror and he starts to . . . well, you know.'

I thought I probably did know. I knew that fleeting moment of deep sadness that almost immediately gives way to numbness. That moment when you know that the safest, sanest thing you can do is to leave your own body.

'So I figure . . .' Tamsin's voice seemed to fade out. She cleared her throat and started again. 'I figure that the smartest thing I can do to get it to stop is to fake an orgasm.' Tamsin picked at her fingernails. 'No big deal. I'm an actress.'

I knew that there was nothing I could say.

'I literally remember thinking – *I'm going to get traumatised – over this shit?* It was . . . it was grubby. When I learned that word here, I was just like, yes, that's exactly it, that's what it was. It was sordid.'

'It wasn't your fault.'

She kept speaking as if she hadn't heard me. 'He'd got . . . It was all over me, so he told me to take a shower. And he just stood there, and I showered in this private jet bathroom while he watched.'

A long, rattling exhale. I kept quiet. She closed her eyes and took a large gulp of wine.

'Afterwards, he wrapped me in a towel, like I was a baby, and hugged me to him and told me what a great girl I was, how he couldn't wait to work with me. That I was beautiful.'

Her voice cracked. It was so unexpected that I flinched. I'd slipped into the cadence of her story, letting the images drift before me. When I looked back at Tamsin she looked tired, drab. Like an abandoned house.

'And get this – while I'm in the shower he takes my clothes away. I guess he wasn't going to take any more chances. This was after all those other actresses – maybe he'd nearly been caught before. Whatever. He tells me that he'll get them dry-cleaned. He tells me to give his assistant my address, so he can send them back to me. And I just . . . I just *give* it to him.'

She was staring at her own hands again, frowning. 'He gave me one of his shirts to wear. You know . . .' She pulled so hard at a piece of skin on her middle finger that it started to bleed. 'The way the woman always does in the movies, right after sex. I've got another outfit in my carry-on so I change into that, but not until his whole team has already seen me. In one of his fucking shirts. Like we're *lovers*.'

She made the word sound so ugly.

'He goes to sleep. I watch a couple of movies. The plane lands. We get off. He goes one way, I go another. And it's over. Kind of.'

'He harassed you?'

'Harassed? Sure. He sends me my clothes back. He sends me flowers. He asks to be my *boyfriend*, for fuck's sake, like we're in high school. He sends me the script for the Nin picture. Hell, he sends me the contract for the Nin picture.' She stared at her empty hand as if it held a pen. 'All I had to do was sign it.'

'But you didn't want to work with him any more.' I tried to make my voice weighty and knowing.

'I would have worked with him.'

'Yeah?' I said it too quickly.

'I just told you how much I wanted that part.'

'But . . . but you didn't end up signing? Right?' Obviously.

'Right.'

'So what happened?'

Tamsin sighed and poured herself more wine. 'I stopped being able to sleep.'

'You were traumatised.'

'I don't know.' She took a great gulp. 'I just wanted to forget about it all, muscle through, do the movie. Maybe get enough exposure from it that I get to make another movie. And hopefully another after that. But all I know is . . .' She yawned, her face distorting, before she resumed. 'I couldn't sleep. Really not at all, or an hour a night, max. For weeks and weeks.'

For the first time she looked like she might cry.

'Everything else just fades into the background when you're that tired. And the lack of sleep . . . it made me start to go a little crazy. I didn't shower. I felt like that shower on the plane in front of . . . It was such a disgrace.'

'It wasn't your fault.'

'Sure.' I clearly hadn't said it with enough conviction. 'Anyway. I had this friend at the time. Couple of years older than me. I had this thing in my late teens of glomming onto people who were a few years older than me – go figure, right? She was in journalism school, and working for this online feminist platform. Bottom of the ladder, and it wasn't exactly an impressive ladder, now that I look back on it. Mostly it's this paint-by-numbers hatchet job on why no one is a real feminist. You know. Beyoncé is problematic. Gloria Steinem is evil.'

'I know the sort of thing.'

'Jesus knows what she's doing now. I think she's some kind of bogus influencer. So, my friend comes over and she sees that I haven't been sleeping, that I haven't washed, that I stink. I'm not her cute little eighteen-year-old friend any more, I'm . . . I'm repellant. And she freaks out. She tells me that I'm having a mental health episode and I need to *reach out*, I need to ask for *help*. She's telling me that I'm sick and I'm going, no, no, I'm just tired from Cannes, no big deal. But she won't stop, and I freak out too. I start screaming about how I'm sorry that I'm not what she wants me to be, I'm not her hot manic pixie dream friend any more.'

I shifted in my seat.

'And she's just staring at me like, Tamsin, what're you talking about, what is all this? I'm screaming and screaming.

I've thought about it a lot – in the pond, in therapy – all that stuff. I was madder at her than I was at Rawlings. A lot madder.'

There was a firm set to her jaw. A narrowing of her eyes.

'Anyway, I just blurt it all out. What happened on the jet. And before I know it, she's planning her hatchet job on Art. I remember she had this look on her face, like she wanted to rip what happened right out of me so she could smear it on a page for people to read.'

Her breath seemed to collapse as she said that. A long pause before continuing.

'Anyway. She's got no physical evidence, right? Nothing except the shirt he made me borrow, and I'm telling her, that doesn't prove anything. All anyone is going to interpret from that is that I slept with him. And she's going, no no no, the shirt is fine, the shirt is plenty, I believe you, blah blah blah. And I'm thinking, fuck this, if she starts publishing shit that she can't prove then I'm the one who's going to suffer.'

'Right.'

'But then I remember something.'

She looked at me expectantly, as if I was supposed to fill in the missing piece. I slowly shook my head.

'Remember when I'd had my fancy actress moment? Remember how I recorded myself reading the speech?'

'Yeah?'

'So as it turns out, I never stopped recording.'

I looked at her.

'Turns out, my phone recorded the whole thing.'

An obliterating silence filled the room.

'Go on,' I said.

'So, I play it back to my friend.' Her pupils dilated slightly. 'It's all there. The corny lines. His piggy little grunting. Even the sound of me getting in the shower. And me . . .' Something seemed to pull at the sides of her mouth. She lowered her eyes. 'Me and my fake-ass orgasm.'

Chapter Sixteen

TAMSIN TOOK ANOTHER LONG gulp of wine.

'Do we have whisky? There's gotta be whisky somewhere in the mix.' She glanced over a mess of bottles on the coffee table. Her eyes fell on the elegant Japanese bottle, the one that she'd said was like drinking silk. 'Perfect,' she said, uncorking it and filling up her wine glass. The dregs of rosé gave it a sickly, pinkish tinge.

'So . . . so you faked,' I filled in.

'Right.' She was smiling at me, blank-eyed, as if waiting for the penny to drop.

'That doesn't mean anything though,' I said quickly. 'It doesn't mean you consented.'

'Try telling that to my friend.' Tamsin's words were beginning to slur. 'I mean, I say friend. Fucking bitch, more like. She's all, "Tamsin, I can't run with this, there's no credibility, why would you even play me this, the shirt would have been fine, people make their own judgements." And I understand why she says that, but at the same time I'm like, what about the part when I told him not to touch me?'

'Even if you faked an orgasm – even if you really *had* one – that still wouldn't constitute consent. You know that sometimes it—'

'I know that. I knew that then. Fucking *she* knew that then too. But she's like, I can't sell this to the public. You know what they say about Art.' She smiled again, but the drink was starting to blur her face like a bleeding water-colour. 'Fucking ladies' man, right?

'So I change tack. I think okay, the media isn't it. But this friend lit a spark in me, something that made me feel like I needed to tell someone, that I needed him to be held accountable. I needed *justice*. It was hearing the recording again. Hearing myself giving that big, fake performance, like the pantomime dames you have here. And hearing him tell me to get in the shower. And he just *stood* there. And watched me.'

She put her wine glass down on the coffee table so carelessly that I thought she might smash it, and I froze, bracing myself for a splintering noise. But it seemed to right itself.

'But until I listened to it again, I'd forgotten that I'd said no, don't touch me, and suddenly there it was. I'm thinking, I'm going to the cops. This girl may not be able to "sell" what happened to me to the fucking "public", but there is clear evidence of me saying no and him doing it anyway. That's sexual assault, right? That's watertight. How many cases have evidence like that? And even if the slut-shaming media don't get it, the police will.'

I didn't scoff, like I would have done if Renee had been recounting this to me at work.

'So I show up at the NYPD precinct and I say, "I want to report a sexual assault." And at first they're great. I'm interviewed by this cool lady detective and even when I tell her that it's Art Rawlings, she's not fazed. In fact, I got the feeling that this wasn't the first time someone had made a report about him. She just goes, okay, tell me what happened, so I tell her. She asks if I've still got the clothes I was wearing and I say no, he dry-cleaned them. I felt like she lost a bit of interest then, but I say, "I've got one better than that." And I play her the tape.'

'And?'

'And at first, when she hears me saying no she looks at me like holy shit, we got him. I could see this look on her face of yeah, we're going to nail the bastard. And even when we get to the faking part I explain that I just did it on a survival instinct, that I just wanted it to be over and she's like yeah, I get that, don't worry about it.'

She topped up the wine glass of whisky.

'So, like a fucking idiot, I don't worry about it. I trust this woman. I go home, I shower, I wash my hair. I start working out a ton, like I'm in a *Rocky* montage. I think okay, I'm getting ready to serve justice to this bastard. And at first the lady detective is great, she keeps calling to check I'm OK.'

A finger of whisky, all in one go.

'So then what happened?' I prompted her partly because I wanted to know and partly because I wanted to distract her from the whisky bottle.

'What happened?' Her eyes swivelled back towards me, but they were unfocused. 'She starts going cold on me. Forgetting to return my calls, you know? And I should have

183

got the message – she's just not that into you, Tamsin. But I'm eighteen, and I'm dumb, and Rawlings is still calling me all the time and sending me flowers and I just want it to stop, so I go down to the precinct again and ask to speak to her. And . . .' She rubbed one hand clumsily across her face, like a tired baby. 'And she tells me we can't proceed further with your case, the evidence just isn't there, we've reviewed the tape and the higher-ups have concluded that the encounter was consensual. And I'm like, what the fuck do you mean, I told you I was just faking it.' She withdrew her hand and looked at me. Her eyes were bloodshot. 'And she goes, "Well, it was very convincing," and I go, "Bitch, I'm a fucking actress." We've all seen Meg Ryan in *When Harry Met Sally*. But I can see it's hopeless.'

Her shoulders caved in.

'I say, "Look, can you at least do something about all these calls and flowers? This guy won't leave me alone." And she says something about how she wishes her boyfriend bought her flowers, and I don't want to be rude, so I just say, ha ha. And, to give her credit, all the communication from Art stopped. Radio silence.'

She seemed to curl in on herself even more when she said that.

I let her stay quiet for a while, before prodding, 'And then what?'

'And then my agent calls and tells me Rawlings wants a meeting.'

'What?' This I truly hadn't been expecting.

'Right?' She rolled her eyes and for a second she was Tamsin again. 'And suddenly it's like the last few weeks never happened. I'm thinking maybe I've got it wrong, maybe it's all just been some kind of misunderstanding and he really did think it was consensual and he's genuinely sorry. And he's going to offer me the part. I really, really think he's going to offer me the part again.' She looked sleepily at me. 'It's amazing what you can make yourself believe, if you really want to. Anyway, I'm broke. Haven't been working at all, and the money from the French movie has run out. I have to go to a thrift store to get a dress for my big *meeting*.'

Her eyes were half-closed, her words slowed to a slur.

'You can imagine it, can't you? Someone high up in the NYPD, maybe even the mayor, calls Art. And he's like buddy, some little bitch is making trouble, we don't need to escalate it any more, just letting you know in case you want to make it go away.' She affected a thick New Yoick accent.

'So we're in this boardroom and one of Rawlings' lawyers is there, and Art is wearing this fucking grey wool suit and he's so clean, so goddamn clean. And I look like shit from not sleeping and my hair's this fucking bird's nest and I've got no makeup on and I know I look disgusting. I'm not real, not like they're real. I'm just this stain, this piece of mould, this lump of flesh. I can see all these men looking at me and thinking is this the face that launched a thousand ships? Is this the chick our boss is making us work late for?'

'I don't think you could ever be ugly.'

My words seemed to bounce off her. 'I want to crawl under the table. I want to hide. I know they all think I'm crazy, and if I didn't have the recording then I'd probably have agreed with them. But here's the thing.' She looked at me again, and her voice became more lucid than it had been since she'd started on the whisky. 'All these guys know is that there *is* a recording, right? They don't know what's in it. And, Art being Art, they know that it could be really fucking bad. You read that article. They all knew the kind of shit their boss was up to, it was their whole job to make it go away. So they're talking very sweetly to me and basically saying you seem like a nice girl, you're early on in your career, you don't want to blow it all by making a name for yourself as a floozy, do you? One of them actually calls me honey and starts talking about how he's got a daughter my age, how he just wants the best for her. And they put this sixty-page settlement in front of me and say all I need to know is that I have to destroy the recording, and I'll be compensated.'

'And did you destroy it?'

'I told them I already had,' she said. Her voice was flat. 'I told them I just wanted to pretend it never happened. And there's this contract in front of me. I know I should read it – you're a lawyer, Emily, I know what you're thinking. But I can't stand the way these guys are all looking at me.'

Her voice seemed to judder and come to a stop.

'And then it's over,' she concluded. 'I've signed. And the next day there's two million dollars in my bank account.'

Chapter Seventeen

I WAITED FOR A long time for Tamsin to say something else. But after five minutes or so I began to hear soft snores, and when I looked over I saw that she was asleep – hand still loosely curled around the empty whisky glass. Her mouth, hanging half-open, only emphasised how sharp her jaw was. She couldn't have eaten properly in days.

I pulled her onto her side so there was no risk of choking and put a pint of water on the coffee table so that she'd be able to see it when she woke up. I ignored the night-shirt, the spare toothbrush, the cleanser, and climbed fully dressed up the white-painted stairs to the mezzanine loft to Tamsin's low bed.

It was made from solid wood, I could see that when I ran my hand over it. Probably teak, or something like that. I based my guess on the way that the word felt in my mouth, not out of any real knowledge. All I knew was that it wasn't the cheapest IKEA bed, the one that I, and half the people I knew, slept on. Couldn't even say owned, because our landlords owned them all.

I hadn't had a drop of the wine, Tamsin had drunk it all. But my head hurt anyway.

The ache at the top of my stomach and the back of my throat was the simple, base note of envy that I felt for her and always had. Even after everything she'd told me, it hurt that she had a beautiful bed to lie on, a ceiling of her own to stare at in the sleepless hours.

I picked up the book by the bed and flicked through it. A biography of Marilyn Monroe. I wanted to be interested, wanted to care about Norma Jean. But all I could think about was the Marilyn that had ballooned out some parts of herself and shrunk others away till they'd stopped existing. I read the same paragraph, over and over. I saw Tamsin where Marilyn was, the white dress, the sexy baby voice. It wasn't the pose that was so surprising, it was the way that men always seemed to fall for it.

It was noisy on the street outside, though it was after midnight. I wondered why a girl with insomnia had rented – or perhaps bought? – a flat in the most nocturnal part of London. Perhaps it was comforting to know that she wasn't the only one up.

I realised that I had no idea whether Tamsin owned her flat. Before, it would never have occurred to me to ask. But now I thought about it, there was a level of personalisation in the staircase bookshelf, in the way that everything hung exactly within arm's reach in the little kitchen. It was hers, in a way that I couldn't imagine a home ever being mine.

I slept on and off for a few hours, dreaming of things that Tamsin owned, of the food she'd cooked for me.

Art Rawlings, lurking behind the table, telling me to enjoy the champagne, that it was his very favourite.

When I woke up, I was lying on my side. I hadn't noticed in the dark, but there was a laptop charging in the place where the baseball bat had once lain. How un-Tamsin-like, I thought, to have technology by the bed. Did she lie there scrolling through Twitter, or drifting aimlessly around Netflix in search of something she might actually want to watch, like the rest of us? Was that what she did all day?

I picked up the laptop and opened it. I needed to check the weather forecast. Tamsin wouldn't mind.

There was no password on the laptop, which seemed extremely trusting, or old-fashioned.

I glanced through the desktop files and saw a folder labelled 'monologues'. The internet browser was taking its time loading the BBC weather page, and my fingers ranged. Each of the audio files inside was labelled by name and date. Working backwards, I scrolled to files from seven years ago. 'Juliet'. 'Nina'. 'Andromaque'.

'Anaïs Nin'.

It was a performance, not a diary. I swallowed, tasting the stench of my own breath. What was the point of a performance without an audience?

I listened to Juliet first, plugging my earphones into the port. It was reasonable, I thought, to want to know how good an actress she really was, after everything she'd told me. I recognised the speech from Mr Hawkins' GCSE English class. It was the one where Juliet is waiting for Romeo after their wedding ceremony, before their first night together. Mr Hawkins had asked Lucy to read it

189

out, saying she was the only one who had a feel for reading the iambic pentameter.

He always used to make me read the Nurse. He said I had a knack for the prosaic stuff.

Tamsin did Juliet's speech perfectly. Breathless, eager, childlike but with a hint of sensuality. She was *brilliant*. I realised, in that moment, that I'd never assumed she was any good as an actress. When you were as beautiful as her you didn't have to be.

The cursor seemed to move of its own accord.

The Andromaque one was in French so I didn't listen to the whole thing, but I got the idea. A woman. Mistreated, scorned, devastated, drowning in a river of tears, a victim of circumstance. Tamsin turned her hand well to that too, considering how young she'd been at the time.

The cursor moved on again. I skipped past Nina. Anaïs Nin.

I sat for a long time hovering on the play button.

She had played it to this other friend, this faithless, grasping friend.

She had played it to the police officer, and it had been played in turn to what sounded like a group of her superiors.

Perhaps Tamsin had intended to play it for me the previous night, if she hadn't been so drunk. I was certain she would play it to me now. If I asked.

I took out one earbud and listened carefully to the heavy, regular breathing that was still coming from below. Tamsin was asleep. There was no sense in waking her. It was easier for both of us if she just stayed asleep.

The recording started with another monologue in French. It was slightly muffled, drowned out by the background roar of the plane engines. I skipped over some of that part and resumed listening at the sound of a little giggle, and then, so clearly, almost as if he'd known he was being recorded, 'What's so funny?'

Her voice – so much brighter than it was now, or perhaps just younger – exclaiming over the beautiful bathroom. The sound of a door closing and a click. I felt like I could hear a change in the quality of the ambient noise, but perhaps that was only because I knew she was trying not to be frightened.

I could have paused it there, turned off the laptop, gone home. I could have made coffee for my friend, cared for her sore head and urged her to eat something.

But then he started to ramble, peppering his words with bursts of French in an absurd, exaggerated accent. He was no different, hearing him talk about his films in that recording, from men I'd been on dates with, from the Stus and the Harrys of the world. Boring on about their electronic music recordings or black-and-white photography.

Then, in a different voice, a low hiss, 'Are they real?'

Even though I knew it was coming it still made me shiver. His voice drew so much closer. There was no coyness in her confusion: 'What?'

And he was rambling again. Just as she'd said he had. 'You know, the sexiest thing in a girl is *realness*. Are you for real, sweetie? You've got to be real, you can tell me, I can handle anything, but I can't work with fakeness. It

191

goes against everything I am. These fake girls, they're everywhere. You're not like that, are you, honey? Let me check.'

A little cry. 'What are you doing?'

And then a sound that might have been 'no', but it's lost in the ambient bellow of the plane.

Rustling. And then sighs and gasps among the rustling – then more rhythmic cries.

She'd made it sound like it had been such a convincing performance of ecstasy, but to me she just sounded like a creature in pain.

Then a guttural moan. Him.

I paused the recording then, my hands twisted into the slept-in sheets of Tamsin's bed. I didn't want to hear the sounds of the shower.

I dressed in the clothes I'd been wearing the day before. I didn't shower. The silken memory of the bed sheets clung to my skin. On another day that might have felt like armour, but now it seemed to weaken me, to turn me into something skinless and in need of protection.

Tamsin was still asleep on the sofa, with all the lights on. I stood there watching her for a moment. Her eyes were closed, and the damask curtain of her hair fell across her face. She looked like a portrait, a Pre-Raphaelite.

I put out the light and left, shutting the door softly behind me.

Chapter Eighteen

FOR THE REST OF the weekend, I read and reread the stories of Rawlings' victims. Some sections of the media were starting to call them victims now. Others: 'the women who have come forward' or 'accusers'. A handful called them 'survivors'. There was a shoot of all thirteen of them in *Vogue*. Larroque and Ortiz and Carter and the rest. They were all dressed in black wisps of silk. None of them were smiling. They were all beautiful enough to get away with not smiling. Everyone online talked about how revolutionary the shoot was.

There were also rumblings, in the think pieces and the talk shows and the internet comments sections, that what Rawlings had done was somehow understandable, or else that it hadn't happened at all. The apologists didn't seem quite clear on which claim they were arguing for. One of his former leading ladies announced that although she couldn't 'speak to other people's truth', Rawlings had always been a perfect gentleman with *her*.

Even Hana mentioned it. She looked at the copy of *Vogue* that I'd gone out and bought – excruciatingly expensive, but cheaper than the paywall – and raised her eyebrows significantly.

'Well. You know what they say. The casting couch and all that.'

She broke off a single square of dark chocolate from the bar she kept in the fridge, and then went back to her room.

I spent the afternoon on the sofa with *Vogue* and a cup of tea, reading an interview with one of my favourite novelists and an article that assured me that the only thing wrong with lip fillers was 'stigma'. I was surprised to learn how little Botox cost, and how much Chanel flip-flops were.

I wondered if Tamsin would call me. She didn't.

I wondered if I ought to text her, to make up some reason why I'd left before she woke up. I didn't.

All Sunday I watched Rawlings' films and observed in every frame how shallow they were, how flimsy his female characters invariably turned out to be, how his misogyny turned every frame rancid.

James texted to ask if I wanted to meet up for a coffee, but I said I had to work.

Over the next couple of days a series of increasingly elaborate fantasies started to form in my mind – when I couldn't sleep on Sunday night, on the Overground to work, then sitting at my desk on Monday, staring idly at my emails. Eventually there was a fully choreographed sequence in my head, well-lit and captured as if by boom mic.

Me, turning up at Tamsin's place, grim but determined, my heart throbbing like a building bassline.

Me, finding Tamsin still in her dressing gown, her strength folded away to make space for her suffering. She, pale and translucent, like a Victorian consumptive. Unspilled tears blurring her steady gaze as Billie Holiday or Amy Winehouse or Janis Joplin howled out their sorrow over the speakers.

Me, speaking to her softly but urgently, laying it out for her – that only she could make a difference, only she could slay the dragon. The fire in her eyes gradually rekindling.

Me, holding Tamsin's hand while she made a faltering call to the police (or the journalist who had broken the story – I hadn't quite settled on that part). The way that she might – at first – break down. Say, 'I can't do it.' With my steady gaze and quiet, firm words, I would convince her. She could. She *must*. There was too much at stake.

She would nod, her shaking hands gripping the phone tighter, her brow creased in resolve. But halfway through speaking to the cop, the journalist, whatever – her throat would dry up as she arrived at the worst details of the assault.

She would, with shaking hands, pass the phone to me.

Me, describing it for her. Teasing out coherence from her chaos as only a lawyer could, threading a way forward.

The three fingers of whisky that I would pour for her when she finished on the phone. The tremulous nod when I told her she'd done the right thing. The renewal of strength and purpose as she leaned forward to hug me. The break in her voice when she said that she couldn't have done it without me.

Me, conveying everything unsaid with simple words, 'You're so brave.'

Us, clinking our glasses against each other, against the encroaching evening, against the sounds of the press that even then began to gather outside. The spiking microphones and blank-faced cameras and calls of Tamsin, Tamsin, Tamsin.

And – maybe just once – Emily.

Then there would be the long-term story. Later, during the *Newsnight* interview, the arty documentary, the limited podcast series, Tamsin would draw on our conversations to explain the moment that the switch flicked, the dawn broke, the sense of purpose filled her heart. Maybe there would be joint interviews, the two of us together a force to be reckoned with. Perhaps I'd quit my job to make time for my activism. Renee would understand. My drive, Tamsin's magnetism – enough of an identity for one whole woman. And everyone would see us, because we would be everywhere. Stu. My old bosses in the City. Harry . . .

'Emily? How're things going with Amina?'

'Yes!' I almost jolted out of my chair. Renee was gulping down a cup of coffee, her coat half on and half off, Molly gambolling happily at her feet. 'Still waiting for her signature.'

Renee's eyes narrowed. 'And you've taken her through the settlement yourself? You might need a translator, that's fine, just expense it. But she needs to be taken through the whole settlement verbally, okay? We need to be sure she understands.'

'Of course,' I said quickly. 'Already done.'

Amina had said she'd understood the settlement. What was there to take her through?

Renee nodded a final time and disappeared through the office door.

My eyes swivelled back to my email inbox, where a single email from myself, with the voice note as an attachment, lay like an uneasy promise.

I didn't click on the email, so it remained bold and unread. There was so much in that email that I couldn't bring myself to acknowledge. That low hiss. *Are they real?* Those wounded animal sounds. The roar of the jet engine, the roar of the shower.

Hadn't Tamsin said it herself? There was no point trying to be perfect. Now I was a person who sometimes did shitty things. No sense in obsessing about guilt.

Chapter Nineteen

WHEN LUCY TEXTED TO check if we were still on for the weekend, I was vague, telling her that the American girl I'd met at the protest (I still felt the need to call her that) was 'going through some stuff'.

And since she doesn't really know anyone else here . . .

I just left the ellipsis.

Lucy replied, *Yeah, fair enough. Maybe see you one evening this week though, at the bakery? I have some news.*

I lingered for a few seconds, not letting myself speculate on what the news might be, grateful to have the abrupt distraction of an email ping. I'd set a Google alert on the Rawlings case.

I was reading a lot that week. Not articles about Art Rawlings, not opinion pieces or profiles of his victims. I'd binged on that stuff and I felt bloated with it – Gabriela Ortiz and Lila Carter had started to feel like people I used to know. Raina Gupta's plastic surgery no longer seemed funny.

Something had happened that week with a UN climate report. Another major battle in Syria. I ignored both and felt little guilt.

But since I was mostly reading on work time, I read about the best ways to support victims. I read about trauma, mostly first-person stuff from women who'd experienced sexual assault. I soaked myself in their pain as if I could peel back my own skin to let the smart of it sink in.

At night I dreamed of Harry, of how his stubble used to graze the back of my neck in the morning. Sometimes I dreamed that I was marrying him, standing there in a white dress, certain that there was something I was forgetting, some reason why I couldn't possibly go through with it.

And on the train to and from work I looked up property prices for flats in Soho.

A clip was circulating on Twitter, already mutating into a meme. Rawlings, making careful eye contact with the (female) BBC anchor.

'One of the things that maybe I haven't always appreciated fully as a director is the power dynamic between a director and his leading lady,' he said, touching the tips of his fingers lightly together as if he was holding some great insight between his hands. 'You know,' he smiled wryly, 'often actresses see us as having all the power, but what they forget is that us schmucks are nothing without them. They are the *conduit* . . .' he emphasised each word with a thrust of his fist, 'for everything we're trying to achieve.'

'Hmmmm,' the interviewer said, as if deep in contemplation.

'Intense infatuations can blossom in that creative space,' Rawlings carried on, 'and, I'm sorry to say it, but Hollywood being Hollywood, the women in question are often at a very different point in their life than I am.' He shrugged. He was just naming the problem.

A few photographs flare up on the screen. Passionate kisses between Rawlings and Gabriela Ortiz.

'Are you referring to your – ah – famously *intense* dalliance with Gabriela Ortiz?' The anchor had a 'gotcha' look, but Rawlings waved the question away impatiently.

'I'm not going into specifics, that wouldn't be respectful to the ladies involved. But they're young. Maybe they're not so able to balance that high-wire act between creative and romantic fulfilment and professional expectations.' Leaning forward with a hand extended as if to soothe the news anchor's personal ire. 'That's not necessarily a criticism of the women – I'm a big feminist, I get it. If anything, it's more a criticism of myself. It's a tough thing to do.' A shrug, a shake of the head, self-effacing despair. 'I should have been a better guide.'

Clip over. Do I want to rewatch?

Comments blossoming underneath.

The bastard's going to get away with it. This whole thing's a farce.

Jeeeesus. All this stuff that he supposedly did happened what – ten years ago? Anyone can see, the guy's changed.

Lol so u think predators just spontaneously stop being predators? It's a ploy. This and all the supposedly empowering films about women.

WHY WOULD A BUNCH OF NOBODY ACTRESSES BE ACCUSING AN INCREDIBLY RICH MAN OF SEXUAL ASSAULT???? It's a real head-scratcher.

He just gets off on our trauma. They all do. It's exhausting.

Lol so UR saying hes shaped his entire film career around covering up a few fucks with actresses who regretted it afterwards? OK . . .

This is it, ladies. This is the moment we've been waiting for. This is the reckoning.

Guy must be doing something right if he tapped Gabriela Ortiz. Spicy . . .

Feminists be like: this is rape culture! Meanwhile, in the Congo . . .

I never liked his films anyway.

Baltimore Holiday was shit. But I'd go for some monkey business with Ije-whatever Nwa-dick-hey

He'd filled me with such a sense of steady warmth on the first date, but as soon as the Rawlings news broke, I'd stopped thinking about him. He'd made his way into my mind as a little bundle of feelings, not a whole person. When I actually saw him again in the flesh, I had to remind myself of his name. James.

I'd almost forgotten that we'd arranged a second date for Wednesday night. But when he texted to say he was looking forward to it and I frantically booked the table at the pub, as I'd promised I would, I told myself that it might do me good to have a circuit breaker, an evening spent on something other than watching YouTube interviews with rape victims.

We'd texted a bit, but my replies had been mechanical, the same stuff I'd say to any boy on Tinder. I'd tried to rally when he mentioned that he'd read a book I'd recommended and enjoyed it, but once we'd agreed that it was good, there didn't seem much else to say. But he suggested we meet up, and I saw no reason to say no.

When he said hello I noticed a burr to his voice that I hadn't perceived on the first date. West Country? I quite liked it.

I didn't kiss him on the cheek this time, and if he noticed, he didn't let on.

I'd picked this pub. I'd been here before and imagined that it was the sort of place that Tamsin might have chosen for a first date, timeless and intimate. But tonight it was too crowded and I could see we'd have to wait for ages at the bar.

The place was full of City boys in their identical blue suits, as if none of them could bear to stop wearing a school uniform. Grinning. Glaring. Laughing so very loudly, loud enough that I had to lean close to James to hear anything he said. He was shorter than Harry, I noticed, but broader in the shoulders.

'Get a bottle of wine, maybe? That way we won't need to go up again for a while, and by then it might have cleared a bit.'

I went to the loo while he was queuing for the drinks, and scrolled through my Twitter feed while I sat there in the stall. New footage was doing the rounds, Ijeawele Nwadike being chased outside her hotel in New York, reporters screaming at her to comment on the Rawlings story. Her face mostly concealed beneath a baseball cap, her lips pressed tight together as if she didn't trust what might come out of them, repeatedly half shaking her head. For a moment the camera angle seemed to find its way around the peak of the baseball cap and you caught her whole face. I remembered that she was only twenty-one years old. Even if she had given the performance of a much more time-ravaged woman.

When I returned to the table James said, 'Sure you don't want to go somewhere else?' Maybe he could see from my face that I wasn't right. I kept squinting, sure that I recognised the back of a head, a casual way of holding a pint. I edged closer to James than I might have otherwise.

'We've already bought the bottle.' I gestured.

'We can still leave if you'd rather.'

One of the blue suits gave a barking laugh too close to my left ear.

'We could drink it in the park. It's no worse than tinnies. It's better, actually. Classier.'

'No.' For some reason the suggestion rankled. 'It's fine.' I winced as the laugh sounded again.

James leaned forward, looking at me carefully. 'I'd even nick the wine glasses for you. Risk a prison sentence. If you promise to represent me in court.'

'I said no.' An edge in my voice.

I told him I didn't want to talk about my week; since he knew what I did. He said no more. I asked him about his instead. He did something at BBC News – technical, not creative.

'I guess it's been a big news week, with all the stuff that's going on?'

He shrugged. 'They're kind of all big news weeks. That's the nature of the twenty-four-hour news cycle. I guess the news is like a gas – it sort of expands to fill as much space as is available. Doesn't make that much difference to me, day-to-day.'

I didn't push it any further.

He was telling me about a friend of his that was having a hard time after his mother died. 'There's this unspoken agreement, I guess – we're all just taking it in turns to do stuff with him. Actual stuff that doesn't just revolve around getting drunk and making him more depressed. We went to the cinema last Wednesday night.' His eyes crinkled at the sides. 'Which was actually really nice.'

'What did you see?'

'The Billie Holiday film.' I went entirely cool inside. 'He really likes her. Loves his jazz singers. Billie, Ella. Sarah Vaughan.'

'I'm surprised that you could find somewhere that was still showing it.' Several of the indie cinemas in London had cancelled their planned showings, on principle.

He gave a little laugh, as if he hadn't thought of that. As if it were just a talking point, an intellectual exercise. 'Most places still are. Maybe Cineworld are just capitalist pigs. Makes sense, given how much they charge for popcorn.'

'Was the cinema busy?'

'Fairly.'

Big gulp of wine.

'Don't you feel like,' I said slowly, 'given everything that's gone on with Art Rawlings—'

'That I shouldn't have given him my money?' he finished quickly. He looked almost relieved that I'd said it. 'I know exactly what you mean.'

'I'm not sure that you do.'

He looked a little confused.

I elaborated. 'I mean, you're a straight white man.' I looked at my lap. 'We come at it from different perspectives.'

He tilted his head from side to side, as if to say 'fair play'.

'I'm kind of embarrassed to admit that I went. Especially to you, knowing what you do for a living and all that.' He shrugged, palms turned upwards. 'All I can say is that my mate wanted to see it. Like I said, big Billie fan.'

'You mean he's a really big fan of Art Rawlings?'

'No.' He took a slow sip of wine. 'I mean, he's liked some of his films. I think most people have.'

'Are we still talking about your friend, or do you mean *you* like his films?'

'What is this?' His voice slipped from its easy, conversational tones, and he was frowning slightly at me. 'Am I supposed to pretend that I never liked his films?'

'I just think . . .' I poured myself some more wine, then added some to his glass too, so he wouldn't think I was being rude. 'It would be nice if "most people"' – quotation marks mid-air – 're-evaluated, given everything that's happened.'

'That's absolutely true.' He smiled at me, and something in me was far too pleased at the affirmation. 'But yeah, I really loved *Emma's Game* when I was a teenager. And I feel like trying to retcon that would be . . . I don't know. Not the point? Admitting that I like bits of his back catalogue doesn't mean that I'm condoning sexual abuse.'

'Doesn't it?'

'Do you reckon it does?'

'I think it's pretty self-evident,' I said quietly. I spoke with the inflection of finality, then backtracked as the wine and my anger brought more words. 'I think that regardless of whether you liked his stuff when you were younger, there's no excuse for giving him your money now.'

He nodded slowly. I knew he was listening to what I was saying. But I wasn't sure that he'd yet caught the note in my voice, the note that I knew was there and perhaps was deliberately swelling, just to make myself feel full of something.

'I mean, you're right, there probably is no excuse. I was just trying to go along with what my mate wanted.' He looked despondent. I noticed that the corner of his mouth looked soft, and wanted to touch it.

'So your mate's feelings are more important than what Rawlings put all those women through?' I said quickly.

He gave a small, quiet sigh and then shrugged.

'I honestly don't know how you want me to answer that.' He looked me in the eye. 'I could say he's grieving and it didn't seem like a good moment to challenge him on his political beliefs.'

'You call it political beliefs,' I said, 'I call it basic empathy.'

206

'That's fair,' James said slowly. 'But the truth is probably just that I was happy to see him keen to do something. And . . .' he shrugged again, 'I didn't really think.'

I stood up.

'I'm going to head off now.'

'You're angry with me.'

'I'm not angry. I just need an early night.'

He reached over and took my hand in his. 'Emily, is there something else going on?'

'What do you mean?'

'You just seem . . . very invested in all this.'

'All women have a stake in this,' I snapped. 'But I wouldn't expect you to understand.'

'Right.' He gestured at himself. 'Straight white male.'

'Anyway, like I said, I'm just very tired.'

'That's a shame,' he said quietly. 'I was really looking forward to seeing you. But I can tell I've blown it.'

I paused. Waiting. But he just shrugged.

'I guess I'll chalk it up to experience. Get home safe, okay?'

As I was walking home I longed to text Tamsin. Not text her, call her. Buy another bottle of wine – why did I not take the wine from the table, as Tamsin did from Stu? – and head to her place.

I could launch into it all, stretched out on her sofa with a glass of wine in my hand. About men and the way that they thought their feelings trumped everything else – yet *we* were supposedly the emotional ones. About moral laziness. About how James clearly couldn't see that his friend – though he might be grieving – was clearly an amoral arsehole who probably hypersexualised Black women.

About his spinelessness, about how he didn't fight for me to stay.

And she would listen, watching me with her cat's eyes. I knew exactly what she'd say about it all. I was getting good at writing her.

I thought about taking a diversion – only a little one – to walk past her flat. But I figured she'd be asleep. Or maybe just not home.

When I got back to my place that night I found the email address of the journalist who'd broken the story. It wasn't difficult – it was in her Twitter bio, with a request that anyone with leads get in touch – *Our best chance of justice is for anyone who knows anything to come forward.*

I made a burner email account on Gmail. No longer Emily, no longer striving. Just 'E'.

I hovered for a long time, and finally attached the voice message to an email, leaving the unexploded bomb in the Drafts folder.

Chapter Twenty

LUCY WAS WAITING FOR me in the same place that we always met, yet it all felt off balance – Thursday evening, not Sunday morning. It didn't seem like the same cafe. She was leaning forward and towards the door, as if she was impatient to see me.

'What's wrong?' She said it instead of hello.

'Nothing,' I said automatically. 'Just a tiring week. Really busy. How are you?'

She ignored the question completely. 'Something's happened, I can see it has.'

'Nothing's happened. Let me go and get a coffee.'

'I've already ordered you one. Andrew's bringing it. It's not Harry again, is it?'

Lucy had been given several versions of what had happened with Harry. The pared-back, post-break-up, still-loyal version. The drunken, overflowing, impressionistic version. Maybe she was even a step ahead of me; maybe she'd pieced together something like the truth.

'Andrew?' I looked over to the counter, where I hadn't noticed Andrew leaning against the wood. He was wearing a thick cable-knit jumper and old jeans, and looked like the most solid thing in the room. He caught my eye and gave a quick, friendly smile. Then he transferred his gaze

to Lucy, and the smile deepened into something that I
didn't understand.

They had News for me. Some small, squalling news
that smelled of sour milk and naked need, and they would
deliver their news holding hands and looking intermit-
tently into each other's eyes. Would they say, 'We're
pregnant'? Lucy and I had always made fun of that
phrase.

'Nice to see Andrew,' I said. I had to pretend not to
know why he was there; that was part of my role. But when
he brought the coffees over Lucy reached down into her
handbag and drew out the third *Game of Thrones* book,
silently handing it to him. He retreated to a table in the
far corner with his coffee and the book, and made a clear
show of settling in. Lucy's eyes lingered on him for a second
as he settled, then moved back to me with renewed purpose.

'You don't have to tell me why you're upset,' she said.

I felt uneasy, both with how focused she was on me
and how pale she looked. Morning sickness?

'You're back on the coffee wagon, then?'

'I didn't sleep last night. Never mind that.'

'Me neither,' I said, staring down into my own stupid
bowl of too-strong coffee.

She was silent in a way that invited me to speak.

I meant to hold back a little longer, protest a little more,
but it was all I could do to focus on sounding casual
when I said, 'Remember that American girl that I told you
about? The one I met at the protest? I mean, I made a
mistake – she's Canadian, not American.'

'Yes.' If she was struggling to remember what I was talking about, she didn't show it.

Maybe because I hadn't slept, maybe because I felt as though the air in that coffee shop needed filling, maybe because I felt guilty about Andrew sitting alone in the corner and wanted to get it over with – I let it come out. The basic plot points of Tamsin, at least.

'You said she was going through something,' said Lucy when I was finished, 'but I wasn't expecting something so . . .' she allowed herself a little, bemused smile, 'globally newsworthy.'

'I know. Going through something doesn't even cover it.'

'I can see why she wouldn't want to come forward,' Lucy said slowly.

'Oh, so can I,' I said hurriedly. 'Don't get me wrong. I understand completely, it's really, really hard for women to come forward. But what I don't understand is, she's normally so unafraid of everything, and you'd think it would be . . .'

'. . . The same with this?'

It seemed far too crass to actually say it, but there it was.

'That would be . . . logical.'

A long pause.

'I don't think people really are that logical.'

We sat in silence for a while, then –

'Do you ever think about all the time they spent teaching us to put condoms on test tubes?' I asked.

'Boiling tubes. Test tubes were smaller.'

211

'Whatever. You know, I don't know if any man I've been with actually knows how to put a condom on himself? They always just seem to assume it's my job.'

'Anyway . . .'

'Anyway. All the condoms on boiling tubes. All that time we spent doing PowerPoint presentations on the symptoms of different STDs.'

'STIs. Yeah. We did gonorrhoea. Do you remember?'

'It was quite a good presentation. We made up a mnemonic for the symptoms.'

'PPUD. Pain while peeing, unusual discharge.'

'Your memory's so good. Anyway, why didn't they teach us about this?' I gestured around the cafe, as if men like Rawlings were lurking behind the velvet armchairs.

'What do you say, I guess?'

'I don't know exactly. But it seems so much worse not to try and say something. Not to prepare us. Or once the stuff has happened, not to tell us what to do with it.'

We'd all been terrified, of course. Of the pain we were assured would come, of the diseases we assumed we would contract. Of the pregnancies that would do their best to creep up on us.

Lucy didn't say anything. She was staring at the patterned knees of her leggings. Then Andrew appeared as if summoned, touching Lucy's shoulder very lightly. She looked up at him.

'Anyway,' I said, too quickly. 'I've been going on and on about me.' I leaned forward, a big, expectant smile plastered on my face. I wondered if they were going to ask me to be godmother. I couldn't really say no. 'Tell me your big news.'

'It's not like that,' Lucy said.

At the same time, Andrew said, 'Oh, I thought you'd told her.'

'No. Wait. What?'

'It's the silliest thing,' Lucy mumbled. 'I feel ridiculous for dragging Andrew along now. I just felt like I needed . . . Never mind.'

'It isn't silly, Luce,' he said, sitting on the arm of her chair and placing a hand on the crown of her head.

'I *feel* silly. I don't know why I'm making such a *thing* of it.'

'Of what?'

In my head I was running through the list of things that could go wrong with people my age. A parent with cancer, maybe? Had she been laid off? No teachers got laid off, not even bad ones, let alone teachers like Lucy. Had they decided to move to the countryside? Were they making such a big deal out of it because they thought that their absence would tear a hole in the life of their poor, single friend?

'I've got a new boss,' Lucy said, in a rush.

'A new boss?' I echoed blankly.

'It's Chris.'

'Chris?' I cycled through the half-dozen Chrises I knew.

'Chris . . . oh Emily, *you know.*'

I looked at her, still not getting it.

'Mr Hawkins,' she hissed through her teeth. 'He's our new Head. From September.'

'Oh . . .' The air puffed out of my lungs. 'That's . . .' Andrew was staring fixedly at the wall above my head, his expression blank. 'God,' I said at last. 'That's really awkward.'

'So awkward.' The words came out of her quickly. I saw Andrew shift on the arm of the chair. I looked up at him, saw a trace of something leave his face before I could catch it properly.

I asked the only question that occurred to me. 'When did you find out?'

'A while ago. Two weeks, maybe?'

I remembered that day on the Heath. The day Lucy called me twice.

'They announced it to staff and . . . yeah. I didn't quite know what to do.'

'Do?' My mind was moving very slowly, and for some reason I didn't want to look at her. 'I guess . . . yeah, I guess you'll have to talk to him at work and stuff.' I glanced up at Andrew. 'Very weird.'

There was that expression on Andrew's face again and this time I caught it. It was a look that I'd never seen before, a look I hadn't known such a mild-mannered person was capable of.

'It's okay,' Lucy said quickly. 'I just needed you here . . . just while I actually got it out. I'm fine now. You go back to your Lannisters.'

'Are you sure?'

She nodded. I began to pick apart my croissant, flake by flake. Once Andrew had sloped back off to the other table and made a show of resuming his book, Lucy took a big gulp of coffee and leaned back in her armchair.

'I didn't know that Andrew knew about Chris,' I said. She stared at me for a second as if she was baffled, but then nodded in a quick, nervous motion.

'Oh, yeah. I told him everything. Very early on.'

'He seems . . .'

'He finds it upsetting.'

'Do you think he gets it?'

She looked at me very sharply, eyes round. 'What do you mean?'

'You know. What that relationship . . . was.'

'Oh, you know what Andrew's like.' Her eyes darted over to him. I had no idea what she meant by that. I'd never formed much of an opinion on what Andrew was like. 'He thinks everything's very clear-cut.'

'But surely he can see . . . you know,' I fumbled for the right thing to say. 'He can see that you're fine? I mean, maybe that sort of relationship might have been a bit much for some girls of our age . . . Maybe most girls our age.'

'Yes.'

'But you were always different from the rest of us, weren't you?'

'Hmm?' Lucy cocked her head to one side, considering. 'I suppose . . . well, yes, I suppose so.' Lucy nodded, looking a little distracted, raising her coffee to her lips again even though there was nothing but the dregs remaining. 'I wasn't some naïve little thing.'

'You consented,' I said. I felt like I was bringing a new concept to the same old conversations that we'd always had about Mr Hawkins, for hours and hours during sixth form, always circling around an idea that we couldn't then have fully articulated. 'And you were over the age of consent. If he hadn't been our teacher then it would just have been . . .'

'. . . slightly unorthodox . . .'

'. . . but fundamentally consensual . . .'

'Yeah.' She sighed. 'You're right.'

'I can see why Andrew wouldn't have understood that. But it's all about consent, at the end of the day, isn't it?'

'And I consented.' Lucy closed her eyes. 'Enthusiastically. As the kids say.'

'You were attracted to him.' I liked being the straight shooter, the truth-teller. It made me feel a little more like Tamsin.

'Of course. I mean . . . yeah.' She frowned a little. 'I must have been.'

'You were,' I said, twiddling a strand of my hair around my fingers. 'We all were.'

'I remember . . . even more than that, I just really liked that he was so attracted to *me*.' Lucy swallowed again from her empty cup. 'It was a bit like . . . I don't know, people go on and on about power, don't they? I'm never quite sure what they mean. But I remember how he . . . even now, with Andrew . . .' Both of our eyes slid to the corner where he sat, legs spread wide, elbows resting on his thighs, head bent towards his book. 'I'm never quite sure that Andrew feels as . . . as intensely about me as Chris did.' She shut her mouth sharply, as if she'd said something treacherous.

I could tell that the time had come to back away slightly, to return to the present. But there was something exhilarating in meeting this side of Lucy again, the girl who had not truly confided in me in so long.

'How did you feel when you saw him again?' I probed, gently.

'I don't know.' She shrugged. 'Like, surprise, obviously, but then kind of nothing. I don't want to make a massive deal of it. I've been so tired recently. Maybe I've got a bit of a bug. I keep being sick.'

She saw my eyes drop inadvertently to her stomach, and shook her head.

'No, it's not that. Definitely not.'

Her eyes slid over to Andrew.

'Definitely not.'

He was back to reading his book, and I couldn't see his face, but there seemed to be something there that was visible, at least, to Lucy.

'But you're okay, aren't you?'

'Oh, I'm always okay, you know that as well as anyone.' Her voice became steely and sharp, and for just a moment her eyes met mine in an accusation.

I didn't look away. I braced myself for something, something that I couldn't put into words but had always suspected might come.

'Lucy, I know I—'

'Never mind.' She took a little packet of sugar from the pot on the table and poured it into her empty coffee cup. 'I'm not myself at the moment.'

'I feel like I've—'

'You were sixteen.'

'So were you.'

'It's fine. Sorry. I didn't mean to bite your head off. Yeah, I'm okay. Like you say, Andrew makes this assumption that it was . . . that Chris is . . . He thinks I ought to try and find another job. I'm not going to, obviously . . . I just sort of . . . well, I wanted you to know.' She balled up the sugar packet and placed it neatly in the middle of the table. 'In case I'm a bit all over the place.' Round blue eyes on me, the pupils very black and hard. 'Because you knew me then.'

'And I knew him.'

'Right. You knew him. And you knew me.'

Leaving the cafe and walking to the bus stop took me past the end of the road where my parents had once lived. It seemed almost ridiculous that I couldn't just take out my key, slink unnoticed into the house, curl up in my single bed and go to sleep. Even the way that my footsteps rang out and bounced down the hill was familiar to the point of being stale.

How electrifying it had been to stumble home from the station the night of the party at Chris Hawkins' house – the wretchedness I felt, the humiliation, somehow seeming to prove that something meaningful had happened. How much older I'd felt, how poisoned and tainted.

The feeling had flooded through me, as if by injection, after a brief moment with Mr Hawkins in his garden. I was drunk – for the first time – and had stepped out for some air. He'd followed me and called out in a bantering tone that surely I couldn't be such a lightweight. I remembered being amazed at how, through the sweet stickiness of drink, I'd still been able to say all the right things, even though in retrospect they couldn't have been convincing.

He'd asked what I wanted to do at university and I'd told him English and he'd said 'good girl'. Then I'd blurted out that stupid poetry at him that ended with the line 'and in short, I was afraid'.

'It feels like a warning,' I'd said, moonstruck by the outline of his profile in the half-light of the terrace. 'To always follow my intuition. Not to be crushed by societal expectation.' That was a line I'd recently become infatu-ated by. 'To have no regrets.'

Then, amazed at my daring, even as I did it, I'd reached out and touched his hand.

For a hanging moment he had said nothing, but looked down at our hands. Turned mine over in his so the palm faced up, as if considering.

'Indeed,' Mr Hawkins had said, the way he always did in class when someone said something perceptive. 'No regrets.'

He'd looked at me for a long moment, that made me feel like he'd never really looked square in my face before. His eyes moved over me, and I remembered thinking that it was as if I were a poem, and he were reading me.

'You're a clever girl, Emily,' he'd said. Then he dropped my hand and went back inside, leaving me to vomit behind the rose bushes.

Chapter Twenty-One

WHEN I GOT TO Tamsin's building, I was a little disconcerted to find that the front door had been left open. This time I had texted her before heading over. She didn't answer my message, which I thought was all the more reason to check on her. Perhaps she'd left the front door ajar for me.

Entering the stairwell I thought I could hear voices. I knocked at the entrance to the apartment, shifting my tote bag on my shoulder. I hadn't brought wine this time, but I'd bought a nice bar of chocolate. Some loose-leaf tea. A paperback book.

Tamsin opened the door and glanced at me so briefly that I could only take in a flash of her face. Then she turned and walked back to the area by the sofa. I followed her, feet skittering and mussing the soft rugs on the wooden floor.

'I have company now. You have to leave,' Tamsin said. I thought at first she was speaking to me and felt as though I'd been punched.

But then I saw. Sitting on the daybed – where I had slept so many times – was Art Rawlings.

It didn't feel like he was truly in the room. It was as if he was realer somehow than his surroundings, like an actor in an old film against a matt painted backdrop. It was all there – the shaggy head, the bowed posture, the careful scruffiness. It looked bohemian in photographs, but up close you could see the craft to it, how carefully the shirt skimmed his pot belly, how the stubble disguised a weak chin.

Rawlings leapt to his feet when he saw me.

'Hello,' he said, his big American voice filling the room. He stuck out his hand and looked me up and down. Then he flushed slightly. Perhaps his publicist had told him to stop doing that as soon as he met young women. 'Art Rawlings. How're you?'

A distant voice at the back of my mind, a voice that sounded like Renee's, murmured, *He's trying to take control.*

I looked down at his unshaken hand and did nothing, until he withdrew it casually.

Tamsin was looking at Rawlings through eyes like shards of green glass.

I brushed off a feeling of being passed over in the playground. *Aren't you going to introduce me?*

Art Rawlings might be sweating slightly, might be carefully rearranging his hair to cover a receding hairline, but fame seemed written into every atom of him. The strangely poreless – though creased – skin. The weave of his linen jacket. The piercing brightness of his blue eyes.

'Art was just leaving,' Tamsin said.

She looked more beautiful than I'd ever seen her before. More sharply drawn. She wore simple black trousers and a black silk shirt, like a blot of ink against the rich colours of the room, which had been restored to its usual brightness. Her face was pale, hair pulled back into a ballerina bun, bone structure starkly extraordinary. She stood in front of her bookcase, her arms folded across her chest.

Rawlings was looking at her, his neck bowed.

'Tammy, I'm a broken man,' he said, and his voice became hushed and intimate. I shifted and the floorboards squeaked loudly beneath my feet, but Rawlings didn't seem to notice. He gave a hunched, uncertain gesture, but the motion was so distinct that it read as a room-filling confidence. Or rather, it might have filled another room, one that didn't hold Tamsin, with her folded arms and unsmiling mouth.

'It's Tamsin, not Tammy,' she said. 'And you don't look too broken to me.'

'All this stuff, it's shaken me to my core. I don't know who I am any more.' He looked piteously at her, and when her gaze failed to yield, he turned to me as if remembering I was there too. 'My psychiatrist, he's put me on all these pills, it's like I'm in a fog. I'm sure you've read certain things in the papers, there's an agenda there, you don't know the half of it . . .'

'Tamsin told me what you did,' I said. 'She was eighteen.'

He nodded. 'I mean, there's eighteen and there's eighteen,' he said, turning back to Tamsin. 'I don't think you realise how self-possessed you were. This little ingénue. Flirtatious. Maybe you weren't in control of it. But there was something there between us, I swear to god. If I hadn't truly believed that I'd never have—'

'Maybe not,' Tamsin said icily. 'But I guess we believe what we want to be true, right?'

'Easy for you to say now,' muttered Rawlings. 'But it takes two – you know that as well as I do. Two sides to every story.'

'I'm sure you'll be fascinating us all with your side of the story on a friendly news network. I guess we'll just have to see.' Tamsin regarded him coolly. 'Maybe it'll work. Maybe you really did believe that all those young, beautiful women found you irresistible. Weird how they all regretted it later, isn't it?'

'Weird?' Rawlings wheeled around wildly, and then strode over to the French doors. They were open to the balcony, but he stopped just before the threshold, as if blocked by some invisible force. 'Nothing weird about it, is there? They're after the money.' He shot a vile look over his shoulder at Tamsin. 'Just like you.'

'Yet you didn't see me in that *Vogue* shoot,' Tamsin snapped. 'What's the matter, Art? Are you mad that we didn't all just stop needing to make a living after you got us blacklisted?'

'Make a living?' Rawlings scoffed and looked around the apartment. 'Is that what you call this? You could have done real work, serious work.' He gestured around, deriding something that I couldn't see. 'And instead you're *here*.'

'I like it here.'

Rawlings ignored her. 'Money,' he was muttering, over and over again. 'That's all women ever really care about.'

223

'It's easy to say that you don't care about money when you have it,' Tamsin said sweetly. 'We'll see how you feel when those legal fees bankrupt you. Now get out, Art. You're not as interesting as you think you are.'

I suddenly remembered the opening frames of *Baltimore Holiday*. A face, gradually illuminated by a spotlight like a rising sun. Eyes closed. A trumpet like a dirge.

'You'll be hearing from my people,' Rawlings snapped, suddenly businesslike.

Tamsin closed her eyes. For a split second she looked exhausted, but by the time her lashes rose again, her expression was closer to insolent boredom.

'No doubt,' she said. 'Goodbye.'

At first I thought there was no chance that he would leave. He sucked in a breath and seemed to draw all the air out of the room as he advanced on Tamsin. I didn't know whether he might try to hit her, or seize her in a passionate embrace.

She simply looked at him, her gaze steady, and then his slumped posture returned.

'Think about my offer,' he mumbled, like he couldn't help himself, getting the last word, and turned to leave.

As he brushed past me I heard him mutter the word 'bitch'. He did it without conviction.

As the door closed behind Rawlings, I more than half expected all of Tamsin's firmness to collapse. But if anything, she seemed to grow taller in the time it took for my eyes to swivel back to her.

'Tamsin . . .' I said weakly.

She looked at me and smiled, a secret smile as if the focus in the room were really me, not her. Even now, even as Rawlings slammed the building's front door and the whole room shook, she was alchemising whatever had just passed into some sort of anecdote to be enjoyed over a glass of something cold.

She crossed to the kitchen counter and took down two crystal tumblers, then poured out two generous measures of whisky.

'That's the last time I'm ever gonna see that guy,' she said. I could tell she believed it was true.

She pulled her hair out of its bun and it fell diagonally across her back like a curtain sweeping across a stage. I had only vaguely registered that there was something different about her, but now I could see that she'd had it dyed, her hair a deep, burnished red. It looked entirely authentic; if I hadn't known what she'd looked like before, I wouldn't have suspected it wasn't her natural colour.

'You changed your hair.'

'It was time for a change,' she said. It shone thickly on her shoulder.

'I liked your old hair. It was part of you.'

'Well, now this is part of me.'

I'd never known anyone with hair like hers before, that beautiful gilt colour. It had been so startling that I thought it had to be natural. But this new colour looked natural too.

'Scotch?'

'No thanks. I've got to be up early tomorrow.'

I didn't, but I was starting to feel tired. Tired of her beauty. Tired of the radiant light falling in from the balcony. The soft tinkle of ice cubes in the cut-crystal glasses was splintering through my head like the sound of a drill. I wanted to drop onto the sofa, but I felt exhausted too by its softness, the way that the cashmere throw would lure me into languidness.

'Actually, I think I'd better head off. Give you some time to process . . .' I waved my hand towards the door. 'Whatever all that was about.'

'I don't need time to process it.'

I looked over to the hand that was holding her whisky and saw a row of four red curves carved into her palm. The place where her fingernails had pressed into her flesh.

'I find that hard to believe.'

She looked at me through slightly slitted eyes. 'If I say I need help processing, will you stay and have a drink with me?'

Chapter Twenty-Two

The sun was setting, casting a shadow of the balcony railings on the opposite wall in a row of rosy stripes, distorting part of Tamsin's face. She came closer – a wave of perfume, different perfume, ambered and heady – and handed me the drink. The cut glass nestled so easily into my hand.

'He came here.' I took a sip of whisky, misjudged in the hope that it would help me to clear the blockage in my throat.

'Yup.' She sipped her own drink thoughtfully. 'I was surprised too.'

'You mean he just showed up?' I geared up for outrage, fear, horror, all of them ready to fill my voice.

'No, no. I told him to come.'

She sat down easily on the velvet sofa, tucking one foot underneath her.

'Had to have it out with him. Now or never.'

'What?' I took another big sip of whisky and realised that I was shaking. As if the fear she was refusing to feel had made its cuckoo's nest in my own body. 'You told ... you told the man ... who sexually assaulted you ... where you *live*?'

'He already knew where I lived, honey.' She gestured with her whisky glass. 'He's had a guy posted in the cafe opposite this place for the last three weeks.'

My head snapped towards the French windows as if expecting to see some spectral, cloaked figure bursting through. 'What guy?'

'Just a guy. He said his name was Alexei. Maybe it really was.'

'What do you mean, he said?'

'I decided to introduce myself the other day. Seemed like the polite thing to do, if we were going to be working together.'

Leave it to Tamsin to behave as though everyday fear was too pedestrian for her.

'That guy on the tube, who took a photograph of me in the pond? That was Alexei. Or whatever his name is. As you might have guessed from how easily we spotted him, he isn't exactly great at his job.' She laughed. 'I bought him a beer and asked him the right questions, and he told me everything. Turns out Art hired this like . . . espionage company to watch me. He's out there right now, actually.'

She crossed the room to the balcony, and automatically I followed her.

In a street cafe below, incongruous among the Soho clientele, sat the man from the train, the man in the parka. A modest half-pint of beer sat in front of him, a book splayed beside it. Tamsin waved jovially. He jumped a little, then waved back.

'Give him a wave, Emily. He has a boring job.'

I ignored her suggestion and turned around to face her as she receded back into the flat and sank onto the sofa.

'Tamsin, that's a hired . . . a hired *goon*.'

'That's harsh. Alexei's not a goon. He had a job at a logistics company, but now his kid needs daycare so his wife can go back to work. This pays better, and he gets to be home at weekends.'

'*Tamsin.*'

'Alexei's not the problem, Emily. Just like you're not the problem, and I'm not the problem. Art is the problem.'

'I don't believe . . . this.' I looked over to the door of the flat to see if the baseball bat was still there. The spot was empty. 'This is unbelievable.'

'I mean, I say espionage company. Alexei wasn't so good at staying undercover, all those old ladies rumbled him straight away.'

The man in the park. Tamsin's fear. Even now I couldn't really bear to look square at the memory.

But this version of Tamsin was smiling.

'In a way, that's actually kind of a good memory for me, now. When I look back on it.'

'There was a creepy guy, Tamsin. Taking photos of you.'

'Yeah,' she nodded. 'There was. Only it turns out he wasn't a creep.'

'Just a paid fucking spy.' My voice was rising.

'Yeah. And a Greek chorus of fancy old English ladies shaming him. One of the greater moments of my life.' She closed her eyes for a second, grinning, as if she was already trimming the memory into an anecdote. She opened her eyes again. 'Very cool.'

'I can't believe he had you followed. That's so . . .'

229

'I've known for a while that Art hires people to intimidate you,' Tamsin said calmly. 'It's part of his MO. He puts a lot of work into this shit.' She paused for a moment, trying to find the right words. 'He's more of a full-time creep who makes movies as a side gig. It's not the other way around. When I told him we needed to talk I kind of thought he'd send someone to rough me up.' She smiled. 'Coming himself was the biggest favour he could have done me. Made me realise there's nothing to be scared of.' She took a considered sip of whisky, and then continued, conversationally, 'We call these guys predators, but that's too big a compliment. It makes it sound like they're lions or something.' She looked off into the middle distance. 'He's just a little boy who stumbled into some power.'

She closed her eyes. Seemed to breathe a little more freely, her inhales slow and sonorous.

'He could still have hurt you.'

One eye popped open.

'Oh, that was what he thought too.' She laughed. 'He told me I was looking good "for my age".' A poisoned smile. 'He offered me a part in a movie, would you believe? A teenage girl. I think it was intended as flattery. I said, Art, honey, if a single studio ever gives you the money to make another movie, then we'll talk.'

I wanted to laugh. To smash the whisky glass down on the coffee table. To step out of the flat and retrace my steps back to my work desk and my scrolling screen, where women feared the men that hurt them. I needed to make Tamsin understand.

'Don't you think he'll go to jail?' I asked. I made it sound like an intellectual exercise, like I was as relaxed as she was at least pretending to be.

'No,' she said at once, shaking her head. The dying light of the day flickered off her burnished hair. 'Not a damn chance.'

'But you could change that. You've got . . .' I almost said *you've got a recording of the whole thing*, but I changed my mind. 'You've got a voice.' I tried to catch her eye, but she was directing her gaze out of the window. She nodded this time.

'Probably, yes.'

'But you're not going to?'

'I don't think so.'

'You don't think they'd believe you?'

'Some people always want to know what the evidence is.' She shrugged. 'I get that. But some people . . . some people don't care even if there is evidence. Because no evidence could change their mind.'

I left a long pause. Tried to calculate the exact measure of time that would give my words their fullest impact.

'I think you should reconsider.'

She looked at me now. Nodded. Her voice was low and firm.

'Yeah. I guess a lot of people will feel that way.'

A silence. She seemed happy to let it wrap around her. I couldn't bear anything as heavy, as lacking in allegiance, as silence. Not between us.

231

'Don't you think you have a responsibility? To the other women?'

A little crease formed between her eyes, like a deliberate mistake in an otherwise perfect artwork.

'The ones that came after you,' I clarified. 'The ones he might assault in the future?'

'Why would I think that?' She poured me more whisky first, then herself. 'I don't hold the women he hurt before me responsible. He never should have done it.'

'I mean, yes, of course.' I swirled the replenished whisky in the tumbler. Around and around, around and around.

'Larissa Larroque wants to testify against him,' Tamsin said. 'If it goes to court. She said so.'

'Yeah.'

'More power to her.'

'She's amazing.'

'But I don't.'

I stayed silent. For as long as I could.

'Tamsin?'

'Yeah?'

Was this the question I had failed to ask so far? The question that would unlock everything? Explain her behaviour?

'Did he try anything with you? Just now?'

She laughed. Laughter that filled the room.

'We're not on a private jet. We're on my turf.' She raised her glass, as if toasting something unseen. 'He wouldn't dare.'

'But how could you have let him in here? Weren't you scared?'

'Scared? Of Art? Why? He doesn't have any power over me. Not any more.'

'You were all alone. You were vulnerable.'

Tamsin took a slow, considered sip of her whisky.

'I don't think I was.'

'He's twice your size.'

'If I stuck my head out onto this balcony and yelled, you'd have fifteen six-foot drag queens breaking down the door to this apartment and poking his eyes out with their high heels. Maybe Alexei would have joined the party too. He's a nice dude, really. I left the front door open for them. Just in case.'

Whether it was true or not, it was clear that she believed it.

'You couldn't yell last time. You were too scared.' There was a little accusing catch in my voice. I smoothed it out as best I could. 'You said so.'

'I'm different now.'

As if nothing else needed to be said.

'But I'm . . . Trust me, I have a legal background. This is going to damage things if you ever want to come forward, Tamsin. If you press any charges against him. If you want a restraining order. You invited him to your *home*. What would a jury make of that?'

'What jury? Anyway, where else am I supposed to talk to him in private? He needs to see that I'm not scared of him.'

'Whether you're scared of him or not, it's going to make the case for harassment harder.'

233

'Who said anything about harassment? I wanted to talk to him. And I did.'

'How could you *want* to talk to him?'

'He's just a guy.'

'He's a predator!' The words burst out of me. 'You've got to keep yourself safe from him!'

'Safe?' She laughed again, but this time it was a thin little thing. 'He's already done his worst to me.'

'You might think that, but—'

'I might think that?' She leaned deeper into the sofa, considering me carefully over the top of her tumbler. She spoke slowly, with careful measure. 'As if I don't know?' Her voice became even more controlled as she proceeded. 'As if I'm not the one who's lived with it for seven years?'

'I mean . . . exactly. So don't you want him to get what's coming to him?'

'Art *will* get what's coming to him, one way or the other.' She gave a slow, feline blink and took a sip of whisky. 'But the guy's never going to jail. Not in a million years.'

'But—'

'*But* – no self-respecting actress will work with him now. Feminism's part of the personal brand, right? It's not edgy any more – collaborating with a known sex offender. So he won't be able to make the kind of movies he wants to make. And you know what?'

'What?' I folded my arms.

'Don't look so *prim*, Emily.' I stiffened. 'In a way, that makes me sad, that he won't get to make movies any more.

Because *Baltimore Holiday* was beautiful, and I was looking forward to seeing what he did next. I'm already missing out on the fruits of this guy's talent because he's a fucking asshole. Who wins in all of this?'

'But you could lose a lot if you don't come forward,' I jumped in. 'You've broken the NDA already, presumably. You've told me. I have no idea who else you've told, but if you're going to break the NDA, you'd be wise to do it in public, where you can be protected. He's got people following you.'

'He's calling Alexei off. He promised.'

'And you believe him?'

'I do.'

I shuffled on the sofa, looking over to the balcony, remembering the leak of Tamsin's murmured words through the curtain in the early hours of the morning.

'And that guy who was calling you, late at night? He's going to stop too?'

'What guy?'

'The guy . . .' I jerked my head towards the daybed. 'I heard you talking to him, the first night I stayed here. You were on the balcony. You told him not to call you again. That was the same guy, right?'

'That . . . Oh. No, that wasn't.'

'So it was another—'

'No, Emily.' She shook her head slowly. 'No. It was the reporter.' I must have looked confused; she clarified, 'The one who broke the story. The story about Art.'

At first I felt the dawning of understanding. But then it stalled. 'But . . . but that doesn't make sense. You told him to stop calling you.'

'Her. Right. Which, by the way, she didn't. Sending me dozens of texts a day isn't really in the spirit of "don't call me", wouldn't you agree?'

'So . . . so wait. So you knew that this whole story was going to come out?'

Tamsin did a little double-take, a tiny motion that might have been perfectly calculated to make me feel stupid. 'Knew? Of course I *knew*. They wanted me to be a part of it.' She snorted. 'I would have made such a cute little centrepiece. Probably the only way I'd ever get to make it into the hallowed pages of *The New Yorker*.' She sniffed. 'Not to worry. There are other literary magazines.'

'So . . . so you could have been part of this,' I said slowly. 'And . . . you decided not to be?'

'Right.' She met my eyes. 'I decided not to be.'

I said nothing.

'At least the reporter had the courtesy to tip me off when the story was about to break,' she continued. 'Gave me one last night on the tiles before the whole world started talking about Art Rawlings.'

'One last night on the tiles?'

'With you.'

That night. The martinis, the fountains, the Savoy bar and the old man. The skyline, the drag queens, the pizza. That glorious night, that final night.

'Excuse me,' I mumbled, slamming my whisky tumbler down too loud and heading for the loo.

Tamsin called after me, 'It's okay, honey. Take some time. *Process.*'

Sitting on the loo I read again the framed cross-stitch hanging on the back of the door.

I rise with my red hair
And I eat men like air.

I flushed the toilet and washed my hands. I glanced in the mirror, but only briefly. I didn't want to look at my own face for too long.

Then I saw that there was a condom wrapper on the shelf below the mirror. Not even hidden in the bin, just lying there. Like the stray cellophane from a sweet.

'So I take it you're sleeping with men again?'

'Huh?' A textbook double-take.

'The condom wrappers in your bathroom.'

'Oh.' The frown on her face unravelled itself like a loose thread from a jumper. 'Gross. Sorry. I've not really been on it with the chores lately.' She waved a hand at the clutter of coffee cups and wine glasses on the coffee table. 'Yeah. I was feeling low the other night. Went out. Met a guy. He was good-looking and he made me laugh. So I brought him back here and fucked him.'

'You were feeling low?'

Why didn't you call me?

237

'So the whole celibacy persona, that whole *brand*, that was a lie, was it?'

'It wasn't a lie. I just changed my mind.' She didn't sound defensive, just surprised that I was asking.

'It just seems strange that you've completely backtracked on an opinion that you were so committed to a few weeks ago.'

'People are strange.'

'What an insight.'

She looked at me and smiled. 'Miaow. You *are* mad at me. It's okay, I can take it.'

'Why would I be angry with you?'

'Because you want me to do something. And I don't want to do it.'

'It's your choice,' I said. 'No one can make that decision apart from you.'

'But you think you know what you'd do?'

I was finding it hard to deal with the way her whisky tumbler was held expansively to one side. How her head was propped up on her hand, all that red hair tumbling around it. The way she was looking at me. Like nothing I could say could hurt her.

'It's just that I think coming forward would potentially help a lot of people.'

'And I don't.' She poured herself and me more whisky. 'I guess we disagree.'

It was as if by saying that she had sliced me in two. Right down the centre of my body, from crown to crotch.

'You're not scared you might be wrong?'

'I've decided not to live in misery by doubting my choices. I told you that a while back.' She shrugged. 'Sometimes that means I'll do the wrong thing. I'm fine with that.'

'It's just . . . this is so important, Tamsin.' I felt like I was back in corporate law. 'What if the case against him falls apart, and you could have stopped it?'

'Does the whole of the Academy have to accuse him of rape before it's enough?'

'Don't you *want* to speak out?'

'Trust me, Emily.' She took a gulp of whisky. 'I'm going to speak out about Art. In my own time, in my own way, in a situation of my choosing, I will make my feelings known.' Then she rubbed the bridge of her nose with her hand, and briefly looked tired. 'But not yet. Not like this.'

'Why?'

'Because I'm not currently a good enough artist to say what needs to be said in the way that I want to say it, and until then . . .' she shrugged. 'I'll wait.'

I found myself shaking my head. 'Sometimes you've got to react to the moment.'

'So you think there's only one way to make your point?'

'I think speaking out about what happened to you, your trauma . . . putting that out into the world at a moment that could make a difference – that's powerful.' I knew it wasn't tactical, but I couldn't hold myself back from saying, 'More powerful than any art you could make.'

'So what you're saying,' Tamsin said slowly, 'is that my voice only matters if I bleed all over people?'

239

'Bleed over people . . .' I felt the same way I had when I'd first met her and she'd talked about her spirit losing all its nutrients. 'That's so melodramatic,' I said.

'No,' Tamsin snapped. 'Having to *see* people suffering to understand that bad behaviour is bad is what's fucking melodramatic.'

She stood up, her movements less precise than usual following the whisky, and began to pace.

'First, it's be a good girl by taking your clothes off for a movie. Then it's be a good girl by letting this important director jerk off on your favourite dress. Then it's be a good girl by signing this and shutting up. Now it's be a good girl by opening up your ribcage and letting everyone rummage around in it for their own fucking titillation. Let everyone see – *hear* – what happened to you. Put it out there where your mom and dad – your little *sister* – can read all about it.'

'Tamsin, please. I'm trying to understand . . .' I paused. I could see she was shaking, and knew I needed to be very careful. 'I get that it's difficult, but it's just . . . Why won't you *help*?'

'Why am I being selfish, you mean?' She stopped pacing and became very still.

'Were you . . .' I stopped. This needed to be done delicately. 'Sit down, please, I . . . Was there some kind of trauma that you had before even Rawlings, maybe when you were a child, that—'

Tamsin gave a kind of howl that turned into a bitter laugh.

240

'Give me a break, Emily. You've just told me what a shitty person I am. Now you want to know if some creepy uncle touched me when I was twelve? Just to be clear, if that had happened would that mean that I was a *good* person or a *bad* person?'

The flat seemed to pull in on me from every side, suffocating me in its luxury.

'This is a really nice whisky, Tamsin,' I said quietly.

'Thanks.'

'No. That wasn't a compliment. What I'm saying is that we're drinking a nice whisky, sitting on a lovely sofa, in a gorgeous flat, in a cool neighbourhood.'

'And what's your point?'

'All of this had to be paid for.'

'I'm aware.'

'With his money. Rawlings' money.'

'Gabriela Ortiz bought a villa with her fee from their movie.'

'It's not the same.'

'Isn't it?' Her face was changing. 'Explain to me why it's not.'

'You only have all this stuff because ... because he bought your silence.'

'Yes.'

'It's ... it's blood money. And you've made me complicit.'

'So?' She gave a derisive laugh. 'What? Now you're going to boycott me?' She gestured at the French doors, as if the wider world was laughing at me. 'Have fun with that.'

'I'm not *boycotting* you, I just—'

'Emily. Honey. Where did you *think* all the money came from?'

I didn't have to answer that.

'Taking money to stay quiet after he . . . It's . . . it's like prostitution, Tamsin.'

I thought the word would land like a bomb, but she just raised one eyebrow. 'I think you'll find that you're supposed to call it sex work.'

She did something that I hadn't seen her do before. She took out a cigarette and lit it. It was one of those thin, gold-tipped ones – a direct descendant of the Hollywood classic in a long holder. Her fingernails were painted red. The livid marks on her palms had faded away.

I said it very softly.

'So did you fuck Art Rawlings before I got here, is that what this was?'

She turned her head slowly to look at me, but made no reply. By the time her gaze reached my face I felt like she'd measured me from every angle, and now knew me better than I knew myself. And she looked so calm, so unmoved.

What would it take to finally make that face crack?

'Did you think that maybe he'd give you another two million dollars?' I looked derisively down at the empty whisky bottle on the table. 'I suppose you've got to do something. The first lot must be running out, the way you spend it.'

Her expression didn't change.

'Get out of my home.'

I nodded, as if that was exactly what I'd wanted her to say. I turned my back on her.

'Oh, and by the way.' Her voice was still even. 'I remembered where I heard the name Radner and Wise before. Your old employers, right? That NDA he had me sign when I was eighteen? That was their work.'

I turned halfway back, and drew in a breath. She was standing there, marble-calm, unflinching.

I half shook my head, then left the flat and slammed the door behind me.

Chapter Twenty-Three

THE TRAIN WAS DELAYED.

I paced up and down the platform, glancing every so often at the pedometer on my phone. I would allow myself to think about Tamsin, I told myself, once I'd hit six thousand steps. Seven thousand steps. Eight.

The train was delayed again, over and over, and every time the mechanical voice came over the loudspeaker there was a collective sigh from the crowd around me that turned, by degrees, into a menacing growl of anger.

My phone rang just as the train was finally pulling in. For the few seconds that it took for me to get it out of my bag, an entire story fell into place in my head as the sound of metal on metal filled my ears. Tamsin, weeping, asking me to help her.

I can't do this alone, she'd say.

But it wasn't Tamsin. It was James.

I declined.

Maybe what didn't kill Tamsin had made her stronger; maybe she truly wasn't scared of Art Rawlings or men in general. But not me. What hadn't killed me with Harry had made me weaker. Unable to take the call of a perfectly nice boy who liked me enough to try to patch up a bad date. There was no trusting him. There was always a chance that he would open his fangs and eat me whole, or his hands would turn into Harry's, and he would squeeze my neck until it all went dark.

I put on my running playlist, the one filled with heady pop tunes that I'd liked since my teenage years without ever admitting it. The sort of music that could have been synthesised in a lab to alter moods.

The train ran along the backs of houses; I thought about the people living in them. I wondered how many had bought their places for a song in the Eighties. Moving in with their boxes of books and furniture from junk shops. The bottles of champagne they must have popped. I thought about the ones who diligently brought lunch to work every day and declined trips to the pub, saying they weren't really into that sort of thing. The films they hadn't watched in the cinema, saying they'd wait till it came out on DVD. The books unbought, the holiday days spent batch-cooking in unheated kitchens.

Then I thought about the bread I'd tried to bake at home, then given up on because my oven burned everything; I ended up buying a loaf of sourdough for £4.50 from a hipster bakery. The bulk bags of red lentils I'd tried to like, the pizza boxes, the free trials I'd failed to cancel. The attempts to be vegan, even though Harry had teased me about it, the tub of cream cheese I'd thrown out as part of the fresh start. The freezer full of chickpea soup I hadn't taken to work, not even once. The endless shop-bought pasta salads, their orange alien cheese and staggering quantities of fat and sodium.

The boys I'd ghosted on Tinder.

The times I hadn't called my grandparents to thank them for the birthday cards.

The texts from old friends unanswered.

The way I used to let Harry buy me dinner all the time, even when I could afford to pay.

The way that when he said *I want to try something* I'd just said nothing and let him take my silence as a yes.

I tried to cast my mind back, to remember the first bit of food or drink I'd accepted from Tamsin's world.

She'd bought the wine and cheese from Tesco. Maybe that didn't count, maybe that had been within the bounds of an extravagant version of normal.

But I couldn't deny the fish. The rich butter. Nor the champagne, the truffles, the whisky. The coffees sipped gazing out together across the rooftops and down on a morning soaked with sun. The drinks in the beautiful bars – not bought by Tamsin exactly, but paid for by her in whatever sense mattered.

Paid for by Rawlings.

I downloaded Tinder again on the train, ignoring the conversation thread I still had going with James, the one that had ended with an exchange of numbers. I swiped feverishly, matched half a dozen times, and spent the evening in front of *Friends*, talking aimlessly to my matches, repeating the same four or five gambits over and over. No bites, certainly nothing worth biting. Maybe my profile photos weren't good enough. I wished I had a photograph of myself from that night out with Tamsin, a photo of the two of us together that I might use.

I swiped through my phone photos, convinced that we must have taken a selfie together at some point. One of the dizzying days together must have been documented in a snapped moment. But no. There was no trace of her image, no trace of anything of her except a couple of texts from a contact that still just said 'Tamsin'. No surname.

I tried to find her on IMDb. It took an hour, and in the photo she had dark hair and a Polish-sounding surname that I could make no attempt to pronounce. It might have been her. I saved the photo on my phone.

Then I googled Rawlings' name, just to assure myself that the man I'd met was the same entity as the thing in the press.

There was a piece in the *Guardian* saying that Rawlings was probably going to get away with it because of a lack of evidence.

A piece in the *Telegraph* saying that there was no chance of Rawlings getting a fair trial because there was a witch hunt against him.

A piece in *The Times* saying that the incidents had taken place too long ago – there was no threat to the public.

A statement from a sexual harassment organisation insisting that predators never changed.

*

I couldn't sleep that night.

I lay there and thought about the ice caps melting, and Brexit, and rape being used as a weapon of war in the Democratic Republic of Congo. And I thought about Amina and her husband.

At three in the morning, I reread my draft email with the audio file. And I thought of Larissa Larroque, and Gabriela Ortiz, and all the others who had risked everything to speak out. They were so far away, and here I was, lying in a bed with broken slats in a rented flat in Streatham, with hard evidence. I wished I could touch it, hold it, feel it. But it was just an audio file, a collection of 0s and 1s on a server somewhere. Everywhere and nowhere, all at once.

And I thought of Harry, and how he always laughed at me when I was afraid.

At four in the morning, my head feeling like it might break open from lack of sleep, my pulse loud in my ears, I pressed send.

On Monday I found that Amina had sent in her settlement with an electronic signature. I printed it off and put it on Renee's desk. She picked it up and sighed, pushing her glasses down her nose to rub at tired eyes.

'It doesn't feel like a victory,' she said. 'Having her sign that.'

'But she wants to go home, right?'

'She does.' Renee straightened the papers so that the edges were neat, and clamped them with a big clip. Then she frowned. 'Hang on, why's the translation in French?'

'You said it was okay to get a translator and expense it . . .' I trailed off.

Slowly, Renee looked up at me and put the paper down on the desk.

'Amina doesn't speak French, Emily,' she said. Her voice was soft and modulated.

'But French is the official language of—'

'Yes,' Renee continued, her voice still soft. Renee always threw swear words and sighs around the office, but when she was really angry, she went very calm. 'But that doesn't mean Amina speaks it. I believe she has a smattering, but her native language is Wolof.'

'Oh.'

Renee pinched the bridge of her nose, then sighed.

'Have a seat, Emily.'

Walking away from the office, my cheeks still hot and my nose blocked from crying, I listened again to the audio of Tamsin's encounter with Rawlings. Renee had made it clear that I had let Amina down, maybe completely sabotaged her chance of justice forever. And then there was Tamsin, with the chance of justice served to her on a plate.

Unless, to her, it hadn't felt like justice? Listening again, her breathy cries sounded different. Organic and animal. Indistinguishable, in fact, from real ecstasy.

And, after all, she'd wanted the part, hadn't she? Even if she had changed her mind when she stopped being able to sleep.

*

Lucy called me when I was on my way home. She'd spoken to Chris Hawkins – only briefly, she said, because there had been other people around. He'd suggested that they meet for a drink that night.

'To catch up, was what he said.'

'To catch up.'

'I'm not sure how I feel about it. I know it sounds ridiculous, but I feel really weird about the idea of being alone with him.'

'What about Andrew? I'm sure he'd go along with you.'

Lucy paused delicately. 'Actually . . . I've been thinking . . . I think it'd be better if it was you,' she said.

'Me?' I felt that she was getting at something that I hadn't yet grasped. 'But he knows you've got a partner, right? He doesn't think you're single.'

'Oh, I assume so,' she said vaguely.

'So you want me to come along and sort of . . . neuter the situation?'

'Not necessarily. I just . . . Well, now I think about it, maybe he doesn't know about Andrew. And I just don't want to get caught up in anything.'

I devised a disguise of sorts, doing my hair as differently as possible to how it had been when we were at school, and borrowing Lucy's big dark glasses. I thought about bringing a book, but in the end decided that a magazine might make for better cover, so I bought another copy of *Vogue*. I ordered a glass of wine – Lucy promising to spot me – and assumed my perch at the table next to her, facing away.

I could understand why she wanted me there, I thought, as I flicked the pages of my magazine. He'd always been so magnetic, Mr Hawkins. I was there, I knew, to stop her doing something she might regret, to stop her getting pulled away by his tractor beam. I was the dead weight.

I saw him coming down the street from behind my dark glasses.

Eight years had taken Lucy and me from Bacardi Breezers to talk of 'trying' and our first anti-ageing creams. I'd expected some similar metamorphosis in Chris Hawkins. He must be forty now, or somewhere around there. I'd hoped for a paunch, a sagging jowl, a sense that he was a little too old for this pub. But when I saw him coming I felt again like the clever girl in an English class, who occasionally earned a rare teacher's smile.

The River Island suits had been traded in for finer linen, and the shoes were now Italian leather. His formerly clean face was fashionably stubbled and framed by sharp back and sides, the hair on top swept backwards and artistically dappled with grey.

Lucy stood up when he arrived, and he leaned forward to kiss her on the cheek. He sat down, and I got the hit of his aftershave. His smell had changed. He used to wear some kind of Calvin Klein-ish stuff – now I was sure it was Tom Ford. He called her babe, and ordered her a white wine spritzer without asking what she wanted.

She asked how he was, and he started talking about someone called Pete at the Department for Education. Pete, I realised, must refer to Peter Roddington, the Secretary of State for Education.

'God, he was hammered last time I saw him,' he said. I wasn't looking at him, I was staring at the picture of Raina Gupta in *Vogue*, but I could imagine from his voice what his face must look like. 'Anyway, this headship's my last tour of duty in the trenches. Then I'm considering more time at the think tank, taking on more educational consultancy work. Independent sector has some very nice opportunities, proper compensation. You should think seriously about it, Luce. Fresh face like yours, and your brain.'

'You haven't seen me teach yet. You don't know if I'm any good.'

'Oh, babe.' A big laugh. 'I know you. You're the full package. The last thing I want for you is to get stuck teaching *To Kill A Mockingbird* to a load of thirteen-year-olds for the rest of your life. But when the new term comes we can definitely have a chat about responsibilities.' He resettled noisily in his chair. 'It's about carving out a role for yourself. But I'm not worried about you. You've got *it*.'

I heard a small intake of breath from Lucy. I knew what she'd say to me if I spoke in that breezy way. She'd take me to task, ask what my evidence was, point out that she loved teaching thirteen-year-olds, that it was what she'd always wanted. But instead she just said, 'So you're excited about the new job?'

'Nice to be back in my old stomping ground, after the carnage I've had over in Hackney for the last few years. I mean . . . excited? It all feels a bit old hat at this point, but at the end of the day it's about getting to where you want to be. And if you can offer a hand up to some old friends on your way . . .' I heard his chair scrape. Was he reaching out to touch her? '. . . Then so much the better.'

'Carnage?'

'Oh, you know. Rough group of kids. At least to start with. But the catchment area gentrified more every year. Between you and me . . .' I heard the scraping sound again, the lowering of his voice. Was he leaning forward? '. . . I wasn't sorry to have a reason to bow out. I'd done my time.'

'What reason?'

'Oh, nothing major. It could have been smoothed out fairly easily, but I ultimately decided it wasn't worth the aggravation.'

'Chris.' Softly.

'Oh.' He sighed. 'God, you've always had the knack for getting the truth out of me, haven't you? It's that bloody Joan of Arc look you give me.'

'What happened?'

'Well.' More scraping of the chair. 'There was never a formal investigation, but I had a chat with the Chair of Governors and we agreed that it was easiest if I just moved on. And I wanted to sell my flat anyway – did I tell you I bought a place after Alice and I split? Made bank on it, incidentally – so it worked out for the best. But yeah . . .' He laughed. 'I mean, babe, this is between you and me, but since we're old friends I'm not worried. Some kid made some utterly ridiculous claims about me. For attention, you know.' He sighed. 'Troubled girl.'

'I see. So there was no truth to any of it?'

He laughed again. 'God, what do you take me for?'

She said nothing.

'I know that look, Luce.'

'Well, you can see why I might ask.'

'This girl is *sixteen*.'

'So was I.'

'But Lucy . . . you don't understand, I get that. You don't have the full picture. But there's just no comparison. You were so sophisticated – absolutely light years ahead of everyone else. And what happened with us . . . it was just a little flirtation while you were still in school, wasn't it? Some crackling chemistry. But nothing ever *happened* until we were both free agents.'

'You weren't a free agent. You were married.'

'Oh, Alice was already fucking around on me by then.'

'You told me it was an open marriage.'

'Did I?' He laughed again. 'God. I mean, this was ten years ago, Luce. You can see why some of the details would be a little fuzzy.'

'I remember it all.'

'Yeah.' His voice became tender. 'Yeah, I suppose it was all quite formative for you, wasn't it? First love.'

Lucy didn't speak.

'Look, I can tell that this whole thing with the girl in Hackney has thrown you, but I'm telling you categorically, it's nothing. Wouldn't have dreamed of it. She's not exactly an oil painting – like I said, troubled girl, wants attention. She actually reminded me a bit of your mate – that gawky girl you used to hang out with.' The waitress passed. 'Another pint of the same, please? Cheers.'

'Emily?'

'Emily? Sounds right. Jesus, I've taught a lot of Emilys over the years. Clever, you know, but not mature. I remember her A-level essays – she thought she was the first person to have ever done a feminist reading of a Shakespeare play. I mean, you've got to be encouraging about that sort of thing, but it's not exactly thrilling. Whereas you . . . you were an original. God, Emily.' He laughed. 'Haven't thought about her in years. But she used to hang around us all the time, didn't she? When we were just dying to have some time alone. She was so gauche. But,' his voice became sober, kindly, 'I suppose she was only sixteen.'

'So was I.'

'Yes.' Contemplative. 'So you were.'

I was certain now that he reached over to take her hand. His voice was lower and rougher when he spoke again.

'I've never forgotten you. There could never have been anyone else like you. And when I first saw you in that staff meeting – god, you don't look any different to the day I met you.'

'You look different.'

'Oh, yeah.' He laughed. 'I'm going for the silver fox thing now.' I imagined him running a hand through the product in his hair. 'What do you think?'

'Chris, you know I have a partner, don't you?'

'A partner?' He laughed. 'God. You're all very strait-laced, your generation, you know that? I guess there's a puritanical streak, all that social media . . . Of course you've got a boyfriend, a girl like you never stays single for long. I can't say I'm surprised. But Luce, it doesn't change anything between us.'

'No.' Her voice was tight and chilly. 'The thing that changed between us was you dumping me.'

'Lucy, I didn't *dump* you, don't be so histrionic. Our paths diverged.'

'You made it so my entire life revolved around you, and then you got sick of me.'

'Is that what you've been thinking all these years?'

'No.' Her words cut through his, clipped and precise. 'No. I suppose, now you ask, that at the time I just assumed you'd moved on to some other girl in one of your classes. That I'd got too old for you.'

'That's . . .' I heard his chair scraping back. 'I don't think you quite understand how insulting that is.'

'No. I suppose that's the problem, really. I don't under-stand.'

I could hear rustling and chanced a look around. He was taking his wallet out of his jacket pocket, throwing down a tenner on the table.

'I guess I'll see you next term,' he said coldly.

'I suppose so,' Lucy replied placidly. 'Good to catch up, Chris.'

I waited until Chris Hawkins' rangy, well-cut figure had disappeared around the corner before standing, picking up my empty wine glass and joining Lucy at her table. The foam from his second drained pint was still sliding down the glass.

Lucy was staring into space. She didn't look at me, but took out her phone and started texting rapidly. 'Sorry, just letting Andrew know I'm okay, he was worried.' She put her phone face down on the table and slid the white wine spritzer across to me. 'Do you want this? I don't like them any more. I just used to drink them when I found normal wine too strong.'

'Are you all right?'

'I'm always all right.' She lifted her gaze determinedly to meet mine. 'But I suppose that could have gone better.'

'How did you want it to go?'

'I don't know. I just . . . He suggested a drink, and it didn't occur to me to say no. He's still so . . . he's still so *Chris*-like.' A wan smile crossed her face.

'I thought he was different . . .' My voice trailed off. I took another run at it, spoke more forcefully. 'Actually, I thought he was a prick.' I hitched in my breath, the pressure in my chest building steadily now that he'd gone. 'He didn't used to be like that.'

'I think he probably did,' Lucy said softly. 'We were just young. We didn't know any men.'

'All that cockiness . . .'

'It seemed like confidence at the time, didn't it?'

'It seemed like he was taking us seriously.' I gave a harsh little laugh. 'Apparently not. Not all of us, anyway.'

'Oh yeah.'

The waitress came and picked up the ten-pound note, then stood there expectantly. Lucy dug in her purse for coins, and automatically I took my purse out too.

'I'm so sorry that he said those nasty things about you.'

'Oh, it's all right.' Another brittle laugh. 'Couldn't give a shit what he thinks of me, to be honest with you. But, ha . . . interesting that when he said "your gawky friend" you knew straight away who he was talking about.'

'Come on, Emily.' She handed the waitress a two-pound coin, and the woman bobbed her head curtly and disappeared. 'You know perfectly well that you were my only friend at school.'

'You make it sound like you were the loser.'

'Well, wasn't I? By any technical definition? Too awkward for boys my own age? I ended up caught up with someone like *that* . . .'

'You know how he said . . . that the two of you didn't do anything till after you'd left school . . .'

'Yes.' Lucy narrowed her eyes and pursed her lips. 'Well, maybe that's how he remembers it.'

And how did I remember it? How did *she* remember it?

And, more to the point, what the hell actually happened?

The gulp of spritzer seemed to turn to vinegar in my mouth. Lucy. Not preternaturally poised, remote Lucy, but

Lucy at sixteen. A girl as naïve as she was precocious. And me, somewhere in the background, half envious and half dizzy with the idea that something was really happening, something vast and adult and unknowable.

'So what are you going to do?' I remembered Andrew's suggestion that she might want to consider changing jobs.

'I tried to talk to the deputy head about it at school. Discreetly. You know. I didn't quite ... I thought she understood what I was telling her, but maybe she didn't.' She half frowned. 'I mean, I probably wasn't very clear. I'm not very clear on it myself, really. The deputy head, she just kept saying what a breath of fresh air he is. How we don't need any trouble.'

'Trouble?' I frowned. 'How can she call it trouble?' I thought of Chris Hawkins, calling me gawky and gauche. Chris Hawkins, saying *you were so sophisticated*. I thought of Art Rawlings, and tried not to think of Tamsin. 'It's justice.'

'We don't all get to be full-time crusaders, you know,' Lucy said, her words as tight as a drum. 'Some of us have got a hell of a lot of other stuff to be getting on with.'

I stayed quiet for a few moments, slightly stunned. Lucy never talked like that.

'Anyway,' she continued, in a firm, brisk voice. 'I don't want to talk about it any more. How's your Canadian friend?'

'She's ...' I let out a sigh, not wanting to answer too swiftly. 'To be honest ... I'm not sure I'd call her a friend any more.'

Lucy considered me. 'Did something happen?'

'I don't know if I should tell you.'

'You don't have to.'

I took a breath, then I was in full flow. It felt like putting the facts to a more dispassionate version of myself. Lucy kept listening intently, even when I paused for her to interject.

'She takes this moral stance – or rather, *amoral* stance – and tries to pass it off as ... I don't know. Nuance. Enlightenment. Whatever.'

'And what would you call it?'

'I don't know ... laziness?' I took a gulp of the spritzer. 'No. Okay, that's not fair. It must be fear, but fear that she's intellectualised and that she's trying to depict as something lofty. Like coming forward would be ... unoriginal or something.'

'What would it gain? For her to come forward?'

'I don't know.' The words were limp and lacking in force, but I spoke them as if they were a battle cry, smacking my hand down on the table so suddenly that Lucy flinched. 'I don't know what would happen, and *she* doesn't know what would happen. But if stuff stays inside you, it rots. You never know who might be hiding something, and could come forward because you did. You never know.'

I lowered my voice. 'And it looks like she never will, now,' I finished.

Lucy was frowning, but just as she opened her mouth to speak, her phone rang.

'Sorry, Andrew ... yes, honey?' She turned away from me. 'No, I'm fine ...'

260

I took out my phone and glanced through my emails, which I couldn't have managed before the spritzer. A severe talking-to from Renee, explaining that we could move on this once, but if I made another mistake like that then she wouldn't be able to keep trusting me.

Lucy was still talking to Andrew. About what they were going to cook for dinner that night. I logged into my burner account.

I hadn't been seriously expecting a reply to my letter in a bottle. My fingers began shaking so much that I could scarcely click on the email, the moments of loading stretching themselves out into great gulfs.

Hi there 'E',

Thanks very much for the tip. This is potentially really important evidence, assuming that I can use it on the record, but I'd need to talk further to the woman in the audio before I know exactly how important. I do hear what might be a 'no', but then I later hear indications that make it seem as if she's participating consensually in the encounter.

I understand that this is delicate . . . let me know if we can take it any further forward. Of course I'll need to follow up with her. I suspect that I may know her identity.

I deleted the email and cleared my internet history, my face hot and my fingertips ice-cold. I thought of Tamsin at eighteen, suspended thousands of feet in the sky where there was nobody to protect her. Tamsin in the shower,

261

Tamsin unable to cover her nakedness as Rawlings leered from the other side of the glass.

I suspect that I may know her identity.

Because who could ever forget Tamsin?

I bought a meal deal on the way to the bus stop, and sat scrolling through my phone until I'd found Stu's number and sent him a text. I apologised profusely for bailing on our date and told him that I'd actually thought he'd seemed like a great guy.

He replied straight away. *I think I could probably find it in my <3 to forgive u. If u want to come round.*

Then:

And maybe bring that little blonde friend of urs ;)

Chapter Twenty-Four

I'M NOT EXACTLY SURE when I saw the news story. I was at my desk, trying to get hold of Amina. As was my habit on the phone, I was refreshing the BBC News page so rhythmically and automatically that I wasn't really looking at it.

It held podium place as the lead news story, at least for this afternoon, and it seemed to expand to fill the screen, even as the words failed to sink in. I was on my feet before I knew what I was doing.

'I don't believe it,' I said to no one.

I started to call out. If Renee hadn't been in her office I probably would have shouted out loud just the same. But she was there. I began to trip towards her with blind magnetism. There was a rushing noise in my ears, like the sound of a shower drowning out the rest of the world.

'Rawlings has got away with it. They've dropped the charges. I can't believe—'

I was cut off by a sudden crash. I looked around and saw a huge coffee stain on the greyish wall, like a blood spatter. Fragments of ceramic lay broken on the floor.

'Renee?'

Renee was sitting at her desk, her head in her hands. She was so still that it was hard to believe the explosive motion could have come from her.

'Renee, are you all right?'

She didn't move.

'I'm sorry. That was a stupid question.'

She stayed still for a long moment. Then her shoulders heaved. She clasped her hands on either side of her nose as if in prayer, staring at the opposite wall.

'Shouldn't have done that,' she muttered. Then she turned to look at me. 'My wife gave me that mug. I loved that mug. Ruined it for the sake of a moron like Rawlings. Bloody silly thing to do.'

'Renee . . .' I took a step closer.

'Not like me at all. You know that, don't you, Emily?'

'Yeah, Renee. I know that.' I felt a descending in my stomach as I looked at my boss and realised that there was a tear, dirtied by mascara, running down her cheek. Renee wore makeup; I'd never noticed that before.

'It's just that the dog's ill.' She heaved a sigh. 'Molly's always been fine, but she's got a lump. The vet says it might just be a cyst. But you never know, do you?' Her head returned to her hands. 'And my wife and I had a row about it this morning. You know, about whether we should get the operation or if we should just wait and see. Might be nothing, you know? And *this* poor girl . . .' she gestured at the screen, 'has been taken out of the country, and chances are it's a forced marriage case. And the government are making all these noises, but they're not training border agents properly

264

because they claim there's no money. The *Tories*. Claim there's no money for *border agents*. And my mother needs to go into a care home, but you bloody try telling her that.'

'I'm really sorry, Renee . . .'

'You'd think . . .' Her head came out of her hands and she heaved in a big breath. 'You'd *think* cases like Rawlings would be open and shut, wouldn't you? It's bloody obvious that he did it. The women accusing him are as good as any victims can be. There are so many of them, telling the same story. And *still* . . .' Her head returned to her hands. 'If they can't convict *him*, how the hell am I supposed to look a woman like Amina in the eye and tell her there's hope?'

'I'm sorry, Renee.' A lump in my throat. It was my response to everything. 'We'll work harder. I'll work harder.'

'Oh Emily.' She smiled at me, a teary smile. 'If this could be sorted by bright young girls working longer and longer hours, we'd have done it by now.'

'I've let you down.'

'You cocked up. We all do.'

I hovered.

'Nope.' She gave a great sniff, and then stood up. 'Come on. We're going for a drink.'

I blinked. It was only two in the afternoon. Okay, it was a Friday, but this still wasn't like Renee at all.

'A proper drink, in a proper bar. Not around *here*. I don't need to be any more depressed. Come on.'

She hailed a black cab in the street, her arm flung wide in authority, like a statue holding out the scales of justice.

She gave the cab driver the address of somewhere unexpectedly glamorous. She saw my look of surprise, and smiled. The suddenness of her smile made it seem impossible that she'd been crying only a few minutes ago.

'You can take the QC out of chambers, but . . . oh, you know. To hell with it.'

She spent most of the cab journey tapping out emails, which gave me an excuse to stay quiet and put off saying the thing I knew I needed to say. But when we got stuck in traffic and she put away her phone to stare out of the window, I could delay it no longer.

'I'm sorry, Renee. Again. About how I handled things with Amina.'

She didn't reply for a while. I almost doubted whether she'd heard me. But then she said, 'I understand that you feel guilty, Emily. But you need to understand that your guilt, in itself, isn't useful.'

The justifications were hurling themselves up my throat, but I clamped my lips shut.

'It's not your fault, the appalling way NDAs work in this country. It's not your fault that some bastard was able to have her sign her life away without breaking the law. But if we're going to claim to help women, then first we need to do no harm.'

'I know,' I muttered.

'I think you do know. You know you fucked up.' The cab pulled up outside an elegant bar. 'All I ask is that you don't do it again.'

*

The bar was already buzzing. Mostly men with matching suits, matching designer stubble, matching pints. Renee eyed them with distaste before making a beeline for a small booth, slightly tucked away from the hum and roar.

'Right. What're you having? No rubbish about the cheapest glass of wine on the menu. Get a proper cocktail, Emily. This is my treat.'

I started to murmur an objection but she shook her head.

'It's no good, Emily. I know precisely how much you earn. These are on me.'

I hesitated.

'If you don't tell me what you want I'm going to get you a dirty martini. That's what I'm having.'

'I'll have a martini too.' I thought of Tamsin, of that beautiful bar on that final night of glory. 'But vodka. Clean,' I said quickly.

Renee smiled at me.

It occurred to me about halfway through the first drink that this might never happen again. I couldn't imagine Renee's veneer cracking again any time soon.

To my horror, my phone pinged with a Tinder notification. *Heyyyyyy.* Nikolai, 26. I'd only swiped left on him because I thought it was a cool name.

'God, I can't believe what you young people put yourselves through.' She shuddered theatrically. 'Tinder.'

I hastily blocked Nikolai and put my phone face down on the table. 'How did you meet your wife?'

Renee smiled. 'She was a journalist. I'd just been called to the bar. She took me out for lunch. Courting me as a contact, you know. Two women in a man's world.' She shrugged. 'And it just went from there. But we didn't bloody *date*. We just ate lots of cheese on toast and drank cheap red wine and eventually moved in together.'

'That sounds . . .' I puffed my breath out. 'That sounds really lovely.' I stared at my martini. 'It's hard. Dating men.'

Renee gave a snort of laughter. 'It wasn't much fun being a pair of black lesbians in the Eighties, either.'

I felt my insides wither. 'Sorry, I . . .'

'That wasn't . . . what is it you girls call it? A call-out. I'm not trying to make you feel bad for the sake of it. All I'm saying is that you can't go around comparing people's lives as though one were simple and the other complex.'

'But yours was harder.'

'Yes, it probably was.' Renee raised an eyebrow, as if in admission. 'But it's not a competition. And I don't mind telling you that I don't much fancy dating men either. Not that there aren't some nice ones, but I do think it's difficult for you girls now. And . . . you know, in a sense, I was lucky.' She tilted her head to one side. 'Once I met Grace, that was it. No worrying about all the choices out there, just me and her. Neither of us ever gave a shit what anyone thought. We had each other. And a growing menagerie of pets.'

'I'm so sorry Molly's poorly,' I said.

'It's the one downside of having a dog.' She sniffed. 'But now you mention it . . .' She rooted in her handbag and took out her phone. 'I'm going to step outside and give Grace a ring. See how the old hound's doing.' She drained her glass. 'I'd better say sorry, too. For being so grumpy.'

'Good luck,' I said.

'Oh, it'll be all right.' Renee stood up. 'Luckily for me, I married a very tolerant woman. She puts up with all my moods. God knows why. Now,' she held out her card, 'do you think you can get us another round? Same again for me. And don't bloody think about paying for it yourself, I'll know if you do. Just tap it, okay?'

I stood up a few seconds after her, swaying slightly. She'd draped her violet raincoat over her handbag, but I eyed it anxiously. Had she meant for me to leave it unguarded?

I hurried over to the bar, glancing to my right at the City boys dotted along its mahogany surface at intervals.

And there he was.

His shoulders. Not devastating, but certainly gym-honed. Broad enough. Set off by the tailoring of the jacket of a suit I'd bought him for his birthday.

There – his easy smile. Languidly challenging the whole room not to like him.

The long arms, the strong arms. Arms that had held me down and held me when my cat died, when I got promoted, when I was too drunk to walk home unaided.

Without thinking, I quickly slipped my grandmother's emerald ring onto the fourth finger of my left hand, just as he turned his head and saw me.

'Emily!'

'Hi, Harry.'

My voice was stony-dry. He didn't seem to notice.

'Long time no see,' he said, as if I'd moved cubicles to a different floor. 'How are things?'

He was smiling, his face boyish and open in that way that always made people comment on what a nice man he was.

'Yeah. I'm good,' I said.

'Heard you were working for some sort of women's organisation,' he continued casually.

'Yeah.' I blinked, as if I wasn't convinced of the truth of it. Then I remembered how fascinated Tamsin had been when I'd told her about my work, and straightened my shoulders slightly. 'The Women's Advocacy Centre.'

'And how is it?'

It was the *and* that got me. 'Yeah, it's good.'

'I heard Renee Walcott could be a bit strident.'

I laughed. 'Yeah, I guess that's true.'

Because it was true.

'Still, it sounds really cool.' He looked down at me with what I was sure was affection. 'I'm glad you've found your passion. Corporate world was never for you.'

I'd never thought of working for Renee as my passion. But in his mouth it seemed to make sense. Like it had been true all along.

'What about you?'

'Yeah,' he grinned. 'I'm fully domesticated now. Engaged. Kid on the way.'

'You're serious.'

'Absolutely.' A great slurp of his pint. 'Little boy. Due in January.'

'That was quick.' Bile flaring at the back of my throat. We'd been split what – ten months?

He just nodded along, as if in surprised delight. 'You know. Things can happen quite quickly.'

I said nothing. He didn't seem to need me to.

'But I'm excited,' he continued. 'I think that's probably my purpose in life, that's what makes it all make sense. Being a dad. Having a son.'

I had a feeling that if I didn't move away quickly he was going to start showing me ultrasound photos. Tamsin wouldn't put herself through that, Tamsin wouldn't stay to be humiliated.

'And I've been promoted,' he was saying. 'So it feels like things are really falling into place. Anyway . . .' He glanced back at the group of guys he was with. 'Anyway, it's good to see you.'

He leaned down to kiss me on the cheek, as if he had a standing invitation. Then he was gone and I was left leaning against the bar. I had wanted to be the one to cut off the conversation. To leave before he was ready to say goodbye.

When I turned to face the barman I realised that I was crying, even though what I wanted to do was scream with rage until all the glass in the bar shattered.

The barman pointed over to the still-empty booth and said, 'You're sitting there, right? Same again? I'll bring them over.'

271

I nodded. Went back to the booth. I angled my body away from where Harry was standing with his gaggle of colleagues, one hand clasped around his pint, the other in his trouser pocket. Feet planted far apart.

He was right there. Right there.

As if possessed, my fingers began to tap out a note on my phone.

Harry

You're a nice person. And everyone thinks that being nice makes you good.

A burst of laughter from his group.

I stilled my shoulders and glanced up at him. I thought maybe he would be looking at me.

I continued.

But I know you.

I wrote everything down, in that note. All of it. All the things he'd done or not done, the tiny ways he'd taught me that my body wasn't my own and therefore couldn't be taken from me. And I wrote down what had happened that night, that night I picked up and handled so often in my mind that it had become unrecognisable under the smudges of my fingerprints.

The thing he'd done – it wasn't unusual, I knew that. It was like Tamsin had said. If you said it out loud, it wouldn't seem like something worth changing your life over.

There's something I want to try. Spoken so gently.

And I hadn't exactly said no. But I knew damn well that I hadn't said yes.

The way he'd been afterwards – I wrote that down too.

Tamsin might have gone over and said the words aloud. Then again, she might have remained silent.

He was putting down his empty pint glass now. 'Got to get back to the missus, haven't I?'

Had he always talked so loudly? Always been so sure that the rest of the bar wanted to hear what he had to say?

He was coming towards my table, his eyes on the door, his face still wearing the traces of a grin.

'Harry?' I tried to call out to him, but it emerged as a croak.

'Nice to see you, Emily,' he said, over his shoulder. Then he paused. 'Sorry, did you want something?'

'No, no,' I said quickly. I pressed the home screen button on my phone so that the note disappeared. 'Nice to see you too.'

And then he was gone, but not before he'd held the door open for Renee, who gave him a little nod of appreciation.

She sat beside me and took a big sip of her drink, her face glum.

'Molly's not doing so well,' she said.

'Oh, Renee.'

'I'd better be getting back. I'll just drink this and . . . Are you all right?'

'Yeah,' I said.

I knew I wasn't all right. I also knew that if I told Renee that I'd just seen my ex at the bar and was feeling like I'd come through a hurricane, she would listen carefully and say all the right things. But I could see the little traces of bled mascara around her eyes and knew I wasn't going to say anything.

'Tell me about things with Molly,' I said instead.

We clinked our glasses to four-legged paralegals. I said I hoped that Molly would be okay, but I didn't try to stuff the cracks in her composure with reassurances. She started to tell me about the first dog that she and Grace had got together, a three-legged Labrador they'd named Mahalia.

I didn't speak much. I just listened, and after we'd finished those drinks I told her that I'd see her Monday.

I was wearing noise-cancelling headphones and the push of the city felt distanced from me, held at bay by the quiet and the alcohol. I reread the note on my phone, editing a word here and there, trying to be precise, fair, beyond reasonable doubt. I tried to use words that were neither diminishing nor melodramatic. But I couldn't find them.

And all I could see, as I reread, was that I'd passed so lightly through this world. This world that took so much from women. I could barely claim to have a scratch on me. Yet what had happened with Harry – I'd still failed to get over it. I still couldn't work it out in my head – the precise delineation between *no* and *yes*.

I diverted from my original platform, and got a train out to Kent.

Chapter Twenty-Five

STU ANSWERED THE DOOR wearing joggers and a basketball-style top. I could smell him. His deodorant had started to wear off.

'No friend?' He craned his neck to look around me. I decided not to ask myself whether or not he was joking.

'Ha ha.'

I stepped into the flat.

'Shoes off,' he said. Glancing down the hallway, I saw why – there was a thick white shagpile carpet on the floor. I felt a laugh bubbling up in me and covered it by bending down to untie my laces.

Stu was already walking down the hallway.

'Drink?' he called.

'Water. Thanks.'

The fitted kitchen was steel-laced and shiny. There was the coffee machine. There was the protein powder. There were the remnants of the evening's supermarket stir-fry. A plastic container that had once held chicken breasts stood next to the sink, the white netting spotted with blood.

'Decided to have a quiet one. Mad week. Then I got your text.' He uncapped a bottle of craft beer with a hiss and took a long swig, then looked back at me. 'Oh yeah. Water. You been out drinking?'

'Just a couple. With my boss.'

'Nice.' He stepped closer to give me my water, and looked at me carefully. 'I don't sleep with drunk girls. Don't want to leave myself open to any aggro down the line.'

I didn't say anything.

'Mate of mine had a drunk girl piss in his bed once.'

'I'm not going to piss in your bed.' I didn't put any particular effort into making the statement sound like a joke.

'Hey, don't get mad at me. I'm just putting my cards on the table. I'm one of those people – honesty is, like, really important to me. Like that night we went out.' He raised his beer bottle to his lips again, making eye contact with me the whole time he swigged the contents. 'Like, if you'd just said you'd wanted to go, that would have been cool. Just be honest, right?'

'Right,' I muttered. I turned away from him and looked around the open-plan kitchen and living room. 'Great place.'

'Yeah. I moved in a couple of years ago.' The coffee table was an upturned wooden crate, and there were no chairs, only beanbags. 'I'm taking it slow, doing a few carpentry projects. I want to get it right. Do you want to watch a film or something?' He sat down on the sofa, putting his feet up on the wooden crate.

'Not particularly,' I said.

I went over to the sofa and straddled him. He looked disconcerted for a second, but then smirked.

'Well, that was easy.' He put the hand that wasn't still circled around the neck of the beer bottle on my hip. 'Honesty. That's what I'm talking about.' His eyes swivelled briefly to my breasts and then back to my face. 'You know I'm not looking for anything serious, right?'

'What? Oh, right.'

'Because you didn't really seem like the hook-up type,' he continued conversationally, his eyes returning to my breasts and his hands sliding up to grasp them.

'No?'

'Prove me wrong.'

I kissed him. His beard smelled of coconut.

He did have a rain head shower, and lots of Kiehl's products with the word 'fuel' on the label. And he did let me borrow his dressing gown. It felt huge around my shoulders but a little tight on my hips.

I stood in the bathroom for a while after I'd peed, sniffing his beard oil and trying to figure out how his safety razor worked.

When I went back into the bedroom, he was looking at his phone. The familiar motion of his fingers told me he was back to swiping.

'Wasn't too rough for you, was it?' His voice was careless, but he looked at me sharply.

'I told you, it was fine.'

'Good. Feedback's key. You were pretty game,' he said.

He seemed to be waiting for me to say something, but I just got into bed.

'Oh. I assumed you'd be heading off.'

I looked at my watch. 'It's after eleven.'

'Not afraid of the dark, are you? Plucky girl like you.'

'If you'd rather I left, you can say so.'

'Okay. It's just that I've got five-a-side with the guys in the morning and . . .'

'So you want me to go?'

He squirmed for a minute. I waited. Finally he said, 'Yes.'

'Okay.' I picked my bra up off the floor and turned my back on him.

'But we could do this again some time,' he added, his voice magnanimous.

I looked at him over my shoulder as I twisted my bra around.

'I don't think so.'

'No?' His voice cooled.

I pulled my dress over my head and turned to face him, and he motioned me towards the bed.

'Come and look at this.'

He was holding out a picture of a blonde girl – a match on Tinder.

'Look at her tits. They're huge compared to yours.' He looked at me appraisingly. 'She looks a little bit like your friend, actually.'

I looked at the picture again. There was no resemblance.

'No, she doesn't,' I said.

He shrugged, and sat tapping away at his phone while I ordered a cab. It was going to be fifteen minutes.

'Fucking countryside,' I muttered.

'The commute's great, actually. Train straight into Charing Cross.'

'Yeah, you said last time.'

'Sounds like you found me pretty memorable.'

I didn't bother replying.

'Oh, don't be like that,' he said. 'It's been fun, hasn't it? What else were you planning on doing with your Friday night?'

I shrugged.

'You've got a few minutes. Watch a bit of telly with me. Have a choc.' He held out a box, and then mimed pulling it away. 'Only one, mind. I'm guessing you're probably trying to lose some weight.'

I didn't wait for the cab. I walked to the station in the dark, remembering what Tamsin had said about refusing to be afraid to walk alone at night. Because if a woman was going to be raped, she'd said, then she probably already knew her rapist.

I bought some chips from a kebab shop by the station, reasoning that I hadn't eaten anything since lunchtime, and I'd saved money on the cab. I sat on the train platform for nearly half an hour, watching the steam from my chips unfurl into the evening and be swallowed up by the night. There was a drunk man at the other end of the platform, periodically howling as if in pain. Every time he howled, I shrank a little further into my seat.

There were six other people in the carriage, all couples. I stared out of the window, feeling a little calmer as the lights of London greeted me back into anonymity, the carriage starting to fill up.

There had not been a moment with Stu that I had not consented to. Not a muscle twitch, not a skin cell, not a heartbeat. He'd kept saying 'is it all right if I', and I kept saying 'yes'. Annoyed that he kept asking, when I'd already decided on my answer.

And when he said, 'Apologise for running out on me, you little whore,' and I'd said no, he'd suddenly looked very young and shaken his head like a wet puppy.

'I just got carried away,' he'd said hastily. 'I didn't mean it.'

I reread my note to Harry, before gazing out of the window once more. I wanted to see the backs of houses and outlines of great buildings in the half-light, but my own tired, pale reflection was getting in the way. I wondered if he was home now, if his beery breath had slowed into sleep as he lay beside his new girlfriend, his prone hand resting on her nascent baby bump. And I began, again, to write.

It wasn't exactly your fault. Just like it wasn't exactly mine, I added at the bottom of the note.

You're not going to get away with saying I blame you for everything, Harry, because I also blame myself. More than I could ever blame you.

But I also blame you.

But I also blame myself.

I stayed on the train until the end of the line, reading and rereading my own words.

Then I deleted the note.

The following Monday morning I had arranged to debrief with Renee in the Caffè Nero on the bottom floor of our office building. It was the closest thing to a treat that fitted into the brief half-hour that we'd set aside to talk. It wasn't much, but Renee had promised that it would happen every single week, for as long as I needed it.

I'd googled a photo of Renee from the Nineties, in her silks, great gold earrings protruding from under her horsehair wig, her smile both scholarly and defiant. I thought about how much her time cost then, and what it was worth now.

She left me reviewing a write-up of Amina's case ('Add anything that you think is important') and went to buy the coffees. The queue snaked almost all the way out of the shop.

I was focused on the page, but I glanced up when I noticed someone standing beside the table, and started to say 'sorry, but that chair's taken', before I realised it was Tamsin. Instinctively, I looked away, but not before her image had burned itself onto my retinas. I shuffled my papers, hands shaking.

'Hello.'

She looked simultaneously prettier and more ordinary than I'd ever seen her before. Her hair was bundled back and I couldn't tell whether it was still red, or if it had dulled down into brown. This wasn't the rosy light of her apartment or the half-light of evening, but the full glare of a Caffè Nero crammed with people on their brief breaks.

'I looked online,' she said. 'I saw this was where your office was.'

'You found me,' I said. There was something else I could have said, an accusation that I could have levelled, but it wouldn't have been right or true and we both knew it, so I kept quiet.

It was the only time I had ever seen Tamsin in a context that didn't suit her. In her shorts and t-shirt, she looked childlike, uncertain.

'How are you?' I said. I knew I had to say something, and that was the only suggestion that my mind offered.

She looked at me like it wasn't a question worth answering. There was something indistinct in her face, as if its usual determined lines weren't converging as they always had. I couldn't make sense of it, couldn't see what I had seen in it before.

'I got another call from that journalist,' she said. A voice perfectly controlled from its theatre training. 'And another call, and another.'

'Okay.'

'You know why.'

'. . . I . . .'

'It's out there now,' she said, her voice cutting across mine. 'It'll always be out there.'

'Tamsin, I—'

'That's your boss, isn't it? Renee Walcott. I read about her. She seems cool.'

I looked over to where Renee was standing at the counter, already midway through making friends with the barista. 'Yes,' I said.

'I could just go over and tell her what you did.' Her voice rasped, as if her mouth was dry. 'You do understand that, don't you?'

I looked up at her quickly, and for a second I felt as if something of her old quality had re-emerged.

But then it dissipated again.

I tried to nod, but my head would only move in a single jerk. 'Yes.'

There was something in the silence that followed that felt like those old moments, like we were something else again, not friends but sisters long-lost and reunited.

'And you also know that I never would.'

As she said the words, they became true.

Yes, I did know that.

'What are you doing?' She jerked her head at my pile of notes. Spread out across the table in bold typeface, beneath my hands, my work looked official and office-ready.

'Trying to help someone,' I said.

She paused for a moment, her head tilted to one side. 'I guess I'd better let you help them, then.' She reached down and picked up the photo of Amina, the one Renee had handed to me on the first day of the case. 'Help *her*.'

'I'm doing my best.'

'She's a person. Not an abstraction, not some intriguing idea or worthy cause. She's a *person*.'

'I know,' I said, my voice tight. 'I'm trying.'

'You try very hard, Emily,' she said quietly. 'I get that. I do.' She half smiled, head tilted to one side. 'Industrious, right? Striving.'

She'd remembered. Those stupid offhand words from that first night.

'People listen to you,' she continued, putting the photograph of Amina carefully back down on the tabletop. 'More than you realise, I think. I did, anyway.'

I looked up at her. Her face was a little red from the sunshine, a little raw-looking.

'Tamsin, I'm sorry.'

She left a pause, as if considering. Then she blinked at me, catlike.

'Don't do it again,' she said.

And then she left.

I looked through the plate glass window to try to find her, to get a sense of her, but she had already blended into the slurry of the London pavement and faded away.

Renee returned a few moments later with the coffees.

'All right, Emily?' She looked at me intently, and I stared down at the mess of papers.

'I'm fine.'

'You're sure?'

I reached for the papers that bore Amina's name, the signature that I should never have allowed to happen.

'Let's get to it,' I said.

Chapter Twenty-Six

I CROSSED THE HEATH in bright morning sunshine. It had been perfect weather almost every day since that first evening with Tamsin, but it was late summer now. It would have to end soon. But as long as it lasted I knew that I ought to be savouring it, listening to birds and observing the quality of the light through the trees, not hurrying across the grassy slopes as if on a mission.

I looked around at the swimmers, thinking I might see one with her bright hair. I wondered if it was still red. But everyone apart from me was wearing a proper swimming cap, so there was no spotting her at a glance. This wasn't the post-brunch crowd of a lazy Saturday morning backstroking into afternoon. No hangover cure or lifestyle tourists. This was the older woman, her wrinkled and sagging body held in by a swimsuit that fitted her like sealskin.

The water, which had been blackish last time, was iron grey in the early light of morning. When I got in, it gripped my wrists and ankles and made me gasp.

'Get out if you can't handle it,' the lifeguard called. Then, maybe as an afterthought – 'I'm trusting you to know your own limits.'

I fought to turn my gasps into steadying breaths as I struck out, and suppressed a shriek when something uncannily soft touched my hand, like the billowing hair of a dead girl. When I brought my hand up, I almost laughed with relief to see the green weed.

It took a few minutes, but I started to see, hear, feel more fully than I could at the first shock. The survival chill was ebbing; there was space for something less definitive. The leaves rustled overhead; I allowed myself to listen fully. It was strange to hear something in such a sustained way, without music or a podcast, without Tamsin calling out to me to hear whatever she was hearing. What I heard, in the pull of the wind and slap of the water, was a soft, off-balance cadence. A whispering refrain.

I continued to push through the dark water.

Maybe Tamsin was too broken to come forward.

Maybe she didn't need things like justice and closure. A duck slid past. It eyed me with scepticism, but no fear.

Maybe she thought there was no chance of getting justice.

Heave in a breath.

Maybe she thought there *was* a chance, more than a chance, and didn't want to be responsible for putting a man behind bars. Even him.

Spit out a little pond water.

Maybe she was just too tired of it all.

Maybe she was biding her time until there was less background noise, so her voice could be heard clearly.

Maybe she thought she hadn't said no loudly enough. Maybe she hadn't said no at all. Or said no and meant yes. Or the other way around.

Breath ragged now, heart pounding.

Maybe she thought other women would look at her and think, *I wouldn't have got raped.*

Arms starting to tremble.

Maybe she thought this was just what happened to women.

Maybe she felt ashamed to be talking about herself at all. There were so many girls, girls all over the world. Girls being raped, girls being sold, girls being cut. Maybe she thought the well of suffering was so close to overflowing that if she added one more drop then it would spill over. And we'd all be swept away in the flood.

Dip below the water. Close my eyes to the dark.

Chapter Twenty-Seven

I SAT IN THE cafe with three sheafs of paper laid out in front of me, passing the pen from one hand to the other. Settlements in English, French and Wolof. The buzz and hum was comforting, and outside the rain had begun to pour in earnest, as if making up for lost time.

I saw them coming from a distance. They were an extraordinarily chic couple, him holding an umbrella over her, their silhouettes written sharply against the blur of the city.

'Amina,' I said, standing up and offering my hand to shake. 'Good to see you again.'

She took my hand, but didn't meet my eye.

I gave her a brief smile, and then transferred my gaze to her husband. 'I'm Emily.'

'Youssou,' he said, offering a small smile along with his handshake before reverting his eyes to his wife's face. 'I hope you are very well.'

I mirrored Amina, and looked down. The interpreter had already called me to let me know that she was having transport problems. I busied myself explaining, and then passed them both the copies of the settlement to review. Youssou laid them out side by side, eyes flicking between copies as if to confirm that they all amounted to the same thing. Amina just took the French version, the copy which bore her signature, and flipped to the back page, where she stared at her own writing with her eyes narrowed.

'I'm very sorry about everything,' I said. It was tempting to direct myself to Youssou, as he seemed so much more confident in his English. 'You should never have been asked to sign anything that you didn't fully understand.'

'I read French,' Youssou interjected, although he was so softly spoken that it didn't feel like an interjection. 'I explained it to her.'

'Oh,' I said, blinking. A wild rush of relief. I hadn't retraumatised Amina after all, sending her a document she couldn't understand and demanding that she sign herself into a lifetime of silence.

'We were lucky,' he shrugged. 'We shouldn't have to be lucky.'

The interpreter arrived a moment later, and I smiled blandly through the Wolof greetings.

It took us over an hour to go through the settlement page by page, clause by clause. Amina asked a lot of questions, her brow furrowed, her downcast gaze frequently switching to an expression of interrogation, her speech rapid. The questions themselves, via the interpreter, were sharp and incisive, as if she needed to understand every little corner of the dry, bloodless world that the settlement created.

Youssou said nothing at all, but his eyes never left her face, his hand never moved from the arm of her chair.

When Amina picked up the pen and signed her name at last, she gave a little nod. Her face was tired and resigned, and when she put the pen down and the interpreter bade us goodbye, she stood abruptly.

'Excuse me,' she said, and hurried off to the loo. Youssou turned his head to watch her go, and when the door shut, he took up the pen she had just dropped and began to fiddle with it.

'It cost her a lot to tell me what happened,' he said. 'She was ashamed. She thought it was her fault.'

I said nothing.

'And I have read this document,' he indicated it, 'in three languages. Not one of them tells the truth.'

Reflexively, I picked up the English copy and began to read, but he shook his head.

'I'm not saying there is a mistake.'

I put the copy back down on the table and bowed my head.

'And the money,' he said, seemingly mostly to himself. 'The money.'

I looked up at him. 'Do you still think you'll go back to Senegal?'

'Back?' He gave a little laugh. 'I was born in France. I have French nationality.'

'Oh. Sorry.'

'I want to go back,' Amina said over my shoulder. She had returned from the loo, and her face was smoothed-out, calm.

'She misses the lifestyle in Dakar,' Youssou said, his eyes straight back to his wife's face, adjusting his chair to accommodate her as she sat back down. 'She's never liked living away from the sea.' He looked out at the street and wrinkled his nose. 'London is very expensive. Very crowded.'

I thought of my parents with their little cottage in Norfolk.

'I'm glad you get to go home,' I said. 'I'm sorry it was under these circumstances.'

Youssou smiled politely again, but Amina said something to him in Wolof and he gave a different smile, an ironic one, this time sliding a hand gently over her shoulder.

'She said, "At least this way we don't have to go back empty-handed,"' he reported to me. 'She's an optimist. And who knows.' He shrugged. 'Maybe we're happier this way.'

The two of them exchanged a glance, and seemingly as one they stood up. They were halfway out of the cafe before I saw Amina square her shoulders, heave in a breath and turn back to me.

'Here,' she said, handing me a slip of paper with a phone number scribbled on it. 'My friend. Also worked with me. Maybe she has a story.' She looked me in the eye at last, unsmiling but not unfriendly. 'There is always one more story.'

Then the two of them walked away, and I watched them go, close under their umbrella, the rain pressing on all sides. They weren't holding hands, but their closeness felt tangible.

Chapter Twenty-Eight

I CALLED HIM BACK, rather than texting. Like Tamsin on that first night, when she'd cooked me the fish and we'd toasted the world with champagne.

There was a lightness in his voice when he answered which might have been pleasure or surprise. He didn't say much, just enough to encourage me through the speech I'd rehearsed.

When I put the phone down my heart was thudding, but the world hadn't ended. On the contrary, I had plans for Friday night.

We met in a pub near James' place. The idea was to have a drink together and then he'd cook for me. He'd mentioned when we first met up that he liked to cook, so I suggested it.

I didn't feel like drinking and decided there was no point getting drunk for the sake of it, so I ordered an artisanal ginger beer and he did too.

'It's actually much nicer than real beer,' he said, and although I agreed, I detected a note of labour in his voice. He wanted me to know that whatever choices I made were okay with him. I appreciated the sentiment, but didn't crack any bigger a smile than I felt.

The friendliness between us reinstated itself in pieces of the same silence that we had shared that first afternoon. The pub was full to a low hum. But there wasn't too much noise to make space for our quiet. We talked too – about old films we both liked, which pubs in London had the best chips. We looked around and identified the couples on their first dates.

'I'm hungry,' I said after a while. 'Are you still okay to cook?'

'Of course.'

His flat was on the top floor of an old building that used to be a bank. We stepped inside and I could see the bedroom opposite the front door – the bed visible from the hall, neatly made and covered in soft grey jersey sheets.

He turned left, leading me into an open-plan kitchen/ living room. The walls were painted a warm, glowing white and sloped on either side so it felt a little like being in a tent. There were windows on either side, boxes with herbs growing. It was sparsely decorated but very tidy. Much tidier than my room at home. Velvet cushions on the sofa, and lamps, not just an overhead light. The coffee table was from IKEA, but it wasn't the Lack.

He put on music. I didn't recognise it. An older man with a voice like a cello.

'Do you want some water?'

'Thanks.'

A chilled jug in the fridge. Ice and lemon. As he handed it to me, he looked very deliberately into my eyes and said, 'So are we going to say hi to the elephant in the room?'

'Which elephant?' I didn't want to be angry any more. I liked him, and I liked myself with him. I glanced around. 'I see no elephant.'

'You were angry with me the last time we saw each other.'

I bit down the refusal, the denial, the smoothing over. The *I wasn't angry with you, it was just a super intense week.*

'Yes,' I said. I ran my hand through my hair, imagining it was glowing red as Tamsin's had been. 'I was angry.'

For some reason, a lump formed in my throat.

'I was angry, and I'm not sorry that I left when I did.'

'I wasn't angling for you to say sorry. *I'm* sorry if that's how it came across.'

'I know. But the point is, I'm not sorry. Not for being angry.'

'I know.' A pause. 'For what it's worth, I talked to my friend. Told him that I don't want to see Art Rawlings films any more.'

'What did he say to that?'

'That I was probably right.'

A long quiet between us. That thick, heavy quiet.

'Well, I suppose that's all right then.'

'I'm not saying it is. I just wanted you to know.'

Another long pause.

'So what are you cooking for me, then?'

'Pasta. Everyone loves pasta.'

I glanced at the kitchen and half expected to see a bag of penne and a jar of shop-bought pesto. Instead I saw fresh tomatoes, chillies, garlic, basil, a bottle of red wine open but still full.

He sounded confident, but then he faltered when he said, 'Do you like pasta?'

'I thought everyone did.'

'So you don't?'

'Stop worrying. It looks good.'

'Hope it is. If it's not, there's always takeaway as a backup.'

He was moving less confidently than he had before, the easy flow gone from his voice. He put on an enormous pot of water and arced a tea towel so it sat over his shoulder. The motions were practised, but I saw uncertainty weighing them down. The discomfort spread to me. Was this how I made other people feel?

I walked over to the kitchen.

'Let's have a glass of wine,' I said. Touched him gently on the elbow. He went still for half a second, then carried on chopping, as if he'd barely noticed. His movements were smaller than before, less overstated.

I found the glasses and poured the wine. Moving around the kitchen, I kept forgetting which glass was mine.

He produced a plate of cold cuts from the fridge and we ate them with our fingers and listened to the music.

'So how come you live alone?' I looked at the kitchen, with the customised hooks and rails that placed everything within easy reach. The good-quality cooker, the soft, friendly white of the walls. 'Do you own this flat?'

'Yes.'

'Did you parents give you a deposit?'

'Yes. Half of one, anyway.'

I waited for the mitigation, but there wasn't one.

'So you're part of the problem.'

He mirrored my half-smile. 'Pretty much.'

We both knew we could pierce the space between us with a laugh, but we didn't.

I asked what I could do, and started to tear mozzarella to pieces over an olivewood board. It would have been easy for our shoulders to brush against one another. He touched me lightly on the back so that I moved out the way for him to get to a drawer. I washed my hands and, looking around for a tea towel, took the one from his shoulder.

Rain started to fall outside, so heavy that we could hear it pounding off the roof. Louder than the music, louder than the hiss of the gas stove, loud enough that I didn't hear his footsteps when he went over to open the doors on to a tiny balcony and rid some of the steam from the kitchen. The steam unfurled itself into the dark, becoming part of the rain.

I went over to stand beside him, feeling bold yet calm.

'Did you order this rain specially?'

He nodded. 'Of course.'

My arm around his waist, his across my shoulders. A waning moon, circle-light from the street lamps blurred. The edges between us diffused just a little; we started to kiss.

Chapter Twenty-Nine

The first time we had sex was like a telegram. Kisses, one two three. Stop.

Pull back. Check his eyes for any sense that I'd failed him. Angered him. Deprived him of his birthright.

Nothing.

Then lean in. Me. Not him. Touch his hair lightly. Grab it hard. Play with the idea of wanting.

Stop.

'Is this okay?'

I couldn't ask if he felt like he was watching himself from the outside, if he was burrowing deep into a part of his mind that wasn't in his body. I didn't know how I'd say all that.

Our native tongues would never be quite the same. I think he knew that we came from different countries. I think he knew that words wouldn't do, that they meant something different where I came from.

He just nodded. His eyes were round and darker than they had been before, and his breathing just a little shallow. But his smile was wide and easy. It was a smile that said that not only this is okay, but I am okay.

And more besides.

Kiss harder. Arms wrap around.

Stop.

No beseeching eyes. No hand brutishly grabbed and placed to show what I'd done to him, how I owed him.

None of that. Just another smile. Arms around my waist, resting his head gently on my shoulder.

Several times I felt my centre of gravity slipping. Several times I started to leave my body, to go somewhere else, somewhere sterile and humdrum with no place for extremes.

He pulled me back. Not harshly, with a yank. With the way he brushed my hair from my eyes, the way he placed his hand on the back of my head to stop me from bumping it on the headboard. The laugh when I found myself tangled up in the duvet and unable to move. The way he helped me to free myself and cast it aside. The way, when it was over and the air around us had started to cool, he covered me up, so I was warm.

I woke up and he was sleeping. His mouth was slightly open, one arm flung above his head. Hairy armpit exposed. Eyes closed. Long long lashes.

He gave a little snore and turned over.

I got up. I pulled on his t-shirt and my knickers. The t-shirt didn't envelop me the way it does in films – he was slim and narrow-shouldered. My crotch was exposed. I looked like Winnie-the-Pooh. I paused in front of the mirror, but moved on quickly.

The sun was falling easily through the windowpanes and the tread of my feet against the carpet swelled luxuriously in the silence. The air felt freshly washed.

I curled up on the sofa with a glass of water, my arms wrapped around one of the velvet cushions. A distant part of me was frustrated. I hadn't walked an untrodden path to this feeling. I'd found it in the bed of an ordinary boy.

I looked for Tamsin standing by the stove, or curled up in the armchair with a cup of coffee. I looked for her leaning against the balcony rail, letting the wind play with her hair. I looked for her to gather the strands of the morning together and weave them into something whole and golden. I looked for her.

My chest widened and ached. She wasn't there.

She would never be there.

I found my handbag, where I'd left it unsuspecting on the chair the previous night. I opened Twitter. A new hashtag trending: #henevershouldhavedoneit.

Don't judge victims on how they behave after they've been abused #henevershouldhavedoneit

Women don't need to be perfect in order to be believed #henevershouldhavedoneit

Sometimes, when someone does fucked up things to you, you act in a fucked up way #henevershouldhavedoneit

I was about to put my phone back in my bag when I saw a WhatsApp notification from Lucy. I looked at it straight away, before the habit of ignoring kicked in.

A link to a news article, with a small caption. *You were right.*

My heart spiked.

A BBC news article, in its maroon and white livery. Not national news, local to south-west London. But news, still.

AWARD-WINNING HEAD SUSPENDED PENDING INVESTIGATION INTO GROOMING ALLEGATIONS.

The picture was Chris Hawkins looking angrier and greyer, his tie undone, ducking his head as he went into his house. But the video was a freeze-frame. Lucy's face. Lucy's large, clear eyes, looking straight to camera.

I pressed play. The TV-ness of it seemed so strange with Lucy at its centre, as if she'd been superimposed. Her calm, her lack of fuss, her need to speak of things as they were.

'For a long time I stayed quiet,' the video Lucy said. The image was framed by half a dozen microphones. 'For a long time I felt like I'd instigated the whole thing, that I was at fault. From the outside it might have looked like I was fine, that I was over it. It was only when I myself became a teacher that I really understood the transgression. I was sixteen. I thought I was mature. The duty of care was with him. When we met again I tried raising it through the normal channels at school, but it became clearer and clearer that nothing was going to be done, so I've decided to speak publicly.'

Then the disembodied barrage from the news crews began.

'Lucy, do you think he'll go to prison?'

'I don't know. It's my word against his. For now.'

'Lucy, did you encourage Mr Hawkins' attention?'

'I was a *child*.'

'Lucy, were you in love with Mr Hawkins?'

I saw her brow furrow just a fraction and her lips form the word '. . . *Love?*' But then she recovered. 'I don't think I can really be expected to answer that.'

'Lucy, are you angry with Mr Hawkins?'

No hesitation. 'Yes.'

'You seem remarkably composed.'

'Would you prefer me to cry?'

'Would you encourage him to seek therapy for his behaviour?'

She looked blank. 'I suppose that's up to him.'

'Lucy, would you say you were traumatised by what happened to you?'

Lucy's face didn't change. 'That's not the point,' she said. 'He never should have done it.'

Three wavering lines. Another message from Lucy. This time a screenshot, a message from Chris Hawkins. One word.

Bitch.

Then Lucy's caption.

Hahaha. Fuck him.

One last message – a picture, dark and blurry. I couldn't see it at first. Then I squinted and thought, yes, there it is. The head, the promise of fingers forming. An imperfect rendering of something still so small and secret. And a smoke signal, too, that something was over, something that was partly hers and partly ours.

I was happy for her. I also knew I didn't want what she had. Later I would call her, and her voice would reveal at its core the girl I knew when I was eleven, the girl who might never have been fearless but was, in her essence, unafraid. Later, I would call her.

But for now I put on the radio. I stepped from side to side. Nothing special. But from the deliberate roll and dip of my body you couldn't call it anything but dancing. I made coffee. I whisked eggs and sliced bread and cooked with exuberant amounts of butter and salt, as Tamsin always had. Nina sang on the radio that she was feeling good.

Chapter Thirty

Speak of me as I am.
Nothing extenuate, nor set down aught in malice.
                                    – Othello, Act 5, Scene 2

THE LAST TIME I saw Tamsin was on the news.

A background character in the footage for a protest. Her hair wet, her face smudged in anonymity. Chained to a railing, a banner clasped in her hand, There Is No Planet B. I knew it was her, this little white-faced, voiceless collection of pixels, her banner battered by the wind and rain, a padlock around her narrow waist.

A lot had changed by that point.

Lucy's baby was a girl.

She and Andrew named her Elinor. When Lucy handed her to me for the first time, and I felt her weight in my arms, it was like meeting an old friend anew.

I suppose Harry's baby must have been born too, around the same time. I got rid of him on Facebook. If he uploaded a picture of himself holding his boy, his freshly hatched son, I didn't see it. I wouldn't have to see Harry's red-raw face covered in exhaustion and happiness. I wouldn't have to see a tear glistening in the corner of his eye, caught perfectly. Cameras are so good these days.

It didn't make sense to put myself through that.

Lucy left her job not long after Chris Hawkins was arrested. She said she was just taking early maternity leave, but once the new term started, she only ended up going back for six weeks. A lot of parents had written in, expressing their concern. They said that someone who had behaved the way she had as a teenager clearly didn't have an appropriate sense of boundaries between pupils and staff.

The deputy head said it was all about perception. That it was 'a distraction'.

When Lucy told me, I started to rage and pick holes in the argument, as if winning *that* was all that mattered.

'It's okay,' she said. 'I'll find something else.' Her face was composed, but when she turned her head I saw, in the light, the dried remnants of tear tracks on her cheeks. Lucy, who had wanted to teach for as long as either of us could remember, who only ever cried when someone else was in pain.

When I walk around Soho, I always get the sense of revisiting a place I used to live. But you don't ever run into anyone you know in a city of eight million. I could still feel the absences in the places where we had parted. There was no dried blood left there, only stretched scar tissue.

The last time I saw her – saw her in the flesh – she was starring in a play. It was a year after the Rawlings affair. The world had changed. Everything had changed. Rawlings was still a free man.

I'd read the reviews ahead. I'd heard that Tamsin had made a 'shimmering debut' on the London stage, that her 'willow' scene was 'perhaps the most affecting in recent memory'. The theatre was underneath a pub, but my snap judgement on that turned out not to be quite right. Even though it was so small, it was a famous 'space'.

I was with James by that point. I had held off on it for a long time; we were just two people, I insisted, who sometimes shared a meal, or a bed, or a quiet look. It took me longer than it should have to detect it, but I started to see it in how he made me cups of tea, and listened without needing to get his word in. The way he quietly picked up some books and equally quietly discarded others. The way he spoke to his friends about things which it would have been easier not to. He did it, even when he had better things to do. He ushered chaos from my home and made the sky seem larger. I started to wonder if he might, in his own way, be someone. Someone honourable and courageous.

And I was different, when I was with him. A little quieter. A little easier.

The first time I referred to him as my boyfriend it was at work, speaking to Renee. I screwed up my face as I said it, and a little line formed on her forehead.

'I didn't know you'd met someone,' she said. 'How lovely.'

I opened my mouth to tell her that I wasn't sure if it was serious, that I wasn't sure I even wanted a relationship with a man, that I knew it was pathetic of me to feel like I needed someone, that I was perfectly okay on my own. But I was interrupted by Renee's mobile ringing. By the smile that spread across her face as she glanced at the screen. She angled her body away from me to put the phone to her ear and say, 'Hello, darling. How's your day been?'

I didn't tell James about Tamsin at first, when we booked the tickets. I just said that I knew her a bit. But I told him the truth when we were having a drink in the pub before the play. He listened without interrupting. I told him what I'd said, what I'd done, what I'd tried to do.

He stayed quiet for a very long time, passing his beer bottle from hand to hand, a little crease in his forehead.

'It's just strange,' he said at last. 'Because that's not how I think of you.'

'But I did it.'

'Yeah.'

I wanted to demand something from him, maybe an indication that he might have done the same thing. But I cared too much about what we had to ask him to lie like that, so I just said, 'I did some awful things.'

He went back to his silence until I asked him to say something, anything. And he agreed that they were awful things, but I wasn't an awful person.

'You're a great person. I think so.'

He asked if I wanted to go backstage after the play to see her, to make amends. I shook my head. I said there was no way to apologise, I wouldn't get the words right, that I never could. That she would be too busy anyway.

I knew that wasn't quite right. I knew that if we had gone backstage she might have opened her arms to me again, her smile might have been radiant and measurelessly wide. We might have drunk whisky. She might have forgiven me, looked me in the eye in the knowledge that I had listened to those cries that came out of her, and the white noise of the water as it washed it all away. It would have been a meeting based on forgetting, but no less precious for that.

Maybe I would write her a letter, I said. James nodded. I could tell he believed I'd do it, one day. And because he believed me, it didn't need to be today. I knew from looking at him that after the play we would get the tube home and make tea before bed, and watch an episode of something as we drifted off to sleep, together but not touching.

In the morning there would be coffee and toast and honey and oranges on James' balcony. Then the train to work, and calls to Adriana, Amina's friend, a young Brazilian woman with a story of her own, who had still more friends, with more stories. It still made me anxious to pick up the phone, but now, when I did it, I thought of Tamsin.

The first time she came onstage, I tensed up; James felt it and took my hand.

Her hair was back to blonde. Not the olive-tinged, glistening old gold that it had been when I'd known her, but a bright, pale blonde, like a Swedish princess. It worked well, the way that the golden head shone, the dark one bent over it.

The actor who played Othello gazed at her like there was nobody else in the room, even when he was supposed to be appearing in front of the senate to give testimony.

He talked about how he'd fallen in love with this girl, because she listened to his stories.

I thought she must be able to see me in the audience. It was such a tiny theatre. She had always seen me. Seen me enough when we were lying in that rain-soaked street to understand that I was afraid. And take my hand.

But if she did see me, she didn't let on. She was a pro. And after a while I forgot that she was Tamsin, and watched thinking maybe this time Desdemona wouldn't die. Beseeching him: kill me tomorrow, let me live tonight. And he paused and brushed the hair from her face to look into her eyes.

'It is too late,' he said. Tenderly.

Then he killed her. And the lights went down.

Acknowledgments

First thanks must go to my extraordinary agent Marilia Savvides, who has been my rock through all the turmoil of the past two years, and who gave me permission to write something that made me happy.

We did it.

I miss your face.

Secondly, to Jeanette Winterson, who encouraged me to try an experiment. You said I'd know 'by the solstice', and you were right, as always. Thank you for everything.

Thank you to all my early readers: Lena Stamm, Joss Kelvin, Carys Lapwood, Leo Balthasar. Sometimes it takes a coven to write a novel.

Thank you to my mum, for reading many drafts and supporting me all the way. Thank you to my dad, for believing in me and instilling me with good music taste. My sister, for reading an early draft. My brother and all my in-laws for their unfailing support. My grandparents, John and Audrey Cunningham. The loss of you is still fresh, and I miss you very much. You would have been so excited to see this book published. But there are rude bits, so I wouldn't have let you read it.

Thank you to the kickass team at Bonnier for bringing your extraordinary vision to this book – first of all, to

Sophie Orme for finding me. Thank you to Felice McKeown, Katie Meegan, Clare Kelly, Vicky Joss, Jenna Petts – and Sophie McDonnell, for the gorgeous cover. You really are a dream team. Thank you also to everyone at 42 Management, and Alexandra Cliff.

To my friends, this is my love letter to you. If isolation has taught me anything, it's that I can't do without you. You can make a tinny in the park feel like champagne in the Savoy.

Thank you, Bernie and Mort, for allowing me to feed you and pay your vet bills.

And last of all, thank you to Jason Gwartz. Thank you for seeing my despair but refusing to engage with it. I really will do my best to marry you this year.